MYSTIC
MADNESS

THE WITCHES OF HOLLOW COVE
BOOK EIGHT

KIM RICHARDSON

FABLEPRINT

FablePrint

Mystic Madness, The Witches of Hollow Cove, Book Eight
Copyright © 2021 by Kim Richardson
Cover by Kim Richardson
Printed in the United States of America

ISBN-13: 9798786959919
[1. Supernatural—Fiction. 2. Demonology—
Fiction.
3. Magic—Fiction].

BOOKS BY KIM RICHARDSON

THE WITCHES OF HOLLOW COVE
Shadow Witch
Midnight Spells
Charmed Nights
Magical Mojo
Practical Hexes
Wicked Ways
Witching Whispers
Mystic Madness

THE DARK FILES
Spells & Ashes
Charms & Demons
Hexes & Flames
Curses & Blood

SHADOW AND LIGHT
Dark Hunt
Dark Bound
Dark Rise
Dark Gift
Dark Curse
Dark Angel
Dark Strike

MYSTIC MADNESS

THE WITCHES OF HOLLOW COVE
BOOK EIGHT

KIM RICHARDSON

CHAPTER
1

I blinked at the letter. It didn't matter how many times I read it. It always said the same thing.

> *To the residents of Davenport House,*
> *On behalf of the Hollow Cove town administration, I would like to extend a warm invitation to attend the Annual Hollow Cove Pie Festival on Saturday, the 25th of April. The festival begins at noon in the downtown core and will continue until 9 p.m.*
> *We are looking forward to the festive day. May the best pie win!*
> *Addendum: Due to your niece's track record of destroying property, Tessa Davenport is banned from participating in any of the contests.*
> *Yours Sincerely,*
> *Gilbert Gilderoy, Mayor*

I stiffened in my chair, gritting my teeth as anger welled inside me. It wasn't news that Gilbert had it in for me. Ever since I'd *accidentally* burned down the town gazebo, it seemed the little shifter went out of his way to make me pay for it, by any means he could. This was his payback. But excluding me from a town festival? This time he'd gone too far.

Ordinary people celebrated spring with Easter bunnies, giant chickens made of chocolate, and egg hunts. But Hollow Cove's celebration was the polar opposite of normal, and we celebrated with an annual pie festival.

For the past few months, I'd been preoccupied with trying to find Lilith (a.k.a. Queen of Hell), searching for her during the day, and training with my father at night, as he worked to hone my demon mojo. Gilbert's continued animosity toward me was the least of my worries.

Winter came and went, giving life to spring, and still, I had no idea where Lilith was. I'd searched everywhere for the queen of hell, but I'd come up short. Iris and I had even returned to the funeral home in hopes of finding some more DNA or evidence that we could use to track her. We'd even searched the bedrooms hoping to find some clues as to where the queen of hell might have gone. But all we found were copies of spells for transfigurations and glamours, the magic that gave the Sisters of the Circle their fake bodies.

After that, I'd turned to the internet, searching for global disasters or supernatural occurrences that couldn't be explained, anything out of the norm for the human world.

And still, I found nothing that would give me her location.

"Who locked her up?" I'd asked my father on the very first night we'd started our training after I'd filled him in on the whole, "I let the queen of hell escape into our world to save Dolores" fiasco.

My father had been quiet for a while. "Her husband. Lucifer."

My eyebrows practically sailed off my forehead. "That sounds like an excellent story. Should I get some wine?"

Obiryn, my demon father, gave me a small smile. "It's not. It's a terrible story."

"I'm still getting the excellent story vibes. What did she do to piss him off?" I smiled knowingly. "She slept with his best friend. Didn't she?"

My father shrugged. "It's not so much that she made him angry. It was more of a question of dominance."

I raised a brow. "Let me guess. He wanted to control her, and she didn't want anything to do with that, so he locked her up and threw away the key?" It wasn't that I felt sorry for Lilith, but

I didn't think it right for any husband to try and control their wife, goddess or not.

"I'll give you the short version." My father grabbed a chair and sat. "You have to understand who Lilith is first."

"She's the queen of hell. I think that says it all."

My father crossed his legs at the knee and leaned back, looking like a college professor. "Yes. But more accurately, she's one of the Old Gods, a race of immortal entities created by God. Each served as a prime authority with ancient human religions. The thing with these pagan gods or deities is that all of them are petty, cruel, unfeeling, and only concerned with themselves."

"Sounds like Lilith," I said.

My father pursed his lips. "They lack empathy. They're psychopaths. They enjoyed the many human offerings, the virgin sacrifices, and many of them were known to have a taste for human flesh. They enjoyed torturing and killing humans."

"Nice."

"Lilith was no different, but she excelled in creation and magic, and she helped Lucifer build and shape the Netherworld to what it is today. For thousands of years, she assisted him in creating demons and all the other creatures, helping him mold the Netherworld."

4

I crossed my arms over my chest. "I'm sensing we're getting to the good part."

Obiryn gave a soft laugh. "Lilith outrivaled in creation. She was better than Lucifer. Her skills as a goddess grew, empowered by her gift, and so did her magic. She became the very first witch."

"No kidding? I'll admit—that's interesting."

My father nodded. "As such, Lilith's abilities in creation surpassed Lucifer's. She became more popular too. And Lucifer wouldn't have it. He became jealous. When he saw a shift in his people, saw how they preferred Lilith to rule in his stead, he appointed a team of the best mages and wizards to strip her of her magic and hide her away in that cage."

"I'd ask for a divorce." I shook my head. "I know why she's so angry. Lucifer's a bit of an ass. Isn't he?"

He shrugged. "Never met him."

"And everyone in your world knows this? Wouldn't those who favored Lilith look for her or something?"

"Not everyone knew about it," answered my father. "Only the older demons, such as me and a few younger demons. But Lucifer had an answer for that too. He spread lies about Lilith. He had the demon communities believe that she'd abandoned them, that she preferred the company of humans over demons."

5

"So, he made them believe she was here? In our world this whole time?"

"Yes."

I shook my head, remembering that cold, intense stare Lilith had when I spoke about the ones who'd imprisoned her. "I thought she did something terrible like… I don't know… killed an entire nation or something? But she didn't. Basically, she was innocent."

"I wouldn't go as far as calling her innocent."

I looked over at my demon father. "Why didn't you or your demon pals help her if you thought she was imprisoned?"

My father raked his beard with his fingers. "It's too late to get into all that. But Lucifer has many allies, armies loyal to him, and her whereabouts weren't known to us. A small group of us searched for her. We knew the risks. If Lucifer found us out, he would have destroyed us. We looked for many years. We only managed to find her location about three hundred years ago, but getting close enough to let her out was impossible. Not from the Netherworld."

"But possible from our side." I nodded. "Which is why Lilith needed that coven of quacks to help her."

"You are correct."

The pieces started to take shape. I had a much better idea of who Lilith was and what had happened to her. Her revenge would be directed at her husband. I had no doubt about that. Because if it were me, that's exactly what I'd be doing: looking for his traitorous ass.

What was Lilith planning? Who knew? That was the Netherworld's business. I just didn't want her to take out her rage on us, on this side of the planes.

My conversation with my father had put my mind at ease somewhat. I didn't think she wanted to annihilate the human population anymore, but I still wanted to keep tabs on her, just in case she changed her mind. She did mention that she loved to torture mortals. And the fact that she'd been imprisoned for so long had to have affected her in many ways. She was definitely not the same goddess coming out as she was going in.

The rest of that night had been focused more on channeling and controlling my demon mojo. My father had been an excellent teacher and very patient, even after I'd burned off his beard and his eyebrows. Whoops.

"You're going to ruin your eyes if you keep staring at that letter so close like that." I looked up to find Ruth standing next to the table. "It happened to our Great-Aunt Flora," she continued. "She went blind as a bat."

"That's because she got ink poisoning from eating the letters afterward," snapped Dolores.

Ruth ignored her sister and put the steaming cup of coffee on the table next to me. "Here," she said, the skin around her blue eyes crinkling with her smile. "Have some coffee. I put in a bit of cocoa and cinnamon, just like you like it."

"Thanks, Ruth." I took a sip and moaned. "Devine. You spoil me."

"Nonsense." Ruth dismissed my praise with a wave of her hand, her grin just as adorable as the witch.

I sighed. "I can't believe Gilbert would write that. He just can't let go of what happened with the gazebo."

"Give it here. Let me take a look." Dolores slipped on her glasses and snatched up the letter before I had a chance to give it to her. Head bowed and brow furrowed, she kept her attention on the note until she read it thoroughly, possibly four or five times. Finally, she looked over her glasses at me. "He really does have it in for you."

"Tell me about it," I growled. I set my mug on the table and rubbed my eyes with my fingers. I blinked and looked up. "Is it me, or do the powers that be not want me to participate in this festival?"

"Shh!" Ruth lowered next to me, her eyes on the ceiling as though some superior entity was about to strike us down. "Don't say things like that. You don't know who's listening."

I smiled. I had to. I loved my Aunt Ruth even though she was a little on the nutty side at times. At least she eased some of the tension.

"Can he really do that? Keep me from participating?" I didn't think I'd wanted to participate, but the fact that he'd singled me out like that… well, it just made me want to be in this damn festival even more.

Dolores let out a sigh, pulled the glasses from her nose, and held them in her hand as she gestured. "He is the town mayor. I can't be sure, but I do believe he has the right."

Ruth made a face. "He's going to win again this year."

"Win?"

Ruth looked at me, and her smile vanished. "The pie competition. He's won it every year for the last eleven years."

I made a face. "Gilbert makes pies? I thought all he could make were those yappy sounds that come out of his mouth every time he speaks."

Ruth narrowed her eyes, her mouth set in a firm line. "I'm going to kick his butt this year. Just you wait." She rushed over to the kitchen island, her bare feet slapping the hard floor, and pulled out a heavy orange leather-bound book. She slammed it on the counter and began flipping through the pages.

Dolores's eyes pinned me from across the kitchen table. "I'll see what I can do. It's a long shot, but I might be able to persuade him to change his mind." I could still read some of the guilt from the whole Sisters of the Circle debacle behind her dark eyes. She was still trying to make up for it, but she really didn't have to. I'd let it go that night. It was all in the past.

"I can poison him if you want," offered Hildo. The black cat was up on the counter next to the stove that boasted pots of steaming stews and whatever Ruth was cooking. He was always close to the food, that furry beast. His yellow eyes were luminous and had that lazy-cat look of any lounging feline.

I smiled at him. "Uh, thanks, but I'll handle Gilbert my own way." Dunking him in one of Ruth's boiling cauldrons came to mind. Or maybe I'd use him as target practice for my demon mojo. That sounded fun.

Ruth rubbed the top of Hildo's head, and the cat closed his eyes and purred loudly. "It's okay, Hildo," she said in that unique voice she reserved for only tiny creatures. "Don't you worry. I'll find you someone you can poison."

Yup. It was going to be one of those days.

Dolores hit the table with the edge of her glasses. "I've always said Gilbert was the wrong choice for mayor."

"Was there another candidate?" I asked.

Dolores pursed her lips. "There was."

"And?"

She looked at me and said, "He died."

Okay then. I took a sip of my coffee. "Don't worry about Gilbert. It's fine, really. Besides, I still have lots of work to do. I doubt I'll be able to make it on Saturday for the festival."

"Why in the cauldron would you want to miss the festival? It's fabulous." Beverly sashayed her way into the kitchen. Her slender figure was wrapped in a pair of straight-legged jeans and a light-blue blouse, which accentuated her tan skin and shoulder-length, blonde hair. Her kitten heels clicked on the floor as she made her way to the coffeepot. She looked amazing and put together as usual with her perfect makeup.

Yet, something was different about her.

Something major.

"What in the cauldron did you do to your breasts?" cried Dolores.

That major thing.

"Mmm?" Beverly turned from the coffee machine, pressed her hands on her hips, and stuck out her chest, her features molded in what she hoped was an innocent look. The buttons on her blouse were about to pop, the material stretched so thin we could see her belly button.

Though my Aunt Beverly wasn't known for her ample bosom, she still had a nice rack. Now? Now it looked as though she'd gotten a triple-D boob job overnight.

Holy crap. My Aunt Beverly was Dolly Parton.

I wanted to laugh and say "good one," but something in Beverly's face stopped me. This wasn't a joke.

11

Dolores's mouth fell open, showing all her bottom teeth. "Have you gone completely mad? You'll poke someone's eyes out with those things."

Ruth was jabbing one of Beverly's boobs with a green spatula as though to see if it was real, or maybe she was hoping it would pop.

"That's some serious push-up bra," I said.

"It's not a push-up bra. It's a weapon," retorted Dolores.

I cleared my throat. "Um… is this a new spell you're trying?" It was hard not to look at Beverly's new cleavage and not to laugh. They were so big, they were overpowering the petite witch. If she wasn't careful, she might tip over.

Beverly beamed and curled a strand of loose hair behind her ear. "It is. It's one of Martha's. It's called Boob-Booster. It increases your breast size naturally."

"There's nothing *natural* about them," Dolores scoffed. "Ask for your money back."

Beverly narrowed her eyes, her lips tight. It wasn't often I caught a glimpse of her angry. "Well. I think I look great." She spun around and poured herself a cup of coffee.

I stared at Beverly. Something didn't fit. She wasn't one to change her appearance. She went on and on about how fabulous she was naturally, how the goddess had blessed her with her perfect body. So why the change?

"You going somewhere?" I asked, not giving up.

Beverly joined us at the table and stood with her cup of coffee in her hands. "As a matter of fact, yes. Derrick is taking me out for lunch at the Sunset Grill in Cape Elizabeth."

Slowly and very carefully, Beverly slipped into the chair next to Dolores. Her new boobs kept hitting the table's edge, so she had to pull her chair out to be able to fit.

I'd never heard of this guy, but then again, it was hard to keep up with all the men she dated. "He said something about your... *appearance*. Didn't he?"

Color showed on Beverly's face. "I don't know what you mean."

Dolores leaned forward. "She's right. I can see it all over your face. Out with it. What did he say?"

Beverly whirled in her seat, her boobs smashing her coffee mug against the sugar cup and sending cubes scattering over the table.

She scrambled to pick them up. "He might have mentioned that in a woman my age, things are not so tight and perky anymore." She shrugged like it was nothing. "We all know that as we age, gravity is our enemy. We don't bounce back like we used to."

The sudden silence hammered in my ears. "And this is someone you want to date?"

Beverly's head spun around so fast it reminded me of the little girl in the original *Exorcist* movie.

"Of course," she said, staring at me like I was a scuff mark on her new leather shoes. "Why wouldn't I? He's gorgeous. Has a high-paying job. He's a real catch."

"And ten years younger than her," commented Dolores, tapping her nose with her finger.

Ah-ha. Now I understood her ginormous, magically enhanced boobies. Still, the fact that she felt she needed to do this made me feel sorry for her and pissed at this new guy.

I sat there stunned and a little ticked off. Any man who made a comment like that and caused my aunt to feel like she needed to change her appearance was a prick, in my book. I didn't have a book, per se, but you get the general idea.

Seeing as Dolores and Ruth weren't saying anything, I decided to drop it for now. But I was going to look into this Derrick guy.

I stood and pushed back my chair. "Okay, well... I've got work to do. So I'll see you later." Which was true. I had three customers waiting for their romcom book covers. I'd stayed up late last night working on them. They were really good, and I was proud of them. Getting my creative juices flowing would definitely lower my blood pressure.

Although, I could think of something else that could help reduce my stress. Something big and strong with eyes that could light me on fire just by looking into them.

Marcus.

Marcus naked.

Marcus naked, kissing me, and rubbing his big manly hands all over me.

A grin spread over my face as I walked out of the kitchen and climbed the stairs to the attic. I could already feel the loss of tension, though my lady bits were thumping just at the thought of some sexy time with my wereape.

With a stupid smile on my face, I pushed open my bedroom door.

"What the—"

A woman with red hair and red eyes, who was no mere woman at all, sat in one of my chairs.

"Hello, my little demon witch. Miss me?" said Lilith, the goddess of hell.

Oh… crap.

CHAPTER
2

What does a witch do in the presence of a fierce goddess? She starts blathering like a fool.

"Lilith? What? In my room? How did you get in here? The house? Where have you been?"

Lilith inclined her head and smiled. "Everywhere. Done everything... and everyone."

Yeah, gross.

The goddess looked like I'd seen her last in the basement when she'd left Dolores and me to deal with the Rift. The thirtysomething woman had long waves of glorious red hair that shimmered like it was on fire. She wore a black leather ensemble with tight leather pants tucked inside knee-high boots and a bustier top under a short black leather jacket. I had to admit, she had style.

She lounged back in the chair with a glass of red wine hanging lazily in her hand. I caught the scent of her perfume, something rich and spicy and lovely.

"A bit early for wine. Isn't it?" Fear and mistrust rose so fast, it was giving me a headache.

Lilith's eyes sparkled. "It's never too early for wine, dearest."

When I realized I hadn't moved yet, I willed my legs to take me closer to her. "What are you doing here?" If she was here to kill me, that was it. I wasn't naïve enough to think I could fight a goddess and win.

Lilith sipped the last of her wine, and when I blinked, her glass had vanished. "I heard you were looking for me. Well. Here I am." She crossed her legs at the knee, bouncing her right foot.

I took another step closer. I didn't know if goddesses could read people's minds to see if they were telling the truth or not. If she could, and I lied to her, she'd probably kill me.

So I opted for part of the truth.

"I felt responsible for your… escape. I wanted to make sure you wouldn't harm anyone. I get it. You were in that prison for a long time. You were pissed. I'd be pissed too. But I had to make sure you didn't seek retribution on the innocent." There. I'd said it. All I had to do was wait and see.

Lilith's brows rose in surprise, and she leaned forward, her eerie red eyes pinning me. "You did, did you? How interesting. And why would I, as you say, *seek* retribution on the innocent?"

I swallowed, feeling my bowels churning. "I know about Lucifer." Her eyes blazed with a cold, violent rage, and for a second, I thought she was about to burn me on the spot like she did the Sisters of the Circle. When she didn't, I continued. "I know he put you in there. Doesn't sound like a very nice guy."

Lilith looked away for a moment. "He wasn't always like that. He was a gentleman once upon a time. Treated me like a queen, as he should. He was the most beautiful male I'd ever seen. Clever. Fierce. Powerful. Complicated. He was my match in every way." Her red eyes were full of hate and back on me. "And then he betrayed me."

The room buzzed with energy, the temperature dropping by a few degrees. A furious fire burned in her eyes, cold and unforgiving.

A sudden surge of magic sent sharp pricks along my skin, like hundreds of tiny needles.

Instinctively, I drew up my will and focused on Lilith, on the magic emitting from her. She almost seemed to be covered in magic, invisible to the eye, as though the magic was in her blood like us witches, yet different.

Magic *was* her.

And the words from my father came back to hit me. Lilith was the first witch.

Her magic was way out of my league.

I released my hold on my magic. "You should divorce him." I had no idea if gods and goddesses got divorced. Maybe they just killed each other off and considered it an annulment. "Castration? That's always a winner." I smiled at her.

Lilith blinked.

Awkward. "Um. So… how did you get in here? Davenport House is protected from dem—beings from the Netherworld. Just curious how you were able to slip through."

A smile spread over Lilith's face. "You mean your tiny witchy wards? That can't keep me out, Tessa darling. Nothing can."

Yeah, I really didn't like that. "What have you been doing all this time—apart from the sex stuff. Where do you live? Do you even have a place of your own?"

Lilith stood up and I took a step back. I'd forgotten how tall she was. "I have a penthouse in New York City. Love that city. I can find males by the dozen willing to satisfy my sexual appetite at any time, day or night."

Nice. "And what else?" Lilith was a horny goddess, but she wasn't stupid. I was pretty sure she was up to something—planning her revenge and gathering new followers, no doubt. Creating new covens. Sisters of the Circle take two? I was sure of it.

The goddess walked over to my bed. "Aren't you full of questions today? This is where you had sex with that beautiful male of yours. He knows how to pleasure you. Doesn't he?"

Heat rushed to my face. "I'm not talking about that with you."

Lilith laughed and, to my surprise, crawled into my bed, fully clothed.

That goddess was a weird one.

It gave me the courage to ask the one question I'd been dying to ask. "Are you here to kill me?"

Lilith laughed, and it was troubling how natural it sounded. "Of course not, silly. Why would you think that? You need to invest in better quality sheets. What is this? A polyester mix? Oh no, no, no. You can do better than that."

A frown crossed my face as I felt my tension easing, but my heart was still thumping along like I'd run up the stairs. "So, if you're not here to kill me, why are you here? I doubt you came here because you heard I was looking for you when you could have sent an email or a text." I could be wrong, but I had the feeling the goddess was sufficiently up to date with our technology.

Lilith spread her arms over my pillows, closed her eyes, and moaned. "I'm here to make sure you don't forget the favor you owe me. I will collect, you know, little demon witch."

"I'm sorry, what?"

Lilith grabbed the pillow next to her and sniffed it. "You know, saving your life. Not killing you. That."

"I don't remember agreeing to this. All I remember is you leaving us alone to deal with the Rift." I realized as the words escaped my mouth that it was the *wrong* thing to say to a goddess.

Her hand moved. Some unseen force jerked my body still until I couldn't move as though I'd been turned to stone. Oh shit. This was bad.

When my eyes focused on hers, they flashed a ripple of reds, and I felt the force of her mind, her will, glide past my defenses and into me. I strained, trying to fight it, but it was like trying to push water up a hill. Nothing to struggle against, nothing for me to focus upon.

I couldn't do anything. Not even my ley lines or my demon mojo could save me. And she knew it.

I stood helplessly against the invisible solidity of her power, which she'd imprisoned me in.

Strangely enough, I should have been frightened, scared out of my mind, but I wasn't.

I was angry. A fool, yes, but I couldn't help it. Goddess or not, I hated bullies.

I felt a sudden release and I could move again. My breath came in with a ragged gasp as her power lifted from me.

Okay, so she was powerful and could kill me with a wave of her hand. I'd have to watch my big mouth around her.

I let out a breath, trying to calm the storm of emotions welling in me. "So what's this favor? You're a goddess. You can do anything you want. Why me?" Whatever it was, I knew I wasn't going to like it.

Lilith pulled herself to a sitting position on my bed. "I'm not going to tell you yet."

"Why not?"

"You're not ready."

I wasn't sure what to answer. "I'm not ready?"

Lilith cocked her head to the side. "Would you ever consider loaning me your male?"

I think my eyes bugged out of my head, and a sense of deep possessiveness overwhelmed me. Images of Marcus and the queen of hell bumping uglies rose in my mind. "What? Are you kidding? I can't do that. No way. Are you out..." Yeah, I had the smarts not to finish that sentence, though the sharpness in Lilith's eyes told me she knew what I was about to say.

I stood for a beat, waiting for her to bestow her wrath on me, but she didn't.

Lilith watched me, her expression unreadable. "Really? Not even for me? Not even for the one who saved your life?" Her red eyes gleamed with that mischief I'd seen before.

"Uh... *I* saved *you*. Remember?" I gritted my teeth. "Marcus isn't a plaything. He's a person. And my boyfriend. I'm not about to lend him out for sexual favors." Weird how I was referring to him like I owned him.

Lilith let out a puff of air, looking disenchanted. "How disappointing. There aren't that many males with that amount of perfection in this world. He is quite rare. Wild and strong. And I'm sure he's just as strong and wild in the bedroom. Am I right?"

I could feel my cheeks burning with my embarrassment and irritation. "I don't think we're at a stage in our friendship for that kind of sharing." I didn't think I'd ever share my intimate moments about Marcus with her. I didn't even talk about it with Iris, who was my closest girlfriend. Some things were supposed to remain private.

At that, the goddess perked up. She looked at me for a beat too long, which was uncomfortable. "Maybe you'll change your mind. I can wait. I'm a *very* patient goddess."

I seriously doubted that, but I wanted to steer the conversation away from Marcus. "You're really not going to tell me what this favor is?"

"No."

I sighed. "Does it involve a certain king of hell?" I didn't want to get tangled with something that would draw the attention of the demon leaders in the Netherworld. They'd tried to kill me once. I really didn't want them to start up again so soon.

"Are you worried about your little secret getting out?" asked the goddess, reading my thoughts.

"I thought I might take a break from all the wanting-me-dead business."

Lilith grabbed the other pillow, mine, and smelled it. "You better go," she said, letting it go. "They need you downstairs."

I glanced over my shoulder, expecting to see one of my aunts, but the door stood ajar, empty. I turned back around. "How do you know?"

Lilith raised a brow.

"Right. Goddess and all that."

Her face spread into a brilliant, dazzling smile. "Exactly."

This was a great excuse to be rid of her for a while, though I didn't know how long she planned on staying. I walked over to the door. "Guess I'll have to introduce you to my—"

When I looked over my shoulder, Lilith was gone.

"She does that a lot."

I climbed the stairs, thinking of what I was going to say to my aunts about Lilith. I knew they'd be upset at the notion that the queen of hell was in Davenport House, uninvited, and had managed to get through their defenses. Dolores, especially, remembering how she had glared at me when I was about to release Lilith into this world to save her.

"You guys need me for something?" I stepped into the kitchen to find my aunts huddled around the kitchen island, staring down at something. It occurred to me that Lilith knew what this was about and had decided not to tell me. She was a strange one. I couldn't figure her out. And this favor of hers didn't sit well with me.

If said favor involved her spending time with Marcus, I might have to kill her. And die in the process.

I joined them and saw the cue card in Dolores's hand. "A new job?" Excitement rang through me at the prospect of work, the magical kind.

"It is." Dolores removed her reading glasses and rubbed her eyes.

I angled my head to try and read the card, but the writing was too small from where I was standing. "From your collective frowns, I'm guessing it's not what you were hoping for. How bad is it?"

"The worst," mumbled Ruth, her forehead wrinkled to match the frown on her mouth. But something in her eyes looked a lot like sadness.

My gaze flicked to each of them in turn. "Now I really need to know what kind of job this is. Does this have to do with the pie festival? Is this Gilbert again?" I was going to strangle that owl shifter if he'd decided to remove my aunts from participating in the festival. I couldn't care less, but it was clearly something they enjoyed and wanted to be a part of.

"It's not Gilbert," said Dolores. "It's a case."

"We haven't had a case like this in thirty years," said Beverly, as she tried and failed to pull her blouse down to cover her belly button. She yanked down hard, only to be hit in the face by the girls.

I bit the inside of my cheek so as not to laugh. I leaned forward, wanting to grab the card and read what it said, but I didn't have to.

"We need to go to Pine Forest," informed Dolores, grimacing with her upper lip quivering.

I placed my hands on the cold, hard marble surface of the island counter. "The small wooded area next to Sandy Beach?" Though I'd never been to that small patch of forest, I knew where it was, seeing as it was so close to the beach.

Dolores nodded. "That's the one."

"Okay," I answered, my heart hammering with the suspense.

My tall aunt swallowed, which looked painful. "But you need to be prepared."

I dipped my head. "Be prepared for what exactly?"

Dolores let out a long sigh, her face twisting into an agonized grimace. "Because teenagers have been found dead, their bodies torn apart."

CHAPTER
3

The drive to Pine Forest from Davenport House was about ten minutes. Seeing how distraught my aunts were at the concept of these dead teens, I didn't complain when Dolores sat in the driver's seat, nor did I complain about how fast she took her corners, sending Ruth and me sliding in the back seats like we were on waterslides.

Dolores drove the old Volvo station wagon down the main road and then wound around Lakeshore Drive, past the big houses and the sprawling estates that looked out at the Atlantic Ocean. Rows of fruit trees were in full blossom, their white and pink flowers standing out against the dark brown of their branches. We twisted through tall trees and rolling hills down to the shore.

I bounced in the back seat as we hit a patch of gravel before driving deeper into the forest that bordered Sandy Beach. The dirt road wasn't large enough for a two-car lane and I wondered what Dolores would do if we came face-to-face with another car.

But then the road widened somewhat, enough to park a car along the road and leave enough space for another to get through, which was precisely what we did. Two SUVs were already parked in such a fashion. I recognized Marcus's burgundy Jeep Grand Cherokee parked behind a gray vehicle.

Dolores pulled in behind Marcus's Jeep, and we all climbed out.

"This way," ordered the tall witch as she pushed her way through trees and shrubbery toward some unseen path.

I looked over my shoulder. We were deep in the forest, so I had no idea how Dolores knew where we were supposed to go. But seeing as Ruth and Beverly filed in behind her without question, I did as well.

As soon as we broke through the first line of trees, I saw the path. It was rough, and anyone could have missed it if they weren't looking, but it was definitely a path.

Flat stones lay here and there, but it was primarily hard-packed dirt. The path took us under a long line of oak and ash trees, the branches reaching low and tugging on my hair in places. After two minutes, the path became more apparent, clearly laid out as a route and not some wildlife path.

Beverly's heeled ankle boots crunched under last year's leaf fall. The rest of us all wore flats. I had no idea how she could manage without falling on her face. The woman was a walking, high-heeled miracle.

The deeper we went, the darker it got, and it felt more like it was late in the evening instead of barely 9:00 a.m. I pushed some branches out of my face and kept on the bit of path I could see as Dolores led us deeper into the woods.

After three minutes of lumbering through the trees and bushes on our barely-there trail, we came into a clearing. Light rose around us. The density of the forest thinned, and we stepped into a clearing of tall grasses.

Just as we came into the clearing, I heard voices talking in hushed, urgent tones.

"It looks like witchcraft," accused Jeff, one of Marcus's deputies, in his familiar deep voice.

"We don't know that for sure," came Marcus's voice next.

Witchcraft? Why were they talking about our craft with such accusation in their tones?

But when we got closer, I understood why.

30

The clearing was about twenty feet in diameter, and the sun shone down on us, illuminating the crime scene like a beam of light on a theatrical stage. Yellow police tape circled what looked like a small campfire, and I could make out bundles of clothing. Well, they looked like bundles, but I had a feeling they weren't.

Dolores yanked up the tape and passed under it. Then she held it up for the rest of us. We all clambered under the tape and stepped carefully forward.

I met Marcus's gaze, and he gave me a tight-lipped smile. However, I saw no warmth there, nor in his eyes. Instead, his handsome face was marked with ire along with a troubled expression in his gray eyes as he glanced away quickly.

Next to him were Jeff and Cameron. The hulking wereape deputies stood with their hands on their hips, mirroring Marcus's troubled expression, but I also saw the same accusation on their faces that I'd heard in Jeff's tone. I didn't like it.

I took another careful step forward and swept my gaze around the scene as my aunts all spread out. I flinched as the air intensified with a sudden raging, cold energy that I wasn't familiar with. My witchy instincts flared. All my warning flags were sailing into a thunderstorm. Someone had definitely used magic here.

31

My eyes tracked around slowly, and I froze as every bone in my body chilled.

In the middle of the clearing lay a stone circle.

Dark maroon spills and splatters covered the ground. Blood was everywhere. A severed head was propped against a rock, partly hidden by what I guessed was a dark hoodie. I didn't see much blood next to it, though I noticed a dark puddle. Most of the blood had been absorbed by the ground, which told me this happened a few hours ago.

I spotted an amputated arm next, followed by a leg, then three other legs, and a larger lump, which I presumed was another head next to another set of severed arms.

There was so much blood.

From what I could tell, we had two bodies, two victims. But that's not what had the hairs on the back of my neck standing on end.

Writing withered across the surface of the stones in the circle in runes and sigils that looked familiar but weren't Latin. Even in the daylight, I could still clearly see the wave of blue energy flowing through the runes and feel the power buzzing through them like electricity through high-voltage cables.

I knelt next to one of the heads. I wasn't sure why I did that, and I regretted it as soon as I did.

The young man's face was a mask of horror, frozen in time, as though in his last moments he'd endured insufferable pain, so much that his features had immobilized in that way.

I heard Ruth's intake of breath and looked over as she was inspecting what I knew was the other head.

Straining to keep the nausea at bay, I joined her and looked down at the head. Another young man with his screwed-up face mirrored his friend's in perpetual fright.

Bile rose in the back of my throat. These were just kids. Teenagers. No more than fifteen or sixteen years old.

Whatever magic had been used was still here residually, but it was still quite powerful. Which was odd. Judging from the beer cans around the fire, this happened last night, hours ago.

"Thank you for coming." Marcus stood before me, his eyes narrowed and unblinking. There was a definite hard edge to his tone.

"Of course." Dolores rose from examining one of the severed legs. "It's part of our job to investigate possible magical malpractice and abuse of power."

"More like a slaughter," said Beverly as she tugged her coat free from a fallen tree stump. Unfortunately, none of her spring coats fit her new, um, chest area, so she had no choice but to borrow one of Dolores's trench coats. She was drowning in it, the hem dragging on the ground behind her like a cloak and catching on the dirt and twigs.

I couldn't help but notice that both Jeff and Cameron were fixed on her chest, I wasn't sure if they enjoyed the view or were puzzled at the sudden increase in her upper region.

"The evidence points to some kind of ritualistic *séance*," said the chief as he gestured to the obvious stone circle. "The runes and the way the stones are laid out. From what I can see, the bodies were not cut with any kind of manufactured weapon, like a sword or a knife. The wounds appear to be cauterized but not like any I've ever seen. Any light you can shed on this would be appreciated." A muscle feathered along his jaw, and I could tell he was uptight, anxious.

Ha. They thought witches were responsible for this. I doubted it, but I could be wrong. I wasn't an expert when it came to all things witchy, and there were some seriously twisted witches in the world. Like the Stepford witches for one.

The question was, if this was the work of witches, why kill two teen boys? Lots of reasons, that's what. They could have drained their blood to use as blood magic, offered the boys' lives to demons in exchange for more power, and lots of other twisted reasons.

"Do you know these boys? Are they local?" I asked him, searching his face. Boys... because they were just boys, and their parents were about to be heartbroken.

Marcus nodded, and I noticed how pale his face was. "Jace Deschamps and Cedrick McCormack," said the chief, and I saw Jeff and Cameron stiffen, scowling.

My heart gave a tug. "You knew them."

"I did," answered the chief. "We did. Both these kids are werewolves. They were good kids. They didn't deserve to die like this." His face reflected pain and anger, born of guilt and grief. His body shifted, and I could see the strain of trying to keep his temper, his animal, under control. He looked like he was about to beast out and go hunting for these killers. So did Jeff and Cameron.

I wasn't sure if the fact that the victims were werewolves was essential or not, but I made a mental note anyway.

"This whole mess screams demons to me." Beverly's face was dejected as she stared at the head of one of the teen boys. "It's unfortunate, but kids are always playing with trying to summon a demon. They might have summoned a Greater demon, thinking they could control it."

"I hate to admit it, but what she's saying could explain what happened here," I answered, casting my gaze around the crime scene. "These runes are strange to me. I don't recognize the writing on the stones, but this could be a summoning gone terribly wrong." Though what I should have been doing was

35

snapping pictures and sending them to Iris. She was the real expert in demon summoning, being a Dark witch.

I took out my phone and started to take pictures, first the runes and then the bodies. We'd need these for reference as well.

With her face twisted in concentration, Dolores pressed her hands to her hips; her head dipped as she surveyed one of the severed legs.

"But demons usually rip apart their victims," answered Dolores. "Using magic to sever their limbs doesn't seem to fit. Demons are usually enraged at being trapped in a circle. So once they escaped, they would have torn them apart, not spread them out neatly. Very odd."

True. What Dolores said made sense. "If not demon, then what?"

"Stand back!" announced Ruth, her eyes wide as she pulled her hand from her leather satchel and flung it in the air, sprinkling the crime scene with a shower of pink dust.

A boom blasted and echoed around the clearing, like the crack of a rifle. And then the dust fell, covering the crime scene in a sea of pink powder.

"What's she doing? She's contaminating the crime scene!" Cameron moved forward, just as Marcus grabbed his arm.

"Let her work," he said. Cameron backed down, though the frown on his face said he wasn't very pleased with Ruth's methods.

The pink dust glimmered and then turned dark red before disappearing completely. I had no idea what that meant.

"And?" I asked, knowing this was one of Ruth's magic dust scanners for residual magic. Though it was still strong enough for us to feel it, maybe Ruth's dust could pinpoint what type of magic had been used.

Ruth wiped her brow, leaving a long smear of pink dust on her forehead. "It has all the elements of a magical undertaking," she said. My lips parted as the line of pink dust on her forehead shifted to a blue, then a white, then a yellow.

"What do you think it is?" I asked, still watching as the dust on her forehead peeled itself off and began to float around her head in a circular motion, making it look like she had a halo.

Ruth was silent for a moment. "It's Earth magic."

Huh. That was a surprise. For something that caused this kind of devastation, I would have guessed Dark magic or even Black magic. But Earth magic?

"It's Earth magic," repeated Ruth. "But it's not like any kind I've ever felt before."

"Why do you say that?" Dolores eyed her sister.

Ruth wrinkled her face. "I'm not sure. It's just... different. And really powerful."

I didn't need Ruth's dust to tell me that magic like that took a lot of skill, gathering and focusing on raw Earth magic in one place enough to sever a limb. Or powerful spells performed by amateurs. Magic this strong could be a dangerous business in the hands of someone new to the craft.

"Is it possible that they did this? To themselves, I mean," I asked and felt Marcus's attention snap to me. I knew it wasn't what they wanted to hear, but I was going to play out all the possibilities. And one was that these kids might have made the unfortunate discovery of playing with magic that was way beyond their skill.

"I don't see how," answered Dolores. With a twig, she lifted an empty beer can. "They were drunk. I don't see how either of them could have conjured magic of this magnitude while inebriated."

"Well, that's just it," I told her. "Because they were drunk, maybe they screwed up the spell work."

"She has a point," agreed Beverly, still tugging on her coat.

Ruth was shaking her head. "No. These boys are too young. It would take years, maybe even a lifetime to harness this kind of Earth magic. No. Someone did this to them. Their faces…" Ruth swallowed like she was having a hard time with what she wanted to say next. "Look at their faces. It's all in their faces."

She had a point there. They looked like they'd been tortured and died in severe pain. "Okay. So who did this?"

I looked at Marcus, who was looking at me like I had the answer.

And then something that Dolores had said about the body parts being spread *neatly* came to me again.

I'm not sure what possessed me to do it, but I found myself moving away from the crime scene to the very edge of the clearing. A moss-covered boulder sat next to a fallen tree stump. My boots slipped as I climbed it, about four feet off the ground, and looked back.

"Holy shit," I breathed, staring at the scene with my heart hammering against my chest. An icy wave of revulsion hit me as my stomach lurched, sending bile up into my throat.

"What?" Marcus was next to me in a blink of an eye. "What do you see?"

"Dolores was right," I said.

My aunt straightened. "I usually am."

"The body parts aren't spread out sporadically," I said as tiny shivers ran up and down my spine. "They're placed. Organized. They have a purpose."

Dolores frowned. "What are you talking about?"

39

"It's a... symbol," I said, though it really wasn't. "The limbs are placed strategically to draw up a logo."

"What? A logo? Let me see." Dolores came to my mossy rock, grabbed my arm, and yanked me right off. Yeah, she did. I was too surprised to resist, but I doubted I'd have the strength to stop her.

"You're strong," I said, partly laughing and partly irritated as my aunt clambered up the rock with Marcus lending his arm.

"Man hands," said Beverly with a shrug. "She takes after our father."

Dolores blinked a few times. "Oh my. Oh my dear. This is unusual and truly disturbing."

"What is it, Dolores?" asked Ruth. "You have to tell us."

"It's a smiley face," I answered before Dolores could. "The limbs are spaced out to make a smiley face."

A twitch ran through Marcus's face as though the gorilla in him wanted to bust its way out. I saw the rage and the storm of emotions brewing behind those beautiful gray eyes as the chief reflected on what I'd just told him. Basically, someone had most definitely killed these two boys and thought it amusing to take the time and arrange their body parts into a giant smiley face.

Ruth pressed her hands to her eyes and shook her head. "I can't look. I can't look." I didn't bother to tell her that she'd already looked and worked the crime scene.

Marcus's gray eyes searched the grounds below, but he didn't say anything for a long while.

"Whoever did this, it looks like they enjoyed doing it," he said finally. "A really sick individual." Bloodlust flooded him, and rage flashed in his eyes. With a single massive exertion of will, he regained control, though the muscles in his face and neck kept bulging. Damn, he was scary.

"But who could be this evil? This twisted to do such a thing?" asked Beverly, fear and anger flashing in the backs of her green eyes.

If only I didn't know.

Because I did.

I knew of only one person in this world who would derive great pleasure from torturing mortals and then take her sweet time to make a smiley face.

Only one being was that demented and crazy.

And that was Lilith.

CHAPTER

4

"And you believe Lilith did this?" asked Marcus, scowling in disbelief. He stood in the kitchen back at Davenport House with his arms crossed over his chest, staring down at me with tension crawling over his face as I sat at the kitchen table.

I let out a breath, a sinking feeling sucking at my insides. "I do. It's her."

I could have chosen *not* to tell anyone about my suspicions that Lilith was behind the murders of those boys. I could have just played dumb in case I was wrong. But what I'd learned over the past few months was that it didn't do me any good to keep secrets—from Marcus or my aunts. It never ended well.

"This is all my fault," I said, exhaling long and low. "The dead boys are my fault. They're dead because of me. I should have never let her out. Never. None of this would be happening."

Guilt hit, so hard that I felt my gut churning and Ruth's buttermilk pancakes threatening to come up.

My thoughts flashed back to the crime scene. My heart sounded loud like a tolling bell, and I hadn't been able to stop it from thrashing like that since we left the woods. I could never unsee the way the body parts were placed in a sickening smiley face. So wrong. So very wrong.

All because I had let her out of her cage.

My world had halted then, and I slipped through its stillness, frightened and full of culpability of my actions.

I was a fool.

"But Dolores would be dead," said Ruth, giving me a weak smile. "You did what any of us would have done. You can't blame yourself for this. This isn't your fault."

Ruth was the sweetest person I knew, and I truly believed she meant it. But it didn't matter. I was responsible for those deaths. Me and me alone. I had the single most crucial ingredient coursing through my veins that enabled all of this to happen—my blood. I was the only one who could have released her from her prison. I was responsible.

Which is why *I* had to put her back in.

"And why do you think this was her?" asked Beverly, lines etched across her forehead. "We haven't heard a peep about the goddess, not since she disappeared that morning when you closed the Rift. And that was months ago."

Here it comes. "Because I saw her. Just this morning. She just popped into my bedroom like it was a totally mundane thing to do. Like she was an old girlfriend, and it was completely normal to have the goddess of hell pop in for a visit."

Dolores threw up her hands. "Why didn't you tell us? Didn't you think that perhaps we would want to know a goddess was in our house!"

I glowered at her, not appreciating her tone, but it didn't stop the frown on her face from reaching new depths. "Because we'd just gotten word about the dead teens. It kinda slipped my mind."

"A murderous goddess of hell *kinda* slipped your mind!" snapped Dolores. "This is not the kind of information that slips one's mind. It should be carved permanently inside your head."

"Well, it did. No need to rip my head off."

"It explains the unusual Earth magic I sensed," informed Ruth. "How strange. I never thought the queen of hell would be using Earth magic. I'd assumed she'd be using the Netherworld's magic. What did she look like?" asked my aunt, scrubbing a pan in the kitchen sink. "I've always wondered what a goddess would look like."

I stared at her. "Umm… the same, I guess. Red hair, red eyes. A bit unstable."

Beverly shifted in her seat, worry stretched over her face. "Dolores. You know what this means? It means our wards are no longer effective."

"Oh no!" cried Ruth, lifting her hands and sending dishwater all over the floor. "She can come inside!"

"She's already *been* inside, you half-wit," snapped Dolores. "The wards were put up against demons and other lesser supernatural entities. It never occurred to me that we'd have to make it god proof."

"God*dess*," interjected Ruth, smiling. "She's a girl." But her smile vanished at the sight of Dolores's intense frown and the vein that pulsed between her brows.

"Can we add to the wards to keep her from coming back?" asked Beverly, a faint throb of anxiety pulsing through her voice. I wanted to mention that I didn't think any type of magic could keep Lilith out, but this time I chose to keep my mouth shut.

Dolores tapped the table with her finger. "I'll have to hit the books. Some wards can protect us or perhaps shield us from deities, but they are extremely complex. It'll take days to come up with something and that's *if* it's going to work."

"Tessa. Why did she come here to see you?" Marcus's voice was even, but I could still sense the worry hidden there. "Why in your room alone and not with your aunts?"

His voice sent tiny shivers down my spine. I loved that he was worried about me. "She came to collect her favor. Well, not collect as in *this* very moment, but she came by to remind me that she would. And soon."

Marcus let out a long breath through his nose, muscles popping along his neck under the collar of his jacket. "What kind of favor are we talking about?"

I shrugged. "The horrible kind, obviously. I doubt she wants me to do her laundry. When people ask for favors, it's usually because they don't want to do it themselves. So... your guess is as good as mine."

Marcus watched me, his gaze so intense that it nearly made me look away, but I didn't. "Why would this... Lilith... kill two boys and then arrange their limbs like that? For what reason?"

I shook my head. "For the simple reason of being able to do it. She told me she was the best at torturing mortals. She loved doing it. Because

I think she's just that evil and crazy. She's been locked up for over a thousand years. She's enraged, probably insane. And now she's taking it out on us."

"But why?" said Ruth. "We've never done anything to her. You saved her. She should be thanking you, not killing these poor boys. I don't understand why she would do such a thing. It's out of character."

Dolores raised a skeptical brow. "Because you know her so well?"

Ruth clamped her mouth shut and made a face at Dolores.

"Unfortunately, I do." I waited until I had their full attention. "According to my father, Lilith was unjustly imprisoned by her husband, Lucifer. He was jealous. She was getting more powerful than him and had the love of their demons, their people." I relayed most of what my father had told me and hit all the major points, at least the ones I could think of at the moment.

"So, he locked her up and threw away the key," commented Dolores as she nodded.

"He did."

Dolores's eyes met mine. "And you didn't think of mentioning this bit of information to us?"

Here we went again. "I didn't think it mattered," I answered. "I never thought she'd be back. I didn't think I'd ever hear from her again."

"You were wrong," said Dolores pointedly.

"Yeah. I can see that. I don't know why she picked Hollow Cove to start her revenge. But she did. She's angry. She's lashing out. And she's doing something that makes her feel better."

"By killing two boys," said Dolores.

"Yes. This is what she loves doing, apparently." It didn't make me feel any better saying it out loud, but at least they were all up to speed with what I knew.

The tension rose as the silence stretched, and we sat caught in painful silence for a minute or so until Marcus broke it.

"You think she'll stop at these two, or is she going to continue?" asked the chief.

I'd been pondering that on the drive home. I swallowed, not liking what I was about to say. "I pray that I'm wrong, but I have a feeling she'll continue. Like she has a beast inside of her that's out of control. I… I don't think she's going to stop."

"Then *we* need to stop her," announced Beverly, her face alight with fire at the idea of fighting back.

"I agree," said Dolores, "but how do we go about doing that? She's a goddess. And a crazy goddess. That's a combination for disaster."

I had to agree with Dolores on that note. My gut clenched at the image of the dead boys' limbs spread out into a smiley face. She was one sick bitch.

"First, we'll have to find her *before* we even think about stopping her." Dolores narrowed her eyes in thought. "Tessa? Do you know where she is? Is she staying here in Hollow Cove?"

I shook my head. "I don't know. She mentioned a place in New York City. But she could be anywhere." She could be right here in Hollow Cove as well.

"What about Lucifer?"

We all looked at Ruth.

Ruth shrugged and said, "Well, he put her away once. Can't he put her away again?"

I hated that what Ruth said made sense, but I wasn't sure getting involved with the king of hell was a good thing. Maybe he'd asked for a few favors too.

Dolores leaned back and crossed her arms over her chest. "You mean to say that you wish we'd contact Lucifer? And what? Invite him to tea?"

Ruth pressed her lips together, her cute face pulled into a frown. "Maybe he'll be thankful to know where his wife has gone. He's worried about her. He'll come and get her. I'm sure of it."

49

Dolores waved a hand. "He stuffed her in a jail cell because she bested him. I don't think he locked her up for love."

"I've been locked up for love," said Beverly, a seductive smile on her face. "I make a gorgeous, willing prisoner, handcuffed to the bedposts. Blindfolded is better."

"I think Ruth's right," continued Dolores after a moment. "Let him take care of this. She's his wife. His problem."

I doubted Lilith would see it that way. "She won't go so easily, though," I said, not believing I was going with this. "Not a second time. Not when he probably tricked her the first time."

Dolores was rubbing her eyes. "Wait a second. Just wait. We're talking about Lucifer, the creator of the Netherworld. The king of hell. The last I heard when a witch tried to contact him… well… he didn't."

"What do you mean?" I asked.

"Lucifer killed him. All that was left were his clothes. What I do know is that he hates all mortals. If we tried to contact Lucifer, we wouldn't live to talk about it. It can't be done, not without catastrophic consequences."

"What about your father?" asked Marcus, and I looked at the concern on his face. "Could he not advise Lucifer? Tell him where she is?"

"It doesn't work like that. He's never met the guy, god, whatever. Besides, my father was part of a faction that was trying to find and rescue

Lilith. He was on Team Lilith. I don't think he'd want to tell him."

"He will if we tell him what she's done." Dolores eyed me. "It's like you said. She's been locked up for over a thousand years. She's not the same goddess that she was, that he knew. Your father has ties to this world. I don't think he'll like what she's been up to. What if she comes for you next?" She gave me a knowing look. "You tell your father, or I will."

I cocked a brow. "I'll tell him, but I'm not making any promises."

"I should go," announced Marcus suddenly. He'd been reticent this whole time, too quiet, and I hated not knowing what he was thinking.

I pushed my chair back and stood. "You're leaving?"

The chief nodded. "I need to alert the parents. Jeff and Cameron brought their bodies to the morgue. We know who they are, but they still need to be identified by their parents." A mix of emotions twisted his face, his posture tight with stress.

I touched his shoulder. "I'm sorry you have to do this." I was glad Marcus didn't have to pick up the body parts, but it was still horrid, especially for Jeff and Cameron.

"It's the part of the job I hate the most." His gaze moved over my aunts. "Let me know if you find out anything else."

51

"We will," answered Beverly, her eyes flicking to each of her sisters.

"I'll walk you out," I said as I joined the chief.

Together we walked down the hallway, my aunts' voices lost in murmurs. When we arrived at the door, he turned around, his body tense and his gaze fastened on my face.

"What are you going to tell their parents?" I asked, my heart starting to pound again.

"That we're still investigating what happened. I can't tell them that a goddess killed their sons for no reason. I need more to go on."

I nodded. "You're right."

Marcus's gray eyes searched my face. "This isn't your fault. You know that. Right?"

I didn't say anything. I didn't want to lie. Not to him.

He leaned forward with a low murmur in his throat. "I'll call you later." He dipped his head and kissed me. It was quick but enough to send heat pooling in my core as he nibbled on my bottom lip before pulling back.

A small smile played in his eyes with a hint of desire, but he looked tired.

I waved as he got behind the wheel of his Jeep and pulled away from the driveway.

The chief knew how to kiss—no doubt about that—the kind that sent your panties and your lady bits scrambling for breath. But that wasn't why my pulse was racing.

Guilt would do that, combined with the knowledge that Lilith was going to strike again. Because she would. But I *was* going to stop her before she did.

Still, the question remained; how did I stop a goddess?

CHAPTER
5

"You're awfully quiet."

I looked away from the window to find Iris staring at me. "Sorry? Did you say something?"

Iris smiled. "You're miles away. Far away."

"In a galaxy far, far away," added Ronin, checking his hair in my dresser mirror. He picked up a small jar of pomade that Beverly had given me. "Is this any good?" He opened the jar, sniffed it, dug a finger in it, and then ran it in his hair.

I slipped my phone back into my jeans pocket. "I was just thinking about Marcus. About how he has to tell those parents that their kids will never come home."

I'd texted him several times, but I hadn't heard from him since this afternoon. I couldn't even imagine what he was going through. Losing a child must be the worst thing that could happen to a parent. If I had a child, and someone had done this to them, I don't think I could go on living. I took comfort in knowing that Marcus wouldn't reveal all the gruesome details. He might have to eventually, but now wasn't the right time.

"I wouldn't want to be him right now," said the half-vampire as he put down the jar of hair pomade. "But I'd kill for his hair."

"The two of you have been getting close," said Iris, and I turned to see her smile widening. "You're always together. You're like a married couple." She had a twinkle in her eye.

I laughed, thinking that she and Ronin were always together as well and that they were most likely more the "married couple." "Yes. We have gotten closer. It's nice. Really nice to finally have someone in my life mature enough to have a real conversation. No more childish tantrums. No more arguments about why men don't do the dishes or laundry. All these years, I've been missing out on what a relationship with a real man is supposed to be. It's a wonderful thing. Plus benefits."

Iris laughed. I knew she was happy for me. Hell, I was happy for me.

The truth was I had no idea a catch like Marcus would even be interested in a broke, thirtysomething who had to move in with her aunts so she wouldn't live on the streets.

Over the past few months, Marcus and I had gotten even closer. I spent most of my nights over there when I wasn't working, which in a way, was kind of like I had moved in.

And, of course, the more time we spent together, exploring each other—getting to know all of our quirks and faults—the more I was falling for him. Neither of us had used the L-word yet. But it was coming. I could feel it.

Iris moved to one of my chairs. "So, you said she was sitting here." She turned around. "And then went in your bed? She actually took off her clothes and climbed into your bed naked?"

Ronin grunted. "How come I always miss the good parts?"

"No. I mean, yes." I shook my head. "No, she didn't take off her clothes. Yes, she climbed into my bed, but fully clothed." I moved to my bed, remembering the goddess's wicked smile as she sprawled across my sheets. "She smelled my pillows. Actually sniffed them. I'm telling you, she's mad."

Iris made a face but didn't comment. Instead, she yanked out what looked like a magnifying glass from her bag, but instead of one single glass component, this one had three, and the glass had a yellow tint to it. She mumbled a few words that I couldn't catch and leaned over the chair, her face an inch from the chair's headrest as her magnified eye slowly rolled over it.

"Is that a magnifying glass?" I moved closer to get a better view.

"A magical magnifier," answered the Dark witch. "I made it. It lets me see any residual magic particles left behind by a magical practitioner. Sometimes their magical DNA. Hair. Skin dander. Seeing as Lilith is the first witch, like your father says, she's magical. If she left anything behind… I'll find it."

Ronin turned and leaned his back on my dresser. He pressed a hand on his chest. "I've always had the hots for the smart ones. Isn't she sexy when she's all Einsteinish?"

I laughed at the pink that marred Iris's cheeks. "I'll leave you two the room in a minute."

Ronin growled. "Better make it quick. I'm really turned on right now."

I laughed harder as I watched Iris, on her knees now, inspecting every inch of the chair. Every so often she'd look up, only to have three massively large eyes blinking at me. That was creepy.

"I knew letting her out would eventually come back and bite me in the ass. Hard."

"And you're positive she did this?" Iris was underneath the chair on her back looking up at the bottom.

"I'm sure," I answered, hearing the guilt in my voice. I gritted my teeth, trying to keep it together. But it was hard as the images of those two boys kept flooding my mind, pictures I could never unsee, no matter how hard I tried. And I did try.

The Dark witch stood up, brushed herself off, and moved to the bed. She wiggled her fingers in the direction of the bed and raised her eyebrows suggestively. "Have you or Marcus been in the bed since Lilith was here?"

"Uh... no. Because that would be gross." The thought of doing anything but sitting on the bed fully clothed had both rage and disgust rise in me. I wanted to pour bleach all over the sheets and the mattress. I'd order a new bed from Wayfair later.

"Good." Iris climbed over my bed. Once again, the Dark witch moved her magical magnifier along the surface, over the bedsheets, the pillow—

"Got one!" she cried out happily. "No. Not just one. Three. Three long hairs. This is a good day to be a Dark witch."

I chuckled and joined her at the side of my bed. Pinched between her fingers were, without a doubt, the brightest red hairs I'd ever seen. Long, with a bit of a wave in them.

I let out some tension from my shoulders, though I could feel a tightness around my neck. This was a significant find, and my gut tightened in anticipation. "How long 'til you complete the locator spell?"

Iris had tried a locator spell months ago, but it had failed to give any conclusive information, like where the hell the goddess was hiding. We'd thought that meant she was back in the Netherworld, but knowing what we knew now, she'd been in this world this whole time.

Beaming, Iris rolled off my bed and carefully moved to my desk where she'd put Dana, her album of paranormal DNA she'd collected over the years and stored for future curses and hexes. She flipped to a blank page and placed the hairs onto a sheet. "Not long. Maybe two hours. Maybe less. But once we find her, you'll need to move quickly. She'll sense the magic pull and might think it's Lucifer, so she'll bolt. Better jump the line as soon as we have her location."

"Got it." I had no idea what I was going to say to the goddess once I found her. But I still had time to think about a plan.

"We'll use my room, all my stuff's in there," informed the Dark witch, casting her gaze around my room. "It's better that we stay out of your room for a bit, in case I need more samples. Don't wash your sheets just yet. You know, just in case. You should definitely sleep at Marcus's tonight."

I would gladly use that excuse anytime to get to sleep with that glorious wereape. "Okay, good. That should give me plenty of time to talk with my father. I want to know what he knows. Everything. The demon leaders must know she's escaped by now. It's been months. They might even have a search party out looking for her. I don't want to think about what will happen if they find her first."

"They'll kill her," commented Ronin.

I shook my head. "Pretty sure it'll be the other way around." I glanced at Ronin and pointed a finger. "Try to keep your hands off of her while I'm gone. I need her working. All those vampire charms can be really distracting."

Ronin shot me an innocent look. "Me? I would never." He flashed me a smile. "I'll do my best, but I can't make any promises. What can I say? I'm a hot dude. I'm half-vampire. I'm programmed for lovemaking. And not the one-minute kind... the two-hour kind." A smile curved over his clean-shaven features, turning on those vamp charms.

Iris's face turned bright red, and I looked away before she saw that I noticed. Iris was a lucky gal.

"I just hope I find her in time before she goes out and does this again," I said, wanting to change the subject.

Iris closed Dana and looked my way, her pretty features creased in thought. "You think you can reason with her? I mean... she is a goddess. Why should she listen to you, a mere mortal?"

Right. Good question. "I don't have a choice. If I can figure out why she's doing this, apart from just being crazy, maybe I can convince her to stop and negotiate with her. I'll probably owe her another favor."

That wasn't the smartest thing, negotiating with deities, but I was out of options. I didn't want to have more dead teens on my hands. Whatever we were going to do, we were going to do it now, before Lilith upped and killed more kids. I couldn't live with that, knowing I was responsible. It was too much.

Iris's brow furrowed. "Remember what happened when you offered a favor to the Soul Collector?"

"It turned out okay. Didn't it?" I answered, remembering the giant clusterfuck I'd gotten myself into. I'd aged prematurely into the ripe old age of eighty, and the rest of my life had been owed to Jack, the Soul Collector demon. Yet, in the end, it had turned out okay, and I'd made new friends. "Maybe I'll get lucky again this time."

"She might just kill you like she did the Stepford witches," said Ronin, his face serious.

I sighed and scratched the top of my head. "I know," I said, letting my arms fall. "I've thought of that. I'm hoping to catch her in a good mood." If I were a hot male, it would have brightened my prospects. As a female, I had a fifty-fifty chance she wouldn't squish me like a bug.

"And if you can't?" asked Ronin. "If you can't make her stop? Then what?"

I let out a breath, shaking my head and knowing this was a possibility. Why should Lilith listen to me? I was nobody to her, just another mortal, except that I had released her from her cage. "Then we move on to Plan B."

Ronin blinked. "Which is?"

"We trap her."

The half-vampire stared hard at me. "You want to *trap* her? You want to trap a goddess?" he said incredulously.

"Yes. That's what I said. It's been done before, and I'm not talking about what Lucifer did to her. Or maybe I am. Look. I've read that you can trap a god." I just didn't remember where I'd read it.

Ronin placed his hands on either side of my dresser, his head low but his eyes level with mine. "You know as well as I do, summoning and trapping midsize demons is extremely dangerous. And now you want to trap a goddess? Do you know how crazy you sound?"

"A bit."

A scowl pinched Ronin's brow. "It won't work. She's going to kill you, Tess. And she'll kill Iris if she's there with you."

"I'm hoping it won't go that way." But it really could. Lilith had gone mad because of the years she'd spent imprisoned. If she got wind that I was planning on trapping her, in whatever means I could use, she'd most definitely kill me. Possibly my entire family. Possibly the whole town.

"It's going to work," I said again, trying to convince myself as much as Ronin.

Ronin took a deep breath, tension pulling his shoulders tight. "You're going to work a crazy, complicated spell you've never done before, to trap a goddess, no less, and hope you'll get it right the first time? How the hell does that work?"

When he put it like that, it sounded foolish. "That's the plan." If Ronin was reacting this way, Marcus would react worse. Way worse. I was not looking forward to that conversation.

The half-vampire crossed his arms over his chest, looking as angry as I'd ever seen him. "I won't let you," he said, shaking his head. "I won't. It's too risky. I won't let you risk your life for this." A wisp of fear tightened the half-vampire's eyes, his gaze darting from me to Iris.

"You know how well I respond to orders." I pressed my hands on my hips. "And because I know you care about Iris and me, and you're just worried, I won't punch you in the face." I raised my hand to stop his comeback. "I'll be careful. And you never know. It might not come to that. Maybe I *can* convince her to stop. I might not have vampire charms, but I can be persuasive." Cauldron help me if it didn't work.

"Your father can help, though. Right, Tessa?" I pulled my eyes from Ronin. Iris slipped Dana into her shoulder bag and wrapped the strap around her neck. "You think your father knows how to trap a goddess?"

My heart gave a pound and then settled. It was the only thing we could think of. There was no way any of us had the skill or magic level to kill a goddess. I didn't even think it was possible. Trapping her was our only option. It was a stupid one, but it was the only one. Right now, I had to go with stupid.

"I'm pretty sure if anyone knows how to trap a goddess, my father would know. Or at least point me in the right direction. I'm pretty sure we're not the first ones to try it. I know I've read about this somewhere. I think it was in one of Dolores's books. At any rate, I think it's a spell. So it might be just a question of getting the right spell to work, the right incantation, the right runes and symbols, and whatever else we might need."

"I still think this is a bad idea." Ronin's scowl deepened.

Irritation welled. "If you've got a better idea, let's hear it? No? Nothing? Let's not get all worked up about something that hasn't happened yet. We'll focus on finding her first, so I can try and speak to her. At the very least, talk some sense into her. If that doesn't work... then... we move on to Plan B."

I felt my phone vibrate in my pocket, and I pulled it out to see a text message from Marcus.

Marcus: *Sorry. The parents are here. I haven't had a moment to myself. Very sad. If you have a chance, stop by so I can get your opinion on something. Wait for me in my office.*

I texted back.

Okay.

I felt kind of stupid writing just "okay," but what else was I supposed to say? I didn't want to sound insensitive when that was the exact opposite of how I was feeling. But even from his text, I could tell he was a mess. He'd never dealt with something like this before, not with kids, and it was tearing him apart.

"What about Lucifer?" asked the Dark witch.

I shrugged. "Apparently he's really hot."

Iris gave me a pointed look. "Are you going to ask your father to try and get the word out to Lucifer that his wife is here and doing what she's doing?"

I jerked as Ronin clapped. "Yes, yes, yes," said the half-vampire, enthusiastically. "That's exactly what you're going to do. Get your father to tell Lucifer. It's perfect. Let him deal with his crazy-ass wife. Why should it be your problem?"

"Because I let her out." I took a breath and said, "I don't think Lucifer is going to be thrilled to speak to the father of the one who let her out. If Lucifer finds out that I was involved, I'm not sure how well that's going to go for my father. Or me. What if he decides to kill me instead because I ruined his plans?"

"I hadn't thought of that," Ronin said shortly.

From what I'd been told, there weren't many half-demon witches. Hell, I was pretty sure I was the only one, which explained why Lucifer chose the type of spell that only the impossible could unravel. He never thought it would be possible. Never imagined that one day, I would come along.

I knew then in all certainty, that Lucifer was most definitely looking for me. Swell. That was even a worse conversation to look forward to.

It was bad enough that I'd let the queen of hell escape her prison. Now I had the king of hell looking for me. Awesome. My life was thrilling with adventures.

I tried to keep it together, but tension had me wire tight. "Even if my father can somehow speak to his lordship of hell, we still don't know *where* Lilith *is*. She's not stupid. Crazy, yes, but not stupid. She'll anticipate this and won't make it easy for any of us, Lucifer included, to find her."

"Which is why this helps," added Iris, tapping on her bag.

I really hoped she was right.

I rechecked my phone. Unease rattled my rib cage. "It's almost five. I should go before Marcus closes the office."

"Okay then." Iris moved toward my bedroom door. "I'll start. Should be ready when you get back."

Ronin pushed off my dresser. "You're not going to see your demon father? I thought this whole thing was to get his advice?"

I moved to my walk-in closet and grabbed my short black leather jacket, pulled it on, and wrapped a scarf around my neck. As soon as the sun set, it got chilly in April in Maine. "It is. But I need to see Marcus first. Won't take long. He's with the families now. I just want to check on him."

I would jump a line to speak to my demon father, but right now my wereape needed me.

And he came first.

CHAPTER

6

"This way," said the sexy blonde, turning her head around as she swayed her hips. An amused, dangerous smile played on her pretty mouth. I didn't like it.

I also didn't need directions to the morgue since I'd been there on several occasions, so I certainly didn't need Allison's help in finding it. But the damn gorilla Barbie insisted, and I was not in the mood to argue. I might just accidentally kill her. Not that she'd be missed. Not by me.

Marcus's ex-girlfriend had weaseled her way into an HR job in the chief's office, hoping to get closer to him and get her gorilla hands all over the chief. I'd hoped Grace, Marcus's administrative assistant, would have fired her incompetent ass by now, but I wasn't so lucky.

Waves of blonde hair hit her mid-back and bounced off her fitted black blouse tucked neatly into her black pencil skirt that covered her tall, high-heeled boots. I really didn't get the pencil skirts that seemed to be her wardrobe of choice. She had no choice but to walk with short, quick strides to match my normal walking pace. She walked like she had a stick up her ass. I could lend her my broom if she wanted.

Not only did she look ridiculous walking in that, but she also couldn't fight in that, let alone run if she needed to. If she fell over, I didn't think she could get back up on her own, and I was tempted to test my theory.

Together we moved through a hallway in the basement level of the Hollow Cove Security Agency. To the left stood a pair of double doors with the word MORGUE painted in large, black letters on the right one.

As I headed in that direction, I realized Allison didn't slow her tread and was leading me past the morgue to the room at the end of the hallway. I'd never been in there before, which was clearly not the morgue.

As she kept walking, I sneaked to the left and pushed through the double doors. Cool air hit me with the stink of disinfectant as I stepped into the sizeable lab-like room. The morgue was equipped with stainless-steel counters, topped with gleaming, sharp medical tools and devices.

Heart thumping, my eyes settled on the two stainless-steel autopsy tables in the middle of the room. Two white sheets covered the boys' body parts. I couldn't see them, but I didn't have to. We didn't get a lot of dead bodies in Hollow Cove. I knew it was them.

"What are you doing?" came Allison's voice from behind me.

I turned, irritation bubbling up. "Shopping for milk. What do you think I'm doing? I'm checking the bodies."

She raised her chin importantly. "You're not here to check the bodies."

That was news to me. "So why am I here, then? Marcus texted me that he needed my opinion on something." The something being those poor dead boys. "He also told me to wait for him in his office."

"I was instructed to bring you to him as soon as you arrived. Hurry up," she hissed, clearly not intending to answer my question. "Marcus is very busy today, as you might know. Or are you so selfish and self-absorbed that you can't see the pain he's in?"

"Keep it up, and you'll soon find out what size boot I wear," I snapped and hauled myself out of the morgue.

"I don't know why he even allowed you to come here." She kept on blabbing. "You shouldn't be here. This area is restricted for employees only."

"Then you shouldn't be allowed either since you're not a real employee."

Allison halted. The frown on her face when she turned around was pure evil, which made me smile.

"I *am* a *real* employee, have been for the past four months," she seethed.

God, she was so easy. "Keep telling yourself that and maybe it'll come true."

The wereape's jaw twitched, and when I saw her hands balled into fists, my belly did a happy dance.

"Temper, temper." I smiled, knowing that wereapes had tempers that matched their strength. I made a show of looking at her fists. "If you attack me first, I'll have no choice but to defend myself. I might even have to kill you. Go ahead. Please attack me. Please. Please. Please."

Allison scoffed. "I'm resistant to your magic. You can't kill me."

But my demon mojo could. I kept smiling but said nothing. She must have seen something on my face because uncertainty flashed across hers.

"Give it up," I told her. "Marcus picked me. Not you. I win. You lose. Grow the hell up and find yourself another man." Clearly, this female was delusional. Enough was enough.

Allison's face was unreadable. "Nothing lasts forever." She spun around, walked to the closed door at the end of the hallway, knocked twice, and pushed through.

"Marcus," called Allison as she walked in like she owned the building, which I knew she didn't because Ronin did. "Tessa is here. The *witch*."

I followed Allison into a well-lit room with pale-green walls and tall plants nestled between two gray couches. On the couches sat two couples. The men's shoulders were nearly as broad as Marcus's, and one sported a shaved head, while the other had long, black hair tied in a low ponytail. They were burly, built like they spent most of their free time at the gym and then went back for fun. They reminded me of Jeff and Cameron. They sat at the edge of the couch in a predatory manner, like they were getting ready to pounce.

The women were more petite in size but fit and lean with red, teary eyes. It was obvious they'd been crying, and both had crumpled-up tissues in their hands.

Judging by the light wrinkles around their eyes and thinner cheeks, I guessed both couples were in their early forties. The scent of wet dog and the thrum of paranormal energies pegged them as werewolves.

Marcus sat in a chair opposite them, and his gray eyes frowned at seeing me. My eyes swept across his body as he stood and then approached. Every inch of him was stiff and tense.

"Tessa? I asked you to wait in my office."

I frowned, and my eyes flicked to Allison, who gave me a winning smirk. It was tough not to go over there and slap that banana-loving face, but I stayed where I was. I didn't want to disrespect the grieving parents.

I'll get you for this, I told her with my eyes.

The bald male rose very slowly, his muscles taut and body angled slightly forward and low. If I didn't know any better, it looked like he wanted to tackle me. What the hell was going on?

"Jeff said witchcraft was involved with killing my boy," growled the bald werewolf, muscles popping on his neck and a vein throbbing on his forehead. "Only a witch could kill him like that. That's what he said. We all smelled the magic on our boys."

Ah. Now I got it.

The females from the other couple, the darker of the two, jumped to her feet surprisingly fast. Her lips curled in a predatory manner. "I can smell the witch on her. Is she involved? Did she kill my son?"

"What's going on here?" I said, feeling like I'd just stepped into an ambush.

I understood Allison's winning smile and choice of "*the witch*." She made it sound as though I had killed those boys. And by the murderous gleams that reflected in the parents' eyes, they thought I did.

The other two werewolves followed their pack's example and stood, poised for the attack on yours truly.

Well, I wasn't about to let them tear me apart. I pulled on the elements around me, keeping them close. A witch had to protect herself. A wave of cold energy rippled through my core, and the demon mojo in my veins wanted out. That was a huge no-no. If my demon mojo got out now, I'd be hung from a noose by these people.

I didn't appreciate that Jeff was spreading rumors that witches were involved with the killing of those boys. If the rest of the werewolf community believed it, we'd have a full-on war between the witches and the werewolves.

The male with the ponytail growled. "She's pulling some magic. Look at her. She's going to spell us."

"She'll be dead by the time she utters a word," said the largest female.

"If she killed my son," snarled the bald male, "she deserves the same fate." Huge muscles bulged on his shoulders and arms, splitting the seams of his shirt. He was about to beast out.

Shit.

My gaze flicked to Marcus. His face had gone from handsome to feral. A dangerous

MYSTIC MADNESS

expression creased his beautiful features, and his posture remained confident and strong, holding a fit of repressed anger. They'd just threatened his mate, his girlfriend.

Was it wrong that I was kinda turned on by Marcus's protectiveness? Probably.

I had no doubt Marcus would fight them if it came to that—a contest of brute strength with the wolves against the gorilla. Could he beat all four of them in their werewolf forms? I didn't know, and I didn't plan on finding out.

This was not going well at all. I didn't want to slap Allison anymore. I wanted to kick her in the throat.

"Take it easy, Ed," growled Marcus, though his reasonable voice had no effect. "Tessa's not involved. Everyone… just calm down."

"Witches always believed they were superior to us," commented the small female, her large canines showing. "Because of our animal side, they think we're beneath them. They think we're beasts, that we should be kept as slaves."

Whoa. This conversation was going nowhere fast. My heart pounded. "That's not true. Witches and werewolves live together peacefully." Well, it was true for my part.

The smaller female eyed me, tears running down her face. "Did you kill my son? Did you do it?"

My throat was nearly too dry to get any words out. "I'm sorry about your sons. I really

75

am." I couldn't very well tell them that I wasn't involved or that I was directly responsible for their deaths because I was. In a way, I did kill them. At least, that's how I felt.

Whatever she saw on my face made things a hell of a lot worse.

Her mouth parted, and a feral growl that had the hairs on my arms standing on end rolled through that woman's throat. Who knew someone that small could make such a loud noise?

Her jaw fell open, exposing sharp teeth. She spoke a single harsh word I didn't recognize before charging forward.

A power word formed on my lips.

In a blur of astonishing speed, Marcus was in front of me. He pushed the small female back with a single motion of his hand.

"Don't," he said in a low warning growl that had me hold my breath. "Don't do it, Marge."

I moved to the side and looked around Marcus's broad back.

Marge was hissing like a mad cat, and for a second, I thought she was about to slash Marcus with her exposed talons or take a bite out of his jugular. But then she stepped back.

I'm not sure why, but at that moment I glanced over at Allison. She stood with her back against the wall, her arms crossed over her chest with that same winning smirk on her face.

"How can you protect her?" cried Ed. "If she's so innocent, why does she smell guilty?"

I frowned and inconspicuously sniffed my armpit. "You can smell if someone is guilty?" If I wasn't so scared, I might have been impressed.

"See?" said Ed. He took a deep breath, his muscles tight with controlled rage. "She just admitted it. She's guilty of something."

"Guilty of being stupid," I mumbled, though it came out louder than I expected. The bigger female took a step forward, her entire body shaking as a low growl rumbled in her throat.

I focused my will as my power spiraled through me. The pressure of keeping it there felt like a force pushing against the inside of my forehead.

"Down, pooch," I said to the female. "I don't want to hurt you." I really didn't. But if she attacked first, I'd have no choice.

"She's a witch," hissed the ponytailed werewolf. "She's not one of us."

"Why hasn't she been arrested?" cried the other female. "Is it because she's your girlfriend? Is that why you're protecting her?"

The muscles on Marcus's back shifted and tensed. "You know it's not. I need you all to calm down. I know this is difficult, for all of you, but let's not start throwing blame where it doesn't belong. It's just going to make matters worse."

"What are you not telling us?" pleaded Marge. "If you know something, you have to tell us."

I couldn't see Marcus's face, but I knew him well enough to know it was strained. It was his job to protect the people of this town, his pack, if you will, and now he had two dead boys on his hands.

The fact remained. Even if Marcus told them the truth, it directly implicated me. If I hadn't let Lilith out of her cage, their sons would still be alive.

"Tessa. Get. Out." The command in the chief's voice sent tiny shivers rolling up and down my spine.

He didn't have to tell me twice. I should have never come here. I should have listened to my gut and stayed in his office.

Ponytail Guy pointed a finger at me. "It's not over. You'll pay for this."

Yup. I probably would. But right now, I needed to get my ass out of here.

"I'm sorry," I said again, though I knew it fell on deaf ears.

My legs felt like they were made of cement as I willed them forward and out of the tiny room full of werewolves, who wanted to make meat cakes out of my flesh. I didn't even bother looking at Allison, though she would get what was coming. That was a promise.

The tension of holding my magic without a release was making my head spin. Though one thing was clear.

I had to get rid of Lilith. And I had to do it now.

CHAPTER
7

I jumped a ley line as soon as I'd made my way out of Marcus's building and hit the pavement.

My body sped forward in a howl of wind and colors as energy rushed through my head, my body, everywhere. Houses and businesses blurred. I kept pushing, wanting to put as much distance as I could between the Hollow Cove Security Agency and me.

As soon as I was surrounded by forests, I pulled on the ley line and let go until I felt a sudden release. My surroundings slowed so they weren't blurred anymore, and I could clearly see walls of tall evergreens encircling me.

Then I decelerated the ley line until I was at a standstill.

"Dad? Obiryn?" I called, hating how weak and uncomfortable my voice sounded. It sounded guilty.

A moment later, a shape stepped into the ley line with me.

"Tessa? Why's your face all red? What's the matter?" My father rushed forward, his silver, luminous eyes rolling over me like he was looking for injuries.

I rubbed my eyes with my fingers. "I really made a mess of things." I sighed and then relayed the events with Lilith showing up in my room, the dead teenage boys, and the memorable reunion with their parents.

"I knew releasing Lilith from her cage wasn't smart," I said and only then noticed how wet my armpits were. Oh yeah. I was smelling all kinds of guilty. "At the time, all I could think of was Dolores, hanging there. I knew they were going to kill us either way. I don't know. I couldn't let Dolores die. I don't think I could have lived with that."

"You did the right thing." He leaned back and tugged the sleeves of his expensive, dark business suit.

"Did I? Doesn't seem like it. Seems I just made everything worse." I studied his features while he was lost in thought. "What?"

My father tapped his chin in thought. "You're sure Lilith mutilated those werewolf boys?"

"Of course I'm sure. Besides, Ruth said it was an old type of Earth magic. And you told me that Lilith was the first witch. It fits. The evidence points to her. And the fact that she's buckets of crazy says she did it. A smiley face, Dad. She's the only one who would think this was funny. You said the gods had no empathy for mortal emotions or lives. She basically told me that torturing mortals were her"—I made finger quotes—"'fun times.' She did this. I know she did."

My father screwed up his face and crossed his arms over his chest, staring at his shiny black, expensive-looking shoes. "Being locked up has changed her."

"I wouldn't know."

"She seems to be fixated on you."

"What?"

My father's silver eyes met mine. "You rescued her. I believe she formed some sort of attachment."

"Uh… no, she didn't."

"Uh… yes. Think about it. You let her out of her prison—something her followers have been trying to do for over a thousand years. And then you come along… and voila. You set her free. It explains why she's hanging around. She wants to be near you."

My blood pressure spiked. "That doesn't make me feel any better."

A smile curled my father's lips. "You're like her knightess in shining armor."

"Yeah, I don't think so."

"I'm afraid you are."

I shook my head, confused as to why my father was still smiling. "But she was gone for months. I tried to find her. Why is she just showing up now?"

"I couldn't tell you," answered my demon father. "One's mind is never the same after being incarcerated for so long. She is more of a victim than anything else. The experience changed her."

My brows shot up on my forehead. "She's *not* a victim. She's a freaking goddess."

"Who has been locked away for a very long time, unable to set herself free. And I'm certain she never stopped trying. But she was trapped."

"Speaking of trapped..." I swallowed and said, "How do I trap her?"

My father uncrossed his arms and placed his hands on his hips, reminding me of Dolores. "Excuse me?"

"You heard me. I want to trap her. I'd ask if there was a way to kill her, but I'm guessing that's a big fat no. So, the next best thing is to trap her. Stop staring at me like that. It's my fault she's out. I have to stop her. She's killing boys, Dad. I can't allow that."

My father looked away and scratched his graying, trimmed beard. "Trapping a goddess is not an easy thing to do, Tessa."

I perked up. "But it can be done. You just basically told me. And I'm *almost* sure I've read it in one of Dolores's books." I watched him a moment. "So, will you help me?"

"It's a combination of complicated magic and power. And it doesn't always work. Most of the time it doesn't, and you know what happens then."

I made gestures with my hands. "Poof."

My father nodded. "Poof."

"Trapping her is the only way. I have to try."

"You don't understand." My father let out a sigh. "It took Lucifer a team of the most powerful wizards and mages to conjure up a magical cage to trap her inside. He'd been searching for the right tools for years. The right plan. Not to mention he had to trick her into it. It's not like drawing up a few circles and runes, adding some rope, and hoping for the best. It's not that simple."

"I didn't think it would be."

My father's silver eyes pinched in concern as his face went tight. "And you need a place to put her. This trap, well, it needs to be somewhere. In the Netherworld, she was in a pocket dimension, another partition realm within that world. A secret place. You'll need something similar. Have you thought of that?"

Nope. "Yes. I have a few ideas. There's an abandoned barn just up the road."

My father frowned as he spotted my lie. "This isn't funny."

"I'm not laughing either." I raised my hands. "Okay, so I haven't thought it through all the way, which is why I came to you, so you could help me fill in the blanks."

My father began pacing inside the ley line, raking his fingers through his hair. "Lucifer might have been cunning enough to lure her into a trap once, but she won't fall for something of the same nature again." He shook his head and looked up at me. "No. I don't think it can be done."

I drew in a frustrated breath and held it. "If I can't trap her, tell me how I'm supposed to stop her?" I yelled with irritation, desperation, and all the bag of emotions I'd suffered earlier getting the best of me.

"You could just talk to her," volunteered my demon father, shaking out the sleeves of his expensive suit.

I sighed through my nose, trying to keep it together. "That's my first plan. I'm going to try and talk some sense into her. Iris is working on a locator spell right now. Should be ready when I get back."

My father nodded. "I think that is wise."

"But if that doesn't work?" I fumed, my anger fueled by guilt. "She's going to keep killing. It'll be the kids from Hollow Cove first. Then she'll get bored and move on to human kids. Then human women, men, it won't stop. She enjoys the killing. No one stops what they love doing." When my father didn't respond, I blurted, "Then what about Lucifer?" If my father wouldn't help me trap her, the husband was the next best thing.

My father's eyes snapped to my face. "What about him?"

"Well, my aunts seem to think he should know about his wife. Where she is, what she's been up to, and all that. They seem to think he'll take her off our hands." If Lilith hadn't killed those kids, I didn't think I'd ever want her husband to find her. I still didn't like it, but if I couldn't trap her, what choice did I have?

My father's expression went blank. "We can't get Lucifer involved."

I stared at him. "Why not?" When he said nothing, I pressed, "You just said I couldn't trap her, which is the only way to stop her since I doubt I can kill her. He'll come. I'm sure of it."

My father looked at me. "He will. But he can't know."

"I'm confused. Do you want Lilith to go on a killing spree?"

"No. I do not."

"It's because of me. Isn't it?" I watched my father's eyes tighten, knowing I'd been right. "He'll know I did it. He'll know I exist."

My father shifted his weight, his posture stiff with untold emotions. "We can't have Lucifer involved because he'll know *what* you are. He'll want to use you. He'll want you all to himself."

The fear in my father's voice pulled me tight. "What does that mean, exactly?"

My father looked away from me, his shoulders holding a worrying slant. "There's a reason why demons are forbidden from having relations with witches. Because the offspring are usually more powerful than them, having both the magic of demon and witch."

Damn. Now I was curious. "So… you're saying I'm more powerful than a demon?" Yay me!

My father must have sensed the change in me because he smiled. "Yes, in a way. But not all offspring possess magic from both parents. Some only show witch magic, some only demon, and others show nothing at all and could easily pass for human." He clasped his hands behind his back. "You, on the other hand, can master our power while in this world in daylight, something demons are incapable of. And you possess your witch powers, elemental magic, Earth magic, and ley-line magic."

"I knew I was awesome."

My father laughed, and it brought me joy to hear it. "You're too much like me. It'll get you into mounds of trouble."

87

I lost some of my smile. "But I don't get it. Don't they know about me already? Lucifer and his crew? Your demon leaders? They tried to have me killed. Probably will again someday."

My father nodded and sighed through his nose. "At first, since you weren't showing any magic abilities of any sort throughout your childhood and most of your young adult years, you were dismissed as a nonthreatening demon witch spawn."

"Don't think I like being called a spawn. Makes me sound like an insect."

"But then you came to Hollow Cove and began to experiment with ley-line magic."

"Ah. So I became a target when I started to work the ley lines' magic."

"Yes."

"And then Vorkan let me live because of my new demon mojo."

"Precisely." My father's eyes traveled over me. "If you make yourself known to Lucifer, he will come for you. He will recognize you as the one who set Lilith free because of your abilities and because of who and what you are. And he will *never* let you go."

"I never liked the possessive types."

"You're my only daughter, my only child," said my father. "I can't let you do this. Lucifer must never know it was you. Never."

Okay, it made total sense. "This Lucifer sounds like a stalker. Then what? What do we do?"

My father's gaze was intense. "Speak to Lilith if you find her. Try and convince her if you can." The frown on his face deepened as he said, "And I'll prepare the trap."

CHAPTER

8

Technically, I was supposed to go straight home to Iris after speaking to my father, but I had one more trip to make first. I had to make sure things between Marcus and me were fine. I'd kinda left him to pick up my mess with the boys' parents. I made things worse for them and Marcus—thanks in part to Allison. I had no idea what happened after I left, whether they'd fought or someone was killed. I just wanted to make sure he was okay before I went to meet the queen of hell.

Because I might not make it back.

I had two options. Option one, go directly to Marcus's apartment, which was above the

Hollow Cove Security Agency. Or option two, go straight to the Hollow Cove Security Agency and bitch-slap Allison. Hard choice.

What to do… What to do…

When I found myself standing on the landing at the top of the stairs facing the door to Marcus's apartment a few moments later, I knew I'd made my choice.

I dug into my bag and pulled out my keys. Marcus had given me a key to his apartment, which I used regularly. I stared at the silver key in the palm of my hand. Only this time, I didn't think I should use it.

I knocked and waited, my pulse hammering. I listened, but I couldn't hear anything. He might still be downstairs in the office, which was a problem. I couldn't go. I knew if I did, I'd lose my temper, my sanity, and this time I *would* do something to Allison. I would not be liable for my actions. Temporary girlfriend insanity is a real thing.

The tension between us had only gotten worse over the past months, though I had tried to ignore her. I even felt sorry for her at times. What she did today was unforgivable. She'd gone too far, and she was going to pay for that. I promised myself.

A second later, I jerked as the door swung open.

Holy bejeezus.

It didn't matter how many times I'd seen the chief nearly nude, nude, or ready to be nude, it was a glorious, gleaming, golden sight to behold. Hell, I needed sunglasses it was so freaking hot.

Marcus stood on the threshold wearing only a pair of jeans around his trim waist. He was shaped like a Greek statue. I knew every inch of that hard body and the sheer overwhelming strength of it. I was drunk from lust, his eyes ever seducing me.

My thoughts blanked. He oozed sex, sex appeal, sex-o-rama. How could anyone formulate cohesive ideas when such a man was in their presence? I couldn't. Blame it on my lady hormones.

Heat pooled through the rest of my body at the memory of his lips on me and the glorious feeling of his hard, rough hands running over my skin.

A frown creased that perfect visage. "Why didn't you use your key?" asked Marcus.

Because this was so much more fun. "Wasn't sure you'd want to see me."

"Why would you say that?" His voice was silky, a deep, melodious tone, and rolled over my skin as though he were touching it.

"Because of what happened with the parents of those boys." Because of what Allison pulled. "I made things a lot worse for you."

"Come in," said the chief, and I was very aware he ignored my answer.

I stepped through and watched as he shut the door. I rolled my eyes over his chest, his rock-hard abs to his wide shoulders and bulging biceps. "Okay. You don't look like you've been in a fight," I said, though it was really an excuse to admire his perfect physique.

"Nothing happened," answered the chief, "but it could have. And they wouldn't be to blame if it did. They'd just lost their sons. It messes with a person's head."

"I know," I answered, remembering the sorrow and pain I'd seen on the faces of those poor people. "They're in shock. In mourning. A lot of emotions were going around. They also wanted to kill me."

"Don't think about it too much," said the chief. "They weren't themselves."

"Easy for you to say. Why did Jeff tell them a witch was responsible? You know that's going to get out. It's not going to go well for the witches in this town."

"I know." Marcus raked his fingers through his wet hair. He really did have great hair. "I'll have words with Jeff later. But it wouldn't have made a difference if he'd said nothing. The werewolves can smell all types of magic. Jeff and Cameron did their best to remove all evidence from the crime scene, but we can't do anything about residual magic. It was all over their dead sons. Even I could sense it. The fact is, they know magic was involved."

"You still think not telling them about Lilith is a good thing?"

"I do. It'll create a wide panic if the community thinks a mad goddess is out to get them. Until I can figure out our next move, I want to keep that to ourselves." He reached out and pulled me in for a kiss.

His lips were soft and warm, and I breathed in his scent of aftershave and something musky. He pulled back and said, "You hungry? I can make us dinner."

I was ravenous. "I can't stay long," I said, enjoying his closeness. "If you can whip up something quick, I'm all yours."

The chief's eyes sparkled with a desire that had my stomach doing cartwheels. "Consider it done. Come. Let me get you a glass of wine."

I let him pull me into his kitchen. "Can't." I grabbed a barstool and sat at the kitchen island. "Though wine does sound fantastic, I need to be alcohol-free for what I'm about to do."

Marcus was still shirtless, which was how he should *always* cook me dinner, as he looked up from grabbing a wok from under the island cabinet. "What haven't you told me? And why do I get the feeling I'm not going to like it."

"Where do I start?" I laughed, though I sobered up at the concern on his face.

As Marcus cooked, I conveyed everything—from what my father just told me about Lucifer and trapping Lilith to what I was planning on doing with Iris right after I left his place.

The chief placed a hot plate of stir-fried veggies and ramen noodles on a place mat in front of me, next to my glass of water.

I looked up at him. "You're not eating?"

"Not hungry at the moment." He leaned on the counter opposite me, his arms crossed over his chest as he watched me eat. Seeing his frown deepening and his neck muscles shifting, I knew he was trying to keep it together.

I took a bite of my lo mein, and my eyes rolled into the back of my head. "Wow. You should have been a chef," I said, smiling.

"You really think you can talk some sense into her?" asked the chief, his eyes shining with concern.

I swallowed. "I'll do my best. I have to. Now that I know she's got some twisted attachment to me, she's not going to go away unless I ask her nicely and hope she doesn't kill me."

"She's a goddess," said Marcus. "What makes you so sure she'll even listen?"

I took a sip of my water and set the glass down. "I have to try because the other option is a hell of a lot more complicated and dangerous. My father didn't even think it could be done, not after she's been trapped once. It's going to be much harder to do it again."

"But he's confident he can?"

Not by a long shot. "Yes. He's working on it." I lifted my gaze, seeing the worry etching his brow. "Is that what's gotten you worried?"

Marcus's breath exhaled slowly. "That. And the fact that one day you might end up on Lucifer's most wanted list."

I cringed. "Right. That. Who knew I was so popular?" Tracking down the queen of hell to have a conversation was one thing, but having the king of hell looking for the one who set her free, to enslave possibly, was a thousand times worse.

Marcus dipped his head and was silent for a moment. "Could Ruth make a potion that'll conceal your demon blood? Like a glamour or something?"

My brows rose as I stared into those glorious gray eyes. "Good question. I can't believe I didn't think of it myself. It could work. Yeah, maybe. I'll ask her when I get back." Yes, that could totally work. It might not be a permanent fix, but if it'd keep me hidden for a while, I'd take it like a shot.

"Aren't you a clever one?" I grinned, watching the smile curl over his lush lips. It took some serious self-control not to haul myself over the kitchen island and crush my lips on his.

I loved that Marcus was knowledgeable with magic. It made our connection stronger and our conversations very enjoyable. It was refreshing to talk about other things than hockey and football.

I finished my plate and washed the last bite down with some water. "What's going to happen to the boys?" I didn't want to say body parts, and the thought of them threatened to bring Marcus's fantastic lo mein back up.

The chief let out a strained sigh. "There'll be a funeral for them. Tomorrow, I think. Their bodies will be burned and buried in the town cemetery."

I nodded, not sure what to say as I stared down at my empty plate.

"And you're going alone to meet Lilith?" asked the chief. I snapped my eyes back to him.

"That's the plan."

"Wouldn't meeting with her with your aunts be a little bit safer? According to you, she's unpredictable. Ruthless. And extremely dangerous. She might kill you."

The fear in his voice made my chest squeeze. "I know that. But I still have to try. She could have killed me that time just as easily as she killed Jemma and the others, but she didn't. I have to believe she won't. It's all I have to go on."

"It's not much." His voice held an incredible amount of worry.

"What she's done, the boys, it's my fault, Marcus. I need to do this. I can't have her killing

97

off more kids. It's hard enough to function knowing I'm partly to blame for their deaths."

"You couldn't have known she'd do this. You can't blame yourself."

"I can. I do. Listen, I'm going to have a chat with a goddess, and who knows? Maybe she'll listen."

The muscles along his jaw clenched. "I don't like it."

"I don't like that Allison has a better ass than me, but there you have it."

At that the chief laughed, the sound captivating as it moved up and down like music. I could listen to that all day and night. If I could magic his laugh into a cream and rub it all over my body, I would.

"Speaking of your ass," said the chief as he moved around the island and cleverly picked me up off the stool, his hand cupping my butt. "I've been thinking about it all day," he purred, pulling me to him as he kissed my lips and my neck.

I wrapped my thighs around him, holding him nice and tight. "You naughty boy." Heat shot through me, making me jumpy and impatient.

Something glittered in his gray eyes. "Mine." He made a noise that sounded like a cross between a growl and a moan. It triggered something deep inside me, causing my nether regions to pound. An electric burst of pleasure radiated from me at his touch.

"Not sure I have time for this," I whispered, knowing that all the times we'd made love, Marcus always ensured I was *completely* satisfied, more than once, and took as long as I needed.

"Oh," he growled, carrying me to his bedroom. "You'll have time."

My breath came in a ragged gasp as he lowered me onto the bed. "Well, if you put it that way, come and get me."

And he did.

CHAPTER
9

A stupid smile spread over my face and was cemented into place as I made my way down the stairs and shut the side door to Marcus's apartment. My blood still pounded from the mind-blowing sex I'd just had with my uber-sexy chief of the town.

A girl could get used to this lifestyle.

Once I hit the sidewalk, I checked my phone. The clock read 8:00 p.m. I'd told Iris I was coming back straight after I'd spoken with my father. That was two hours ago. I knew she'd been waiting for me, and I also knew she'd be ticked.

I was still smiling.

I walked up Shifter Lane, taking in the sweet aroma of the evening air with a spring in my step. No, I was skipping. Yes. Skipping and smiling. Trust me, you'd be, too, if you'd just spent nearly two hours of horizontal—and vertical—hippity dippity with the chief.

If I could sing, I'd break into a song. It didn't even matter that I didn't know all the words. I'd just invent them as I went.

Black windows stared back at me from the row of shops and restaurants that lined the central downtown core of town. The townspeople were long gone, either having dinner or just finishing up. An orange cat ran across the street, but the road was otherwise still and empty.

The sky was nearly black, completely covered in dark gray clouds. The nearby streetlamps left most of the surroundings covered in darkness and shadow. Leaves from a tall maple rippled in a breeze. Soft, cold drizzle hit, and I blinked through a misty fall of rain.

I was still smiling.

I passed a parking lot, empty except for a metal garbage bin behind the Hairy Dragon Pub. Something stirred in the shadows.

"The cat has a friend," I told myself and kept walking, my smile never fading. If there was such a thing as "the longest-lasting smile award," I was going to win it.

As I strolled by, the gathering darkness rushed in to fill the spaces where the streetlights couldn't reach. I caught another flicker of movement across the darkened parking lot and turned to see a shadow retreat behind a tree.

"Way too big to be a kitty."

Curious, I stepped off the sidewalk and made for the parking lot.

A scream filled the cold night air, followed by a few strangled exclamations that riddled my skin in goose bumps.

"Stop! Please don't hurt me. No, no, no!" screeched a voice, a young, teenage male voice.

I clenched my fists. "Lilith. Damn you."

I acted without thinking and started to run toward the scream, sprinting across the lot. I pulled on the elements as I ran. I was an idiot. I knew Lilith's powers outmatched mine, but maybe I could distract her enough to stop killing more boys, so we could have a chat.

Figures appeared at the end of the parking lot, just beyond the light of the streetlamps. As my eyes adjusted to the darkness, I could make out one lying on the ground with two others hovering next to it.

I felt a cold haze of energies that accompanied a supernatural being when it came into the mortal world, disguised until now by the darkness of the parking lot and cool night air.

I skidded to a stop when the figure on the ground leaped to his feet, tall and fit and not looking harmed in any way. His build, with broad shoulders, like the others, pegged him for a man, not a boy.

Thick dark robes fell over their shoulders, splattered with dirt like they'd been dragged in the mud, and cowls hid most of their features. The parts I could see were unremarkable, neither attractive nor ugly. Not sure how well they could move in those robes, but whatever.

Energies and the vibrations of magic hit, a cold transition of power and a shift in the air that had nothing to do with the wind.

Magic was here. And lots of it.

The hair on the back of my neck prickled. "You're not Lilith. Unless one of you is? Lilith? Is that you under there? You sneaky little minx." I forced a laugh, but it came out sounding like I was constipated.

Nope, these guys were demons. And by the looks and feel of them, they were mid-demons, the powerful kind, like Vorkan. But unlike the demon hit man, these hadn't come alone.

This was an ambush. Were these Lucifer's guys? Probably. Shit. How had he found me so quickly?

A blast of cold terror struck me like a mallet, and I strained to keep the panic from showing on my face. "Well." My pulse throbbed with my demon mojo. "How nice of you to ruin a perfectly good night."

The middle demon stepped from his band of friends, his dark eyes pinned on me. His face was narrow and sour with the voice to match it. "Lilith?" he questioned with a slight accent I couldn't place, and I could tell he sounded surprised.

"Yeah, you know. Red eyes. Red hair. About yay tall," I said, gesturing with my hand above my head. "The queen of hell? The dame of night? Mistress of darkness? I'm assuming it's why Lucifer sent you. Right? Payback?"

Payback maybe, but I knew the real reason why Lucifer had sent his goons. They were going to take me to him.

Not going to happen.

I scanned the demons' faces as they leered. They were savage, cocky, and looking for blood. Mine.

I thought about tapping a ley line and getting my ass out of here. But judging by the number of differential levels of energy in the air, they'd probably disabled my ability to tap into a ley line, just like Vorkan had. I didn't want to waste my energy or any valuable time testing that theory. Any mistake I made now, no matter how small, could mean the difference between making it out alive and ending up in the Netherworld somewhere. Maybe I'd be in Lilith's old cage.

Three against one wasn't entirely fair, but when had I ever backed away from a challenge? Never.

Maybe I had. I just couldn't remember at the moment.

The three demons moved and made a circle around me. Yeah, not cool.

I reached out to the elements around me, pulling in their energy. The power coursed into me, twirling and simmering with a quivering life of its own.

"Do my eyes deceive me," mocked the middle demon, "or are you trying to do a magic trick?"

The other demons laughed, relaxed and insulting. It came off as coordinated and natural, like something they'd done often over the years.

I smiled at him. "I don't know. Are you?"

"Females shouldn't play with power they don't understand," hissed the demon on my right with that same accent. European? Middle Eastern? His voice was slithery, almost serpentine, and creepy as hell. "They're too weak," he continued. "Too stupid to yield magic. They have smaller, feeble brains."

"Huh." I made a face. "Do you understand this?" I gave him the finger.

"You're going to regret that, bitch," snarled the same demon, the words near guttural. His hood slipped, and I could see his pointed features were twisted in a scowl, giving him more of the appearance of an animal. He was the shortest of the three, but that didn't mean he was weaker.

I shrugged. "I know. But it felt damn good. I can do it again if you like?"

The middle demon's dark eyes held mine for a brief moment. "Guess killing you won't make a difference. We'll call it a bonus."

Pissed, I shifted my weight and lowered my body, searching for a glimpse of their death blades but not seeing any. "I'm not planning on dying tonight, guy." What? I didn't have time to come up with a nickname.

"But we'll *play* with you first," said the demon on my left, his light eyes rolling over my body very slowly. It was gross, and a chill took me.

"Bring it, dementors." I called it like it was.

Unthinkably swift, the middle demon extended his hand.

I could do nothing to stop it.

I was slammed with a kinetic force similar to being hit by a car and sent backward at least twenty feet.

I hit the pavement hard and skidded another ten feet. I hissed as gravel tore away at the soft part of my hands while I tried to slow my momentum. Tears sprang up at the pain in my knees and hip. The scent of burnt hair and something else I couldn't make out filled my nose as I got up.

I wheezed as I took a breath, pulling on my magic as I did so. Cold seeped against the skin of my chest.

Instinctively, I looked down at myself.

"What the—?"

My awesome and costly leather jacket was gone, and what was left of my shirt was sizzling. I could clearly see my skin and bra through the giant, burnt holes in what used to be my black shirt. It hung off me in shreds and strings, exposing what was beneath to the elements.

Damn. The girls were practically showing. How the hell did that happen?

Laughter reached me, and I looked up to see the demons walking at a leisurely pace toward me—confident, arrogant, robe-wearing, misogynistic bastards.

And then it hit me. They were trying to humiliate and body-shame me to try and put me—little female—in my place. They were trying to overpower me by removing my clothes. They thought I'd be so self-conscious I wouldn't put up a fight.

I grinned.

These assholes didn't know me. If they thought a bit of nakedness would shame me somehow, they were more stupid than those stupid robes they wore.

Adrenaline pumping, I yanked off my still-smoking, sizzling cloth that used to be my shirt and tossed it. I straightened, sticking out the girls because I wanted them to take a good look, as the cool air sent goose bumps over my skin.

I met their eyes, smiling and giving them my version of "crazy eyes." Look at that. They'd lost some of their smiles.

"Okay. You got me," I said, making a show of cracking my neck. "I was expecting some death blades or your tendrils of black demon mojo, but I'll bite. Sure."

They walked faster. The demon in the middle raised his hand.

Heart pounding in my throat, I spun into action.

"Accendo!"

I hurled out my hand, and a ball of fire soared through the air, a perfect shot, straight for the middle guy.

Said middle guy waved his hand, and you guessed it, my beautiful ball of fire went out into a puff of smoke.

I pursed my lips. "Hmmm. So you've got skills. But… can you do this!"

This time I hurled both hands and shouted, "Fulgur!"

Twin bolts of white-purple lightning shot from my outstretched hands.

With a simple wave of his hand, the middle demon sent my awesome lightning to the left, where it exploded on contact with a tall oak tree.

Seems like these guys had a different kind of magic. I wasn't sure they were more powerful than Vorkan. Perhaps their magic was just different. The demon hierarchy clearly had many more levels that I knew nothing about.

It still didn't mean I couldn't give them a good ol' witch ass whooping.

With my heart pounding in my ears, I stepped forward. "Okay. Enough with the Jedi tricks."

Their shoulders bounced as the three of them laughed. I wasn't a threat. To them, I was just a weak, stupid little female.

"Nice breasts," said the demon on the left. I could just make out the cruel smile on his face. The others snickered, staring at me like I was just a piece of meat.

I flashed my teeth. "Thanks. Aren't they grand? Inflitus!"

A blast of kinetic force hit him in the chest. Completely unprepared, he went spiraling back and hit the ground hard, driven to the edge of the lot with a grunt of expelled air.

Not being a fool, I willed the power of the elements to me again, holding it there and readying myself for the two others, but they were just standing there, waiting.

A wave of nausea hit as the magic took payment. I stilled myself, not daring to show them any signs of weakness though my body shook under the adrenaline.

The demon on the left pulled himself to his feet and dusted off his robe. Tension quivered through him. Oooh. Now he was mad.

"Enough of these games," he said. "Kill her. Kill this maggot."

Did he just call me a maggot? I barely had time to take a breath as spells, dark and fast, shot toward me.

I plunged down and away, screaming, "Protego!" A sphere-shaped shield of protection rose from the ground, up and over my head.

My shield shook as spell after spell hit it. Through the beating of my heart in my ears, I could hear voices raised in a chant of dark and fervent tones.

I yelped as a bolt of blue lightning tore at my shield. Blue light blinded me, and a roar deafened me. The light faded just as my shield stuttered and fell.

Whoops. Now I was in for it.

CHAPTER

10

Something whistled past me, biting the sides of my face like sharp blades, and I hurled myself sideways to avoid getting spelled in the face.

Spells and hexes shot through the air like automatic magical machine guns. Who the hell were these guys? I'd never seen anything like them. The control they had on their magic was awe-inspiring. If they weren't out to kill me, I might have asked them for a few tips.

The three demons stood shoulder to shoulder, their fingers pointed at me like guns. And I shit you not, actual blue sparks shot from their fingertips.

The middle demon caught me staring and blew the top of his finger. They were enjoying themselves.

Rage coursed through my limbs as I rocked forward on my flat boots toward a metal garbage bin. Feeling the stir of adrenaline, I pitched forward and lowered myself behind it, using those precious moments to catch my breath and think up a plan to save my ass.

Trouble was, I was never really good at spontaneous life-saving plans while under attack.

I took a chance and yanked out my phone, hoping Marcus would pick up. The screen was black. Damn. The phone was dead. There went that idea.

Something hit the garbage bin. Metal tore, and the next thing I knew, the container soared in the air and out of the lot as if a giant had just kicked it like a soccer ball.

My cover was blown, literally.

Okay, Plan B. Trouble was, I didn't have one. I'd just have to improvise.

Before the demons could strike, I jumped up, my hands outstretched, slamming my will into my power word and pushing most of the painful power that remained in me.

"Inspiratione!"

It sprang to life.

Fractures of red energy blasted from my hands as I aimed it at any of the three demons.

I held my breath as I watched it hit, but it didn't. The demon on the right swiped his hand across like he was washing a window, and my red energy blackened and dropped to the ground in a pile of dark slop.

Shit. If none of my power words worked on these bastards, what the hell was I supposed to do?

Run. It was my only option at this point. Marcus's place was closest.

Giddyup.

I spun and ran straight for the alley behind the shops next to the parking lot that would take me to his place.

Something slick and dark whooshed past me. Too fast. I dove forward onto the pavement but not quickly enough. Slamming hard onto the ground, pain exploded in my right thigh.

Crap. I'd been hit.

Whirling, I clenched as pain stabbed my thigh. I looked down and saw a trickle of smoke seeping from a large tear in my jeans. A burning sensation slowly began to spread from the wound in my thigh. I felt hot and cold all at once, and a cold shiver slipped down my spine. Then a burning sensation became a more significant presence with each heartbeat.

I had no idea what spell had hit me. All I knew at the moment was pain. No way in hell could I fight with this amount of pain, let alone try to run. Okay, so I was going to limp my way to freedom. It could work.

I had just gotten to my feet as another blow of magic hit me. This time it was my left arm. Then another spell hit, the backs of my legs this time. I staggered but managed to stay up.

Now I was really, really pissed.

I turned slowly. No point in running anymore, was there? A shadow moved into my line of sight. I didn't have to look up to know it was one of the demons. Of course, he would come over to gloat and relish my pain.

"Nice legs," he said with laughter in his voice, and the other two joined him, crackling their loud laughter.

My legs? I frowned and looked down.

"Ah. Right." I stared at my bare legs. Shit. My jeans were gone.

With my adrenaline still pumping and fueling me with heat, I'd never felt the cool night air on my bare skin. I was now standing in my black bra and pink polka-dot panties (no judging) facing an immortal enemy.

But at least I had my boots.

Their laughter continued to roll off them as they advanced. It was funny how they thought being half-naked would diminish my magic or me in some way.

I straightened my fists at my sides. I wasn't ashamed of my body. I embraced my many folds, lumps, and bumps, my flabby arms, my cellulite, and my wine gut. You bet I had one.

The middle demon tsked. "Why don't you just give up? Your magic is worthless. Weak, with empty threats. You're pathetic. You can barely control it. Females have no idea what it means to yield power. You should have stopped at the beginning. Now I'm going to finish you like the maggot witch that you are."

I narrowed my eyes at him. "Yeah. I don't think so. How about you all get naked, and then we can call it a fair fight?"

The demon on the left put his fingers to his mouth and moved his tongue around in an obscene gesture.

Ew. "I think I just threw up in my mouth."

The middle demon raised his brows and said in a sultry voice, "You're not bad looking. I happen to like my females with some extra weight."

I held up my hand. "Wait. Did you just call me fat?"

"More to grab, slap, and pull," he continued, and I really thought I did throw up in my mouth this time.

I raised a brow. "And now you're hitting on me? Which, by the way, you seriously need to brush up on those skills. Still, I'm confused. Here I thought you wanted to kill me."

The demon snickered as he pulled his hands from inside his robe. "Oh yes. We will kill you. But why waste such nice female flesh."

I felt myself go rigid. My blood roared in my ears. "Try and touch me," I said, my face going cold. "And it'll be the last thing you do, buddy. Trust me. I'm an expert at castration."

He gave me a shark's smile. "Yes. You'll do fine. Very lovely."

I cringed on the inside. "What about Lucifer?" I blurted. It was the only thing that came to me. "Won't he be ticked that you didn't bring me to him directly?"

"Lucifer?" He pulled his lips into a cunning smile. "Lucifer isn't here. You're no match for us, little witch. Let yourself go. You might enjoy it."

Below his cowl, I could see the shimmering lust in his eyes. With his hands splayed, he came for me, his lips moving, and I could barely hear the mumblings of a spell.

My heart started to beat faster, trying to make up for the lack of energy. I was tired, barely holding on. Sweat trickled into my eyes, burning them. The only thing I hadn't used yet was my demon mojo. It was still very new and unpredictable, not to mention draining. At the moment, I wasn't even sure I could conjure it due to being injured. I'd been practicing with my father, but I'd never really used it intending to hurt or kill. Let's just say tonight I'd be graduating.

He came at me in a rush of black robes and spells, but I was ready for him.

Something in me snapped. Call it my witchy instincts or my primal drive to protect myself, but it brought out something deep inside my core with a vengeance. Cold surged up, and my rage pulled up with the power.

With my demon mojo awakened, I let the cold, wild magic rush through my veins, waiting to be released. And then I let go.

Black tendrils of demon energy roared forth from my outstretched fingers. I directed it at the middle demon.

For a split second, he halted, and I saw the confusion and then the fear in his eyes as he recognized that power.

Surprise!

It hit.

He shouted a few words, but they were lost as he cried out when the black tendrils wrapped around him, burning and seeping into his skin. He screamed out and collapsed to the ground. His screams echoed in the parking lot as he thrashed violently. Smoke and the smell of burnt flesh rose.

I felt the pulse of his magic stir in the air. White foam sputtered from his mouth, and more words sprouted from his lips as he tried and failed to take control of my demon mojo.

He didn't have a fancy hand move or spell against my demon mojo. Huh? If I'd known, I would have used it from the beginning. But I was still learning and making mistakes.

When he looked at me, his face was red, marred with black veins and his eyes bloodshot. "I know what you are," he wheezed, pointing at me with a black-veined finger. "I know! I know!"

No idea what he meant by that. I looked over at the other two demons, expecting them to help or attack, but they didn't. They just stood there with confused expressions.

Finally, the middle demon released a horrible scream as he thrashed around on the ground one last time. His mouth opened wide with whatever spell he thought would save him. His howl made my skin crawl.

And he stopped moving.

The demon didn't burst into a cloud of ash. He just stopped moving.

I felt movement and looked up as one of the demons pulled a glass vial from his robes.

I stiffened, thinking he was about to throw it at me.

Instead, he smashed it on the ground.

A giant cloud of blue smoke rose from the ground where the vial had broken, blinding me momentarily. I stepped back, not wanting it to touch me and coughing at the scent of something acrid.

The cloud coiled and grew until the demons were submerged under it. It only took about ten seconds, and when the cloud dispersed, the demons were gone.

All of them.

Including the one I'd just killed.

CHAPTER

11

"**W**hat happened to you? Where are your clothes?" Beverly stood in the hallway, wearing a surprised expression and a tented white T-shirt over her recently enlarged bosom. I'd never seen her in a T-shirt before, and judging by its size, hitting her below the waist, it was probably Dolores's. Her usual perfect complexion was tarnished with blotches of what looked like green and blue paint.

Then the scent of incense, candles, earth, and pine trees in the air hit me. I also felt a humming of energy, more so than Davenport House's usual magical presence. It throbbed with a steady, deep strength, as though House was on his sixth cup of coffee. Something was definitely up.

Eyeing Beverly suspiciously, I pushed the front door with my hand and heard it shut behind me. "Long story." I didn't want to add to the recent stress of Lilith killing boys in our town with the fact that Lucifer had sent his goons to either trap or kill me. I'd deal with it later.

I glanced down at my legs. My knees were raw and bleeding. So were my hands, and my elbows looked like I'd washed them with a cheese grater. I didn't have time to clean the wounds. I'd already wasted enough time.

I leaped to the entry closet, yanked out a light blue jacket, and pulled it on.

That's when I noticed the chalk-drawn ward on the wood floor between my boots. Wards were barriers of aligned energy that blocked out physical and magical intrusion, hitting that energy back upon its source. But what was it doing there?

"Uh… why is there a ward here?" I looked up, but Beverly was gone.

"Here. You're missing one. Put one right over there, and there too." I heard Dolores's voice, trailing from either the dining room or the kitchen.

Curious, I carefully picked my way around the ward and turned left toward the living room.

My jaw flapped open. "Oh. My. God."

It looked like a hurricane had come and gone. Books, papers, even scrolls littered the floor, and everything with a surface—like the couch, coffee table, and chairs—had something covering it.

But that's not what had me do a double take. The *number* of wards had my eyes bugging out of their sockets.

Everywhere I looked, wards of green, red, orange, purple, and blue painted the windows, the walls, and even the floors. Within them were runes and sigils of earth, fire, water, ice, and air. Which, if I wasn't mistaken, would deliver bursts of destructive energy about as powerful as your average grenade.

When I glanced back at the front door, green spirally wards and runes were painted on it. I'd been in such a rush to get home, I hadn't even noticed.

"Damn," I said, turning back to the living room. "You guys *have* been busy."

Through the living room, I could see Ruth balancing on a chair with a paintbrush in one hand as the other held a small cup of paint. She was painting the back kitchen windows in elegant green-swirled wards.

Below her was Hildo, sweeping his tail that was doused in red paint over the wall in curved strokes and leaving an expertly drawn red rune.

The kitchen and dining room looked just as disheveled as the living room, with upturned chairs and bowls of paint crowding the kitchen table and island.

"What is all this?" I asked, looking at the back door window with a green and red ward painted on it.

Ruth turned around, her face spotted with green paint. "We're having a painting-ward party. Grab a paintbrush and join the fun!"

I smiled. Ruth always managed to find the fun in every hectic situation.

"What does it look like," growled Dolores, not looking at me as she carefully painted another blue ward above the fireplace mantel. She stepped back to admire her artistic skills, which were pretty darn good. "Perfect. Absolutely perfect. I should be congratulated. I amaze myself sometimes."

"Here we go again," mumbled Beverly, her weight shifting uneasily from foot to foot. Either she had to pee, or her jeans were cutting off her circulation.

Dolores glared at her sister. "What's the matter with you?"

Beverly shrugged and smiled at me. "I'm wearing the wrong kind of underwear."

I shook my head. I loved my eccentric family.

Dolores sighed and glanced over at me. "This here... is a solid layer of defense. Let's see if Lilith can get through now," she said, stabbing her wet paintbrush in the air like it was a knife and sending splatters of paint on the mantel.

"Urgh. I'm feeling a cramp in my hand." Beverly leaned her hip on the side of the couch, rubbing her right wrist. "My hands aren't used to that kind of hard labor." She smiled and said, "Well, depends on the labor," she added with a wink in my direction.

Moving on... Moving on...

"You guys look like you have it covered," I pointed out.

"Of course we do." Dolores pinned her glare my way. "We're Merlins. That red-haired goddess won't take me for a fool twice." She disposed of her paintbrush and cup on the coffee table, spilling a large amount on the wood surface. Narrowing her eyes, she placed her fists on her hips. "If she thinks she can enter now without a scratch, she'll end up with the migraine of the century," she said, her cheeks glowing with excitement and her eyes gleaming with feverish glee. Dolores frowned at me, seemingly only now noticing my disheveled appearance. "Where are your pants?"

"Right. About that... see..."

"Your knees are bleeding," Dolores pointed out. "Why are your knees bleeding?"

"What's bleeding?" Ruth spun around on her chair, sending a spray of paint down over Hildo's back. He didn't even flinch as he continued tracing the wall with his tail.

"She came in wearing only her underwear," said Beverly, yanking down on her T-shirt. "Cauldron knows, I've been in that situation multiple times where I've misplaced my clothes." She giggled. "But it was usually my underwear."

My aunts waited for me to elaborate, and for a second I considered telling them about Lucifer's guys, but seeing House's present state, I decided against it.

I looked over toward the hallway. "Well, since you have the wards covered—good job by the way—I should go," I told them, turning back around. "Iris is waiting for me. And I'm really late." I started walking out.

"Late for what exactly?" demanded Dolores and I halted. "You've got that look again. The one where you're up to no good."

I cocked a brow. "I seriously doubt that. But I'll tell you anyway." I exhaled and waited to get their full attention. "Iris made a locator spell for Lilith." I raised my hand at their objections, specifically Dolores's, being the loudest. "I need to do this. I have to talk to her, or at least try. Who knows? I might be able to talk some sense into her and get her to stop before she kills anyone else."

"Maybe. And maybe not," said Beverly. "If she's as deranged as you say, I don't think she will stop."

I sighed. "Which is why I'm going to find her and talk to her. Maybe she'll listen. I mean, I think she thinks we're friends or something." I wasn't comfortable with that idea, but what my father suggested seemed to fit.

Dolores made a noise like a groan in her throat. "That's all this family needs. A mad goddess who thinks our niece is her plaything. And do you know what happens when gods and goddesses play with their toys? They *break* them. Sometimes they take the head off first," she continued, her eyes distant and unfocused like she was recalling some faraway memory. "And sometimes it's a leg or an arm."

"Thanks. I get it," I said.

"I don't think you should go." Worry etched Ruth's green-paint-splattered brow. "Dolores is right."

"I'm always right," said a smug Dolores.

I pressed my arms on my hips. "Look. I'm running out of options here. My father agrees with me. I have to try and talk to her first."

Dolores arched a brow. "You've been to see Obiryn?"

I nodded. "I have. And he thinks it's worth a shot."

My tall aunt searched my face. "You said *first*. What did you mean by that? What else is there?" Her eyes narrowed. "There's something else you're not telling us. What else are you planning?"

Damn, that witch was observant. There was no way to get out of it now. "If speaking to Lilith doesn't work, if I can't convince her, then… we have to trap her."

Dolores's face went still. "I'm sorry. What did you say?"

I let out a breath and started again, "I said that—"

"I know what you said!" Dolores waved a hand dismissively at me. "I just cannot *believe* what I'm hearing. One does not simply *trap* a goddess. Well, for one, she's a *goddess*."

"I got that part already," I answered.

"It's hard enough to try and keep her from entering our house, and all these wards might not even be enough, and you want to *trap* her?"

"What?" Ruth frowned. "But you said they would."

"Deities have more power than witches," continued Dolores, waving her hand around. "Even if you combined the power of all the witches on this continent, it still wouldn't be enough to trap such a being." She eyed me for a moment. "I don't think you could trap her in this world. No, I don't think it can be done."

"Listen," I began, "I'm not going to pretend that I know how to do that because I don't. At least, not at this moment. But my father is going to help me."

127

Beverly moved closer with faint, pensive lines between her perfect brows. "Obiryn thinks it can work?"

"He does," I said, sweeping my gaze on each of them. "Besides, it worked once. I have to think it can work again."

"I wouldn't be so sure." Dolores lowered her brows in thought. "Where does he think he can set the trap?"

I shrugged. "I don't know yet. He said he'd get back to me."

"Where will she be kept?" asked Dolores, clearly not wanting to let this go for now. "I assume you thought of a place to put her? You can't just lock her in a room or a basement."

My irritation blossomed. "I don't know yet. We still haven't worked out all the details."

"Clearly." Dolores gave me her version of the evil eye. "Your plan has many holes."

Tell me about it. I frowned at her. "You can keep arguing about that. Me? I have to go see Iris."

Before Dolores could keep pointing out the missing elements and the major flaws in my plan, I rushed out of the kitchen and headed up the stairs.

Instead of going straight to Iris's room, I made a quick stop in mine. After using the bathroom—I really had to pee—and attending to my wounds, I pulled on a pair of jeans and a black T-shirt before wrapping a short black jacket over my shoulders. I grabbed my messenger bag and stuffed my little black book, *The Ley Lines of North America,* inside.

Once I reached the second floor, I hurried down the hall to Iris's room. The door was closed. I leaned forward, listening, but I couldn't hear anything.

"With my luck, they're probably having sex," I muttered before raising my hand and knocking three times.

"Come in," answered Iris's voice.

Relieved, I pushed open the door to find Iris sitting on the floor and Ronin lounging at the end of her bed.

I joined Iris. "Sorry I'm late," I said, a little out of breath. Damn. I needed to work on my cardio. "I had a bit of a surprise with some of Lucifer's goons." No point in telling them about my quick, though very hot, stop at Marcus's place. A witch must keep some secrets.

Iris's mouth fell. "What?"

"Are you sure?" asked Ronin, sitting up stiffly.

"Oh yeah. He sent his demon buddies after me. They tried to kill me."

"But they failed, obviously," said Iris, looking frightened. "You don't look hurt. You're all right."

"For now." I rubbed my temples with my fingers. "Lucifer knows it's me. I don't know how, but he does. He knows I let Lilith out, and now he wants to use me or something. According to my father, that's what he'd want." All because of what I was.

"But you just said his guys tried to *kill* you?" said Ronin. "He can't use you if you're dead. How does that work?"

I shrugged. "I might have made them change their plans," I added with a smirk.

Ronin laughed. "I can buy that. Well, at least you're safe now."

"But they'll be back." A chill wrapped itself around my neck at the thought that the king of hell wanted to use me. I pushed it away and tried to focus.

"Then we'll just have to be better prepared," said Iris with a defiant look in her dark eyes. "They're demons. We know how to take care of demons."

"These guys were strong sons of bitches," I said, remembering the battle. "Their magic was different."

"Different, how?" Ronin leaned forward and rested his elbows on his knees.

I shook my head. "It all happened really fast. They were using some demonic spells and not the same type of demonic defensive magic I've seen demons use before. Like my demon mojo. They used spells."

"So they'll be more unpredictable," concluded Iris, which was exactly what I was thinking, "but not invincible."

I exhaled. "Let's hope, for my sake." I stared at her bedroom floor. My eyes swept over a mixing bowl stained with blue powder to the large North American map that was stretched out. "And? Any luck?" I couldn't worry about Lucifer's pals right now. I could only focus on one thing at the moment, and that was to stop Lilith's killing rampage. Then I'd deal with Lucifer's peeps.

Iris beamed up at me. "Yes. It wasn't easy, and it didn't work at first."

"It worked on the third try," announced Ronin.

Iris looked over at him, her jaw set in annoyance. "Yes. Thankfully I had enough of her hair samples to try the spell again." She glanced back at me. "I think with goddesses, their power is so strong it kept destroying the locator spell, like the magic was too powerful to reveal anything. It occurred to me that I was thinking about it all wrong. This isn't just a demon. We're looking for a goddess, and there are numerous differences. Her energy is different, more powerful. Once I understood that—"

"After the third try," interjected Ronin.

She glared at Ronin again. "I had to *change* the spell around a little to adapt it to a goddess." Her eyes met mine and she smiled. "And then it worked."

I beamed at her. "Look at you. Creating new spells. You're on your way to becoming as accomplished as Dolores. She better watch out."

Iris laughed, her cheeks red. "Well, not yet." She leaned forward on her knees, her eyes sweeping over the map, and pointed to the small ball the size of a pea resting on the map. "She's in New York City at Six Fifteen West Forty-Second Street, Apartment Twenty-Nine A."

My eyes widened, impressed. "Wow. You got her apartment number too?"

Iris raised her chin proudly. "Yup. It's a condo. I called the building manager to see if anyone had rented or bought any of the condos in the last four months. Only one. The ball hasn't moved for about thirty minutes. She's there now, but you better hurry. I don't know how long she'll stay there."

"I'm ready." After I'd typed the address into my phone—because I wouldn't remember it as soon as I left her bedroom—I yanked out my *The Ley Lines of North America* and flipped it to the detailed map of the ley lines of the East Coast. Hundreds of them, thousands, were going north and south, east and west. I spotted a few that went from Maine to New York. I'd taken the ley lines to New York City before, to stop Adan the douche from using the Elder ring, so I had some travel experience.

I glanced up from the book. "Eleven stops before I get close enough to Six Fifteen West Forty-Second Street. Okay, guys. I'll see you later." I stood and headed to the door.

"Tessa?"

I turned around. "Hmm?"

"Be safe," said Iris, looking worried for the first time since I'd arrived.

"Come back to us. Okay?" said Ronin, and my chest swelled at their worry for me. I was truly blessed with my friends.

I adjusted the strap of my bag around my shoulder. "I will. Promise."

Adrenaline pumping, I rushed down the stairs and headed for the front door where the ley line waited for me. I heard my aunts shout my name and other remarks that I couldn't make out over the roaring white noise in my ears.

I drew in my will and reached out to tap the ley line. A burst of sudden energy hit, and I could feel its vibrating energy beneath my feet, beneath Davenport House.

I took a breath, trying to steady my hammering heart and knowing this might not turn out as well as I made everyone think.

The truth was, Lilith could very well turn me to ash as she'd done with the Stepford witches. But this was easier than trying to trap her. I had to try. For the town. For the sake of those dead werewolf boys. For all of us.

Maybe this was crazy. And maybe I was just crazy enough to try it.

And then I reached out, turned the doorknob, and stepped through.

CHAPTER
12

Music pounded from inside the door, a low bass, a driving drumbeat, and loud talk mixed in the background. It was a haunting, ghostly baying type of music. Goth, maybe? Dark opera? I wasn't very familiar with that type of music. But I knew something for sure. Whoever was behind this door was throwing a hell of a party.

My eyes moved up to the black stenciled 29A. This is where Iris said Lilith was.

I wasn't surprised she'd be throwing a party, but it did put a damper on my plan of having a one-on-one chat. Still, I wasn't going anywhere.

I raised a fist and knocked. I waited and knocked again, harder this time, until I felt some pain in my knuckles.

I was just about to knock again when the front door swung open.

"You're not Lilith," I said, staring at a blue-skinned female with ram-like horns and a yellow, skintight jumpsuit.

The demon—because I didn't think she was mortal, and the scent of sulfur rolling off of her wasn't an expensive perfume—gave me a lazy frown. "Witch, I think you've got the wrong address. Shoo." She waved me off with her hand.

A few months ago, I might have done just that. Instead, I pulled on the elements around me, holding them there in case she did something stupid, like attack me.

"Where's Lilith?" I didn't wait for an invite. A tide of loud music came crashing over me as I pushed my way through.

"Hey? Who do you think you are?" called the blue-skinned demon behind me.

"I'm Batman," I answered.

I took a moment to look around. I stood in a two-story, loftlike condo. The floor-to-ceiling windows gave me a sweeping view of the city lights reflecting and dancing along the Hudson River. It had a modern flair with white walls and white leather furniture—cold, dull, and totally not me.

My skin tightened as I took in the scene. And let me tell you, it was a scene.

As my gaze traveled the length of the loft, different paranormal energies hit me. I spotted a group of men and women, werewolves from their distinctive animal scent, huddled together, their skin covered in tattoos, reminding me of Silas. A dozen or so stupidly attractive men and women sprawled on white leather couches, their glasses filled with thick, red liquid, which I highly doubted was wine.

A couple of black-eyed demons gathered near the far end of the condo. I caught a glimpse of a few faeries congregating in the kitchen. Their pointed ears gave them away. I felt eyes on me, and I turned to find the cold stare of a seven-foot-tall humanoid creature with skin like tree bark focused on me. Yikes.

It was like I'd ventured into some strange underground demon club. Everywhere I looked, the place was crowded with demons, paranormals, and humans. I wasn't familiar with the paranormal community in New York City, but seeing them hanging around demons was a bit of a shock. However, after closer inspection of the mix of weres, shifters, and vampires, I noticed a hardness to them. It gave off something foul. These were definitely more on the shady side. But I wasn't here to judge. This was none of my business. I was only here for Lilith.

The pull of darkness prickled over my skin. The air was hot, stinking of cigarette smoke, booze, and the familiar stench of sulfur that demons gave off mixed with the scent of old blood that all vamps released, wet dog, skunk, and God knew what else. The combination was making my head spin.

"You can't come in here, *witch*."

I turned my head to see the blue-skinned demon was back. She had her hands on her hips and a deep frown, like that was supposed to scare me.

I glanced over her shoulder. "Where's Lilith. I have to talk to her." My skin tingled with my magic, and I could feel the stares of a few demons. The faster I got out of this place, the better. I didn't want to fight, but if they started…

The demon laughed harshly. "*You* know Lilith?" Her black eyes traveled the length of my body. "You look like a human schoolteacher. No, wait. A *librarian*," she mocked.

I smiled. Librarians were awesome. "I'll take that as a compliment. Look. I'm not here to trash her party. I just need to speak to her. It's important."

The blue-skinned demon scoffed. "Witches. Always a flair for the dramatic."

I dipped my head. "Don't make me do crazy eyes."

The she-demon cocked her head. "I think I'll give you to the vampires. Witch blood, I hear, is a delicacy."

I clenched my jaw. "Listen, you blue asshole. If Lilith finds out I was here and I didn't speak to her… well… she's going to be pissed. And do you know what she'll do to you when I tell her that was your fault? Yeah. You know what I'm talking about."

The demon glared at me for a moment, but I could see the fear in her eyes. "This way."

I followed the blue-skinned demon across the living area and down the hallway where it opened up into a larger room. More demons and paranormals congregated here. They looked up as we entered, and their black eyes said they were ready for anything. Their nostrils flared as we neared, taking in the scent of my witch blood.

We moved into another hallway with a few doors. Finally, the she-demon stopped at the last door down the hall.

She gestured to the door with her blue hand. "Your funeral," she said with a smile and walked off.

My heart pounded as I stood there, trying to come up with the perfect speech. But truthfully, my brain always seemed to malfunction in times of stress. I'd just have to wing it, again.

I tried to listen through the door, but all I heard was the constant pounding of music blaring in the condo.

Resolute, I raised my fist and knocked three times.

"Come in," called a female voice, Lilith's.

Here goes nothing.

I pushed in. "Holy crap on a stick."

The room was huge, like three times mine and decorated with the same cold, boring white walls. The big difference was where my room was expertly furnished, this one was bare and had only one piece of furniture in it.

A bed.

The most enormous bed I'd ever seen sat in the center of the room. It was as though four king-sized beds were merged into one. How did they even make sheets for that bad boy?

Sprawled in the middle of it, under a white sheet barely covering her breasts, was Lilith.

And she was lying between four men.

Yeah, I said *four*.

Two had the large shoulders, chests, and muscles that screamed werewolf while the other two were fit and stupidly handsome. And when they smiled at me, showing off their pointed canines, I knew they were vamps.

I cocked a brow, and a smile twitched my lips. "How does that even work?" I probably shouldn't have asked that, but it was the first thing that popped into my head.

Lilith's red eyes pinned me, blazing with a cold, ageless, dangerous light, and I nearly peed myself. But then she laughed, and I felt myself relax an inch. "Tessa, my little witch-demon. This is a surprise. How did you find me?"

Uh-oh.

I waved my hand around. "You know. Witchy stuff. Um. Listen, can we talk?" I moved my gaze over the men. "In private?" I got that I was being a bit rude and pushy, and I had a fifty-fifty chance I'd be a pile of ash in the next few seconds, but I was praying that her admiration for me, or whatever we were calling it, was my ticket.

Lilith watched me as she traced the long fingers of her right hand over the chest of one of the vampires. I couldn't see her left hand, and I didn't want to know where it was.

Her thick, red lips widened at whatever expression she saw on my face. Whatever it was, she liked it. Fear, most probably.

She wore the guise of a thirtysomething woman. Her skin was a pale white, and her face was as smooth as the most expensive marble, in sharp contrast to her long, glorious waves of red hair. She could have looked like anyone, but it seemed she liked this version of herself. It was the same version I'd seen when she'd popped into my bedroom uninvited. Kind of like I was doing now.

141

"So, I sneak into your bedroom, and now it's your turn?" dared the goddess as though she read my mind. She probably could. I had to be careful.

I swallowed hard. "It's not. Really. I just need to talk to you."

Lilith watched me with eyes much older than the face that held them. "You heard her, boys. Out. Us girls need to have a little chat."

The four males did as they were told and slipped out from under the sheets.

All of them, buck naked with their mighty swords at attention.

"Damn." I turned my head, smiling as my face burned. "A little warning next time."

"Why?" I heard Lilith say. "You shouldn't be embarrassed. There's nothing more pleasing than the naked bodies of the male species."

"If you say so." I preferred just one naked male species at a time. Thank you very much.

The werewolves and vampires meandered my way, their faces shifting with sly delight at my presence. A handsome, dark-skinned vampire dipped his head when he neared me, and sniffed, taking in my scent.

"Careful where you poke that thing," I told him, trying hard to keep my gaze at eye level. "This is about as much fun as a sandpaper vibrator." At that, Lilith let out a peal of laughter.

Okey dokey.

He smiled at me, hunger and desire in his eyes, which had me wire tight and pulling on my magic.

"I can lend them to you, if you want," offered Lilith. "Marco can last all night. Can't you, Marco?"

I clamped down on my jaw. "I'm good. Thanks."

My gut tightened as they moved past me slowly, and I felt myself relax once they disappeared out the door.

I turned my attention back to the goddess. "Nice party. I never thought I'd see paranormals mingling with demons. Are they all friends of yours?"

Lilith blinked at me. "They're entertainment. I don't *do* friends. Well, unless they want me to."

"Right." That explained a lot.

"Okay, they're gone. What is it?" said the goddess. Without warning, Lilith pulled off her bedsheet and stood. And yup, she was buck naked too.

The goddess disappeared into her walk-in closet. I sighed in relief when she came out wearing a red silk robe. She lit a cigarette and lay back on the bed. She caught me staring. "What? Don't mortals smoke cigarettes after they have sex?"

I shrugged. "I guess. I don't smoke."

She took a puff and blew out shoots of smoke. "Well, it's never too late to get some lung cancer. What did you want to talk about? It better be good. Lex was just about to tickle me with his... big dipper."

Oka-a-a-a-y.

I let out a breath, trying to release some of my tension. "Just... hear me out before you make any hasty or rash decisions."

Lilith smiled lazily. "I have the relaxed patience of a well-fed cat."

More like the patience of a mountain lion. "Okay, well, just remember who got you out of your prison." I hooked a thumb at myself. "Little me. Remember that before you go cutting off my head."

The goddess took another drag of her cigarette and crossed her legs at her ankles. "Tell me what's on your mind."

With my heart hammering in my ears, I took a careful step forward, trying to decide what to start with. "I'm here to talk to you about what happened in the forest."

Lilith puffed on her cigarette, dragging in the entire thing in one inhale. "What's that?" She exhaled, shoots of smoke escaping from her mouth. Then she flicked the butt of the cigarette off to her left somewhere.

Nervous, I forced my features into what I hoped was a friendly face and not a constipated one. "The little gift you left for us in the forest? You know... the smiley face?"

Lilith shrugged, which was disturbingly ordinary and mundane. "No idea what you're talking about."

I sighed. She was going to make this complicated. "I'm not sure why you did what you did," I tried again, trying to keep my anger from showing. "They were just young kids. Barely into their teens. They didn't have to die like that."

The goddess cocked a brow. "I'm getting bored, Tessa. Get to the point or get out."

Now, *she* was being rude. "I'm talking about those two kids you killed and left on display. I'm asking you *not* to kill any more kids or anyone, for that matter. I'm asking as a favor." Shit. Guessing from her darkened expression, I didn't think goddesses liked to be told what to do or asked for favors.

"A favor?" The iciness in her tone made a tiny voice inside my head scream to turn around and jump a ley line out of here.

Maybe coming here hadn't been a great idea.

I raised my hands in surrender. "Listen. That came out all wrong. I didn't mean like *you* owed *me* a favor. I was asking you to do me a favor." Damn, that didn't sound any better. Here I went again with the word vomit.

Lilith hauled her legs over the side of her bed and stood. She walked toward me, and I had to crane my neck to keep looking at her face. I'd

145

forgotten how tall the goddess was. Barefoot, she was six feet tall or maybe taller.

Her red eyes gleamed with unimaginable power and rage. They focused on me and then narrowed. Power thrummed from her. The air shimmered and shone as it began to twist and spiral with energy.

Fear jolted me, and my heart started to beat faster. There wasn't a chance that she wouldn't obliterate me at the first opportunity. I shouldn't have come here.

Lilith shook her head at me. "You disappoint me, my little demon-witch."

"I've been known to make that happen."

"Do you know who you're speaking to?" she asked, her hands splayed on either side of her.

I swallowed. "Yes." I hated how weak my voice sounded. But the truth was, I was scared as hell. Her robe slipped, exposing one of her boobs, but I wasn't planning on saying anything.

Lilith stopped about five feet from me. "I don't think you do. Let me show you."

She lifted her hand and snapped her fingers once.

The room darkened like someone had turned off the light. Cold hit, and wind pushed the hair from my face as thunder rumbled, making my ears pop.

This is it. She's going to kill me.

I squinted as a dim light shone, giving me some illumination.

My breath caught.

I wasn't standing in a fancy New York City condo anymore. I was standing on some remote rock island surrounded by black waters, in some dim distant wasteland glinting under a pale-orange sky. Twisted, leafless trees rose between rocks.

Holy. Shit.

Screams went up, as several hundreds of mortals strung up on wires, some in cages, were being pulled and torn apart.

I watched for a moment, sickened and shocked. I remembered her saying she enjoyed torturing mortals. I wasn't sure if this was happening now, or if I was staring at a glimpse of the future or the past.

"Are we in the Netherworld?" I peeled my eyes from one of the wailing mortals, knowing I'd never forget the images and sounds.

"I like you, Tessa," came Lilith's voice, and I turned back to look at her and jerked in surprise.

She wasn't six feet anymore, more like twelve. She looked like a giant, and I was the tiny irritating mouse she was about to step on. Her robe and hair rippled in some unseen power, making her look like she was underwater.

147

"And that's why I'm *not* going to kill you," said Lilith.

"Thanks." I had no idea what else to say.

"For now," she added. Her expression went cold, and I stopped breathing. "You freed me from my prison, and it's the only reason I'm not snapping your pretty little neck."

I nodded my head. "Wise decision."

She watched me for a long moment, and I could feel the sweat drip down my temples. Then with a snap of her fingers, a wind rose and ripped around me; the lights went out again. And when they came back on, I was back in the condo in her bedroom.

Lilith waved a hand at me, sluggishly. "Go now, before I change my mind."

Without a word—because, what was the point, but mostly because I happened to like my pretty little neck—I turned. With wooden legs, I headed for the door. Shaking, I yanked it open and left.

Fear gripped my heart at the recurring thought. I'd tried to talk to the goddess, wanted to make her see reason, and failed. Lilith gave me no choice. I didn't like it, but I didn't have any other options.

I was going to have to trap the queen of darkness.

And try to survive.

Swell.

CHAPTER
13

I stared down at another smiley face of severed body parts. Only this time it wasn't the remains of teenagers. The heads were adults—one female and one male.

I'd woken to the sound of loud voices followed by the sound of a dish shattering as it made contact with the hard floor. I didn't bother brushing my teeth or putting on a bra, or pants, as I ran down the stairs to the kitchen in search of the commotion. When I reached the kitchen, I understood why.

"They've found more bodies," Dolores said as I skidded into the kitchen.

"In the alley behind the Hairy Dragon Pub," Ruth added, which was strangely close to where I'd encountered Lucifer's goons—something I still hadn't told my aunts about, though I knew I would have to sooner or later.

"She's done it again," accused Beverly.

She, as in Lilith.

I'd told my aunts and Iris of my utter failure when I jumped a ley line back to Davenport House last night, angry at the queen of hell but more at myself.

"I'm sorry, Tessa," Iris had said.

"Me too. All that hard work for nothing. It could have gone better," I'd told them, my hands wrapped around my tall wineglass as I sat on a stool at the kitchen island. "If I hadn't said favor, she might have listened to me."

"What possessed you to utter the word 'favor' to a goddess?" Dolores was shaking her head at me, disappointed.

Yeah, not my brightest moment. "It's not like I had a manual on how to talk to a goddess," I said, a little ticked. "It just came out."

Ruth reached out and patted my hand. "You did your best."

"Thanks," I muttered.

"You could have done better," Ruth added, "but it's too late to change that now."

I frowned at her. "Well. She's pissed at me. I don't think she'll be coming around to see me anytime soon."

"Maybe," said Beverly, giving me a one-shoulder shrug. "Or maybe because you made her so angry, she might retaliate sooner than you think."

Beverly had been right.

"This is Marcy Bain and Julian Huxley," said Marcus, pulling me out of my thoughts.

I glanced down at the heads, which Lilith again had used as eyes for her sick smiley face. "You knew them?" Of course he did. He practically knew everyone in town.

The chief's jaw clenched. "Yeah. Werecats. Both of them."

"I'm sorry." I wanted to ask him if they had children, but the question sort of died in my throat, constricting me. I couldn't bring myself to ask.

I cast my gaze over the crime scene. The display was the same. Each body had been torn apart with magic, and then, assuming that Lilith was just as twisted as I thought, she'd taken her sweet time placing the severed limbs in her artful display, probably while laughing.

Anger surged, and my demon mojo coursed through my veins, cold and powerful. Only not powerful enough to take down a goddess. I couldn't help but wonder if I'd made things worse. If I hadn't gone to see Lilith last night, would she have done this anyway?

"When will Obiryn give us news about trapping her," asked Dolores, her eyes on

Cameron as he carefully picked up a severed
hand and placed it in a black plastic bag while
Jeff did the same with Marcy's head.

I wondered if, other than the heads, they
knew whose parts they were picking up. Guess
they were going to separate them at the morgue.

I winced as Jeff's hand slipped, and Marcy's
head thumped to the ground. "He didn't say," I
answered, pulling my eyes around to Dolores.
"Soon, I hope. I'll reach out to him when we get
back."

"Our hopes are resting on him now," Dolores
said. I could hear the terror and despair in her
voice, something I wasn't accustomed to.

I sighed. "I know." My gaze found Beverly
standing by the edge of the alley next to
Marcus's Jeep. She kept trying to cross her arms
over her chest, but they couldn't reach. Her
arms were too short.

"It's the only way to stop her," continued my
tall aunt. "You tried and failed to talk some
sense into that monster," she said, making me
feel worse. "Yes. It's the only way now. We
must trap her."

Ruth joined us, the smell of her White
magic—pine trees and earth along with a
wildflower meadow—emitting from her. "I'm
finished," she said, looking a little flushed.
Worry lines wrinkled her forehead, the skin
around her blue eyes creased.

"It's Lilith," I told her. "Same MO. Who else could be this psychotic?" I didn't need Ruth's magic to tell me the same old Earth magic was used for these killings.

Ruth's silence was my only answer. She glanced away, looking defeated, her eyes sad and shimmering with unshed tears.

Even Dolores looked overwhelmed, her usual confident stance having more of a slouch in the shoulders. This was beyond her skills, her magic capabilities. She knew it. We all knew it.

I felt a hand brush the small of my back.

"You okay?" asked Marcus. The heat of his body was soothing and delicious as he leaned in.

I let myself fall into him, taking in his musky male scent and wishing this wasn't happening. I envisioned being somewhere with him and the only thing between us was—well—nothing.

"No. I don't think I'll ever be okay." My voice faded until it was almost a whisper. I was trying to hold it together, trying not to have a full-on freak-out moment, but damn it, that goddess was making it really hard.

"We'll figure this out," said the chief. The fact that he wasn't saying it wasn't my fault made me feel worse.

We all knew whose fault it was. Mine.

"You were right about one thing," came Marcus's voice near my ear. The feeling of his body next to mine was comforting, and I soaked it all in.

I turned so I could look up at him. "What's that?" I met his eyes, my pulse catching at the sadness I saw there. It reminded me of the vulnerability I'd seen in them that time in the basement when our auras had mixed when we got a glimpse into each other's souls. It had been an extraordinary experience, one that drew us closer until we were a unit.

He pulled his gray eyes away from mine. "That she wouldn't stop. That she'd keep on killing for the mere pleasure of it."

I didn't have anything to say to that, so I kept my mouth shut.

With a heavy heart I stared at Jeff and Cameron, their black bags heavy with the remains of those two werecats. They walked away until they reached a gray SUV and popped the trunk.

"Let's go, ladies," said Dolores, her long face grim as she turned from the scene. "Let's see what Obiryn can tell us about trapping this devil."

We had no need to stay here. We'd be much more productive back at Davenport House with glasses of wine between our hands. We did our best thinking and planning that way. Red wine *is* a superfood.

I fell into step with Marcus as we all followed Dolores down the alleyway toward the Volvo station wagon parked at the curb. Beverly and Ruth walked in silence behind us.

I felt a vibration chime through me just as the light faded as though storm clouds had suddenly covered the sky—just a little too fast.

Curious, I halted and looked up into the sky.

"What the hell is that?" I asked no one in particular.

We'd come to the crime scene under a blue sky, a speckling of clouds, and a warm morning.

But now a cold wind rose with a green horizon.

Well, what looked like a green horizon. Only this one rose from the ground in sheets of semitransparent green.

An icy wave of fear hit me, and my stomach lurched. I stared at the now-green anomaly that was slowly rising, far out in the distance, to what appeared to be circling the entire town. Energy pulsed and hummed, and I could see lightning flashing and sparking within the sheets like an electrical web.

The magic that came off it was cold, old, and just like the magic I'd felt at the crime scenes.

I spun on the spot, seeing it rise from every corner of town. The green sheets continued to grow, about a hundred feet in the air, until they were high above our heads and had come together like a giant half sphere. It was semitransparent, kind of like my shield protection sphere.

But I didn't get the feeling we were being protected.

"It's a dome?" I said, my ears popping as though the pressure had changed. "There's a dome over the town? Why would Lilith do this?" I turned to look at Marcus to see if he was just as clueless as I was as to why this just happened. But his face was hard, and the tension in his posture showed he was uneasy.

I looked at the sky, shaking my head. "This is just like her. This is her idea of a joke."

My temper flared. Lilith was the only being with magic this strong to produce some sort of magical dome or force field. I didn't know what she was planning, but whatever it was, it wasn't good.

"This isn't Lilith," came Dolores's voice, and I turned toward her at the warning in her tone, just noticing the collective fear reflecting in my aunts' faces. The three aunts were looking at each other, communicating in silence the way only tight siblings could.

"This is bad. Really, really bad." Ruth looked around widely, a terrible dread in her eyes. She wrapped her arms around her middle like she was cold.

"How did they find us?" Beverly's face was tense and tight with fear. "I never thought they'd come for our town."

Dolores clenched her jaw. "They have. They did."

I gave Marcus a sidelong look and then glanced at Dolores. "Who's they? What are you not saying? If this isn't Lilith, then who?"

"Dolores?" Marcus's tone was urgent, and I recognized that rage and anxiety in his eyes, like a trapped animal. He swept his gaze from the dome to my tall aunt.

Dolores's eyes were fixed on the green dome. Finally, she turned to me and said, "Only one group is capable of this."

I shrugged. "Who? Who, if not Lilith?" I still thought this was her, but I was open to anything at this point. If it wasn't Lilith, maybe that was a good thing. It meant we could deal with it.

My aunt met my eyes and said, "The Guild of Dark Wizards."

Well, crap.

CHAPTER
14

A few minutes later, I stood at the edge of Hollow Cove bridge next to a very stiff and angry Marcus.

Heat brushed my cheeks, and I wasn't talking about the heat from the uber-hot male next to me.

The dome, because apparently, that's precisely what it was, a magical dome, vibrated and hummed with energy. I could feel the air and the bridge's wood planks beneath my feet pulsating with a low, steady note of power. Through the blazing dome wall, to the other side of the bridge, was the road that led to the next town, Cape Elizabeth. I could just make out the wooden sign with a picture of a lighthouse overlooking the ocean with the words WELCOME TO HOLLOW COVE painted on it.

The edge of the dome stopped at the exact spot where the town of Hollow Cove ended and where Cape Elizabeth started. Coincidence? I think not.

I might not be a shifter or a were or have any animal instincts in me, but I didn't like being trapped either. No matter how big the damn dome was—because it was huge—my gut still clutched with a sudden, intense sensation of claustrophobia.

I'd been staring at the dome's radiating green shield for the past three minutes. It was now or never.

Holding my breath, I reached out, and with my right index finger, I touched the shield.

I cried out and snatched my hand back. Searing pain flared where my finger made contact with it. I stared at my hand, watching a nasty red blister and a welt form at the tip of my skin.

"That damn thing burned me."

"Then you shouldn't have put your finger through it," snapped Dolores, standing about fifteen feet from me, a hand on her hip as she studied the dome. I glared at her as she said, "You can't get through. None of us can. Not unless you want to end up like a fried chicken."

Obviously it wasn't the smartest thing to do, but I had to be sure. The dome could just as easily have been a visual deterrent. I stuffed my hand in my jacket pocket, trying to ignore the throbbing pain in my finger. I knew she was right. Anyone stupid enough to try and make it through would end up as burnt toast.

"Dolores is right," agreed Ruth, standing next to her sister, with Beverly on her other side. "Whatever you do, don't touch it." She pulled out a vial from her bag, and with a determined brow, she threw it at the dome's wall. I felt a blast as a shockwave trembled beneath my feet.

I blinked, hoping Ruth's spell might have created a hole, but I didn't see so much as a mark on the dome. Not even a scratch.

"It's as I thought," said Ruth, her forehead wrinkled in frustration. "I can't break through."

My aunts fell into a collective silence, their brows and faces pensive as they tried to come up with a plan to rid our town of this magical dome.

Right before we arrived at the bridge, I'd hopped into Marcus's Jeep with him, and we drove around the perimeter of the town, following the boundary of the dome. I was right. It was a perfect half sphere, trapping the entire town within its green, blazing borders.

After a brief silence, a torrent of people came rushing into the streets, their eyes fastened onto the massive dome. Then came a chorus of whimpers and cries of shock.

"Well, guess the cat's out of the bag," I said, turning away from the face of a frightened ten-year-old kid.

After we'd left the crime scene, Marcus had Jeff and Cameron drive around town. They selected a few competent townspeople and posted them at different locations around town to deter anyone from trying to leave and hopefully keep anyone from trying to enter until we figured something out.

"The murders… the smiley faces… that was them? These wizards?" This whole time I thought Lilith had been responsible for the murders and the perverse display of smiley faces with the dead limbs.

"It was," answered Dolores. "A scare tactic to instill fear and create mistrust among our community. To divide us. They made it look like witches were responsible. Typical of that guild."

When I'm wrong, I do wrong big. "And you're sure it's the same guild of black wizards that put up this dome?"

"The Guild of *Dark* Wizards," corrected Dolores. "And yes, I'm sure. Not a single doubt in my mind. This… this is them. I'm certain of it."

I'd only heard of the Guild of Dark Wizards once, and that was a few months back when we thought they might be responsible for the Goblet of God, the curse that kept the shifters and weres from transforming back into their human selves. From what I remembered, they hated all shifters and weres. Anything that was part animal, they wanted them gone from the world.

And now, they were here.

Ruth spat on the wood plank near her feet. She caught me staring and said, "For protection."

I joined her cause and spat too. It didn't hurt to try.

"What can you tell me about them?" asked the chief. He crossed his arms over his chest, scowling. His low V-neck shirt parted enough to show his muscles rolling across his upper body. "Do you know how many we're talking about? Do they have weaknesses?"

Dolores's lips were pinched in thought. "I know they're an ancient group of wizards. Male only. Females apparently aren't clever enough to join their ranks."

"More like females were clever enough to avoid them," I added.

"They formed the guild in Europe. Romania, I believe. And began to grow their numbers. I don't know how many are here. Forty. Perhaps more. They're a secretive guild, so they don't like outsiders snooping around. A few years back, I heard rumors that some of them had made the move here, to North America, but where they're established, I don't know." She took a breath. "They're fanatics. They want to kill every single last shifter and were in the world to eradicate the animals. I remember reading such nonsense."

"There's one thing I'd love to *eradicate*, given the chance," I snapped.

Dolores shook her head. "I never thought they'd end up here. How did they even find us? We're such a small community. We pose no harm to them."

"Except that our very presence does, according to you," said the chief. "How do we kill them?"

I raised a brow at the chief. "Straight to the point. I like it."

I knew this one question dominated his alpha brain. He wanted to get rid of the threat. If it meant killing them to protect his town, I didn't doubt he would.

When Dolores didn't answer, Marcus pressed. "They're mortal. Right? Like witches but with different magical attributes?"

Dolores glowered at Marcus, disbelieving. "Don't you go comparing witches to that dreadful lot. They're nothing like us. Nothing."

"Yeah," joined Ruth, her face wrinkled in a frown. "We're *witches*," she said as though that explained everything.

"But they're *mortal*?" continued the chief, and I could see the frustration in his gray eyes and the stiffness in his posture. He exhaled, drawing in more tension as he took another breath.

"Yes," answered Dolores. "They're mortal. Just like you and me."

Marcus seemed confident in that answer. "Then we can kill them."

Dolores eyed Marcus for a moment, her expression unreadable. "It's not that simple. They're an ancient guild of Dark wizards with powerful magic. Magic that…" She hesitated, worry lines etched into her forehead. "Magic I'm not familiar with."

Damn. That wasn't good. If Dolores, the most powerful White witch I knew, wasn't up to par with the wizards' magic, where did that leave the rest of us?

Her words bounced around in my head, moving and flipping while trying to find their place. Dread pulled my shoulders tightly as I took a deep breath.

The sound of a car door slamming shut pulled me around.

"Hey," said Iris, as she and Ronin marched our way.

"Thank the cauldron," I exhaled as relief surged through me. "Phones don't work."

The Dark witch nodded. "I know. I tried calling too."

"No Wi-Fi, no emails, no electricity," added Ronin. "Like an EMP bomb was dropped on us."

Marcus tensed, but Ronin was right. Whatever magical dome this was, it short-circuited a wide range of electronic equipment.

A few moments after the dome had appeared, I'd tried to text Iris to know on which side of the half sphere she was and discovered that my phone was dead. I even tried the landline in Davenport House, nothing.

Iris was staring at the sky, where the tip of the dome covered us, her head held high. I was astonished that she could still walk a straight line. That Dark witch still amazed me.

Iris joined us. "Lilith upped her game."

"This isn't her," I told her, knowing in my gut that my aunts were right. "This is the Guild of Dark Wizards' handiwork."

"You're kidding?"

"She's not," said Dolores. "This is *their* work."

"People are starting to freak." Ronin jammed his hands in his front jeans pockets and looked over his shoulder to a group of middle-aged townspeople. "Most don't do well in confined spaces. I'm not claustrophobic or anything, but I know, sooner or later, the crazies are going to want to be let out of this confinement."

The dome wasn't exactly what I'd call confined, but I understood what he meant. We were captives in some magical prison dome. Before too long, we were going to have problems on the *inside*.

I cast my gaze to my aunts who were in conversation with Martha and another paranormal man with gray hair and a short beard.

"It's some sort of magical force field," said the Dark witch, both her hands up and moving along the wall of the dome without touching it. "An electromagnetic field of energy."

I looked at her. "Like the Veil?"

Iris shrugged and shook her head. "Not exactly the same. But if you mean like demons can't step through the Veil that protects us, then yeah. This dome is doing that. It's keeping us in."

The day was just getting better and better.

"You think the humans can see it?" Ronin was staring at the car that drove by on Ocean Side Road from the other side of the dome. It passed the bridge without slowing down, took the next left, and disappeared.

"If they could, all the reporters in Maine would be here by now. I don't think these wizards are looking for that kind of attention. It's probably glamoured or something." I wasn't sure, but I was betting I was right.

I cursed and rubbed my eyes with my fingers. Then I cursed again because I'd forgotten about my burn.

"You need to put some ointment on that, or it'll scar." Marcus took my right hand and gently turned it to inspect my finger. His jaw clenched in worry, but I knew it was more for the town's sake than my tiny blister. He was responsible for all the people of this town, and he took his job very seriously.

I pulled my hand away, giving him a playful smile. "That's not it. I basically accused a goddess, the goddess of hell, no less, that she was a crazy-ass murderess of kids."

Marcus gave me a tight smile. "When you've got an idea in your head, there's no stopping you."

Ain't that the truth. "Well, me and my big mouth. Serves me right. I mean, how do I apologize to a goddess? How does that even work?"

"I'm thinking lots of virgin sacrifices," answered my half-vampire friend. "Lots of *naked* virgin sacrifices. I can help you with that." He gave me an impish grin.

I cocked a brow. "If only it were that simple."

Shouts and cries rang out behind us as I turned and swept my gaze. Not twenty feet away stood a group of about two dozen paranormals and their families, all staring at the dome with the same scared looked about them. A few worried glances in my aunts' direction said it was clear they were hoping my aunts could bring the dome down.

A kid about seven kept smiling and pointing up at the dome, thinking it was some sort of game.

"This isn't *The Hunger Games*, kid," I mumbled. Maybe it was.

As I stood there, more and more of the townspeople came out into the streets. Some joined us on the bridge until it looked like the entire town was outside, gaping at the massive dome that trapped us all.

A dark shadow of fear swept over them all. Their panic was palpable, and I felt a pang in my chest for them. Hell, I felt the anxiety as well. But I was more ticked off than anything.

"We Davenport witches don't back down from a fight," informed Dolores, anger tightening her eyes as a flash of fury crossed her. When she got that look, someone usually ended up getting hurt. "If they think we won't stand up to them, well, they've seen nothing yet. These black-robe-wearing men don't scare me."

Uh-oh.

"Did you just say... *black-robed* men?" Why did I get a bad feeling about this?

Dolores watched me, and annoyance spanned her features. "Yes. What of it? What does it matter what a person wears?"

Beverly scoffed. "It matters a lot."

I straightened. "It matters because I think I might have run into a few of them yesterday."

Marcus whirled on me. "What?"

168

Iris stared at me. "Tessa?"

I waited until Ruth and Beverly joined us before explaining because I didn't want to shout or anything. "The thing is, I was attacked by three guys wearing black robes last night. Right after I left your place, Marcus." His frown was truly terrifying, and it chilled my guts.

"Is that why you came home in your underwear?" asked Beverly.

"What?" Marcus's voice was a little loud.

Oopsie. My face flamed at Ronin's snort. "Uh... yup." What? What was I supposed to say? "The thing is, their magic was different. Their demon mojo. I just thought they were Lucifer's guys."

Ruth's mouth hung open. "Oh dear."

"Lucifer's guys?" Dolores pressed a fist on her hip. "What Lucifer's guys? And why would they be after you, specifically?" She narrowed her dark eyes. "Does this have anything to do with Lilith? What's going on, Tessa?"

Yes, yes, it does. "Long story. But the good news is, they're *not* Lucifer's guys." That wasn't good news. "The point is, I got an up close and personal view of these wizards. Yeah, they had some skill, but I don't think they're invincible. I killed one."

Beverly's pretty mouth fell open, and the lines of her face looked a little deeper. "You killed one?"

I raised my hands in surrender. "Totally in self-defense." I didn't like the way Dolores was staring at me like I ate all the cheesecake without leaving her a piece.

"Merlins!" shrieked a voice that I knew all too well.

We all turned to the pudgy, red, sweaty face that belonged to our town mayor. He pointed a finger in the air, high above his head, his eyes wide and insinuating as though we didn't already see the giant dome over our heads.

When he got to an approximate five safe feet before us, he halted. "Did you see this?" Spit flew from his mouth, his finger still pointing above his head.

"It's kind of hard not to," I answered and crossed my arms over my chest. This was going to be good.

A large vein throbbed on Gilbert's forehead. "What are you going to do about it? Or are you just going to stand here while we suffocate!" he shrilled, windmilling his arms and milking his entrance for every drop of the drama.

Dolores glowered. "No one is suffocating."

"Yeah?" Gilbert's eyes were round and wild. "How do you know? *What* do you know? Do you know anything?" His gaze found me. "This is you. Isn't it?" He pointed his grubby little finger at me. "This is all *your* fault."

I exhaled slowly, trying to calm the storm that was brewing in my head. "Careful where you point that finger. I'm a nervous biter."

"It's the damn Guild of Dark Wizards' fault," shouted Dolores. "They're the ones behind this dome."

"So why aren't you doing anything about it!" cried Gilbert. "Are you going to wait until we all suffocate?"

"Gilbert, calm down," said Beverly, looking over the small shifter to the crowd behind him, where groups of families were hugging each other and trying to calm their crying children. Tensions ran high. "You're scaring the others."

"They should be scared!" Gilbert's voice rose and echoed loudly around us. I never thought his voice could carry like he had a built-in megaphone. "It's the end. We're all going to die."

"Shut up, Gilbert," warned Dolores, her hands fisted like she was about to clobber him.

Something my Aunt Dolores had said earlier hit me. I stared at Gilbert. "This is *your* fault."

The little shifter sputtered. "What? You're delusional. How could this"—he pointed up to the sky—"be *my* fault?" He laughed.

"Because *you* alerted them with your stupid festival." It all became clear to me. "You even made a website, basically telling the entire world who we are and where to find us. All the

171

wizards had to do was search the net and they'd find Hollow Cove."

"Cauldron help us," muttered Ruth. "Gilbert, how could you?"

Gilbert's face went ashen. "I… no… this is a lie! You're lying!" he cried, though his voice was weak, barely capable of convincing himself.

Yeah, Gilbert, the town mayor, had screwed us.

"Ladies, what is this?" Martha came into view. "I came as soon as I heard you were out here," she added, a little out of breath. Her long, purple-and-black, oversized print dress billowed behind her as she moved to join us on the bridge. "Is this the work of demons?"

The crowds that surrounded us suddenly went very still. A silence ensued as all ears waited for my aunts' answer.

"This is the work of the Guild of Dark Wizards," answered Dolores finally. I heard a few steady murmurs from the gathered crowds, but I couldn't make anything out.

"It is? Really?" asked Martha, pushing her bejeweled glasses up the bridge of her nose. "How do you know for sure?"

"This is how they do it." Dolores shifted her weight. "They trap the town or village with a magical dome. We can't escape. It makes it easier to kill everyone inside. No one can get out, and no help can come in. And the dome will stay until everyone inside is dead."

As if on cue, I felt a sudden rush of energy, and my ears popped at the change in pressure again, only worse.

And then the dome shifted and coalesced as it became black, shutting out the sunlight. Like a blanket had been thrown over the town, all the light was snuffed out.

A growing sense of fear and desperation gave my knees a jellylike feeling. We were left in utter, complete darkness. And I knew what the blackness meant. Fear. All-consuming and overwhelming fear. The kind that tore you away from your life and pitched you into the void, alone in the dark.

As it turned out, this was just the beginning.

CHAPTER

15

What happens when an already scared group of people are suddenly cast into utter darkness? They panic.

Screams poured out from everywhere at once, all around us—high-pitched, panicked, and terrified cries. I heard the unmistakable sounds of flesh pounding on flesh, like bodies crashing into one another as they scrambled around blindly.

I felt big, strong hands grab my middle, and the next thing I knew, I was crushed up against a rigid body. I didn't need light to tell me who this was, the musky scent and solid arms familiar. I couldn't help but let myself mold into him. His hot breath caressed my neck, sending tiny thrills inside my belly. I'll admit, it was really nice to have someone want to protect me. Especially when that someone was stupid hot, stupid strong, stupid kind, and all mine.

Having Marcus shield me from this enemy was fine, but I had a town of freaked-out paranormals to think about.

If I knew of a spell to create light, I would have done so by now. The only one I knew, the one I'd practiced with, I'd done it with snow. All the snow had melted in Maine.

Over the screaming, I heard my aunts' voices murmuring at the same time, and then three globes of light blinked into view and soared up into the sky, illuminating the area like three massive spotlights. Witch orbs—magical spheres that gave off a soft, white light.

Yeah, my aunts were cool.

Dolores raised her arms, her lips moving in a chant, and then two of the witch orbs zoomed behind us, one going east and the other west until they both disappeared, swallowed by the darkness.

Reluctantly, I moved away from Marcus's protective hold, wanting to do something and feeling the sudden rush of cold where his hard body had been a moment ago.

"Everyone, calm down," soothed Dolores as she approached the frenzied crowd of paranormals, though anyone who knew her could see the amount of tension in her posture. "Please. Go back to your homes. Lock your doors. It's the safest place for you now. I promise we will find a solution."

"But we're in the dark," cried a female with a ponytail, a toddler wrapped around her leg.

"Grab all the candles you can find," continued Dolores. "My sisters and I will procure more witch orbs to give the town enough light to be manageable."

"Won't be enough," mumbled Ronin, who I knew could see in the dark. I caught Iris's eyes, and she gave me a worried look.

"Please, go back to your homes," said Ruth. "Please. Go home."

"But what about these wizards?" shouted a male. "You said they did this. They've already killed four of us. How are we supposed to defend ourselves if we can't see them coming?"

He had a point.

"We'll figure this out," called Dolores. "There's no point in panicking. It'll just make things worse. Go home and lock your doors."

"And what?" shouted someone else.

"We can't get out or call for help!" cried another voice that belonged to a big, muscular male with a ponytail, who I recognized as one of the parents of the dead werewolf teen.

"We will protect you," said Ruth, with an encouraging smile. "We will keep the town safe."

"You better," threatened Gilbert as though none of this was his fault. He spun around and walked away, removing himself from any culpability. I was tempted to kick him. The other paranormals joined him as they moved off, hurrying in the opposite direction.

I heard the sound of an engine nearing, and I turned to see the headlights of an SUV stop just beyond the bridge. Two car doors opened and closed, and the large, muscled bodies of Jeff and Cameron came into view.

"Chief," said Jeff. "We have a problem."

Marcus squared his shoulders and straightened. "Tell me."

"A group of werewolves are down near Fairhaven," said Cameron. "And another group of shifters is at Parsons Bay. The idiots are trying to break through the dome. They're going to kill themselves trying." I heard the anger and fear in his voice. And when I looked at both of the deputies, their bodies stiff and the whites of their eyes showing, I could see a nervous energy to them—a fear I'd never seen before.

I exhaled. "I knew this was going to start. I just didn't think it would start this quickly."

"Told you," said Ronin. "And it's going to get worse before it gets better."

"He's right," said the chief. "It's going to get worse. It's what happens when you trap people inside a space, though shifters and weres are different. It's much worse for them. Even if this dome is the size of our town, it doesn't make a difference to them. Nothing is more disturbing to a shifter or a were than being trapped. Think of a wild animal suddenly trapped in a cage. They're going to keep at it. And they're not going to stop."

Well, that explained the fear I could still see in both deputies' eyes. They felt trapped, just as Marcus had said. And probably he was feeling a bit of that, too, though if he were, he hid it well. As the chief, he had to.

"Don't they know it's going to kill them?" I asked, remembering the pain I felt on my tiny little finger. "They'll burn to death if they try to get through."

"They'll do it anyway," answered the chief, a faint note of anxiety pulsing through his voice with the weight of the town on his shoulders. It was as though he knew this would happen.

I had the nasty feeling this was also part of the wizards' plan. Have the people trapped inside go crazy trying to get out and kill themselves in the process. They just had to sit back and wait for it to happen.

"Chief?" urged Jeff as both he and Cameron waited for their boss's orders.

Marcus hesitated and looked at me.

"Go." I ushered him away. "I'll be fine. Go where you're needed."

Though the chief had a worried frown on his face, he spun around and jogged over to his

Jeep. I watched as his Jeep and the gray SUV took a hard right and then drove off toward the east side of town.

"Oh, I do hope Marcus can talk some sense into those weres," said Ruth. "I don't want anyone else to get hurt, especially not until we put our plan into motion."

I looked at Ruth, impressed. "You've got a plan?" Wow, that was fast.

Ruth blinked at me and smiled. "No. Do you have a plan?"

Dolores shook her head at Ruth. "You are the reason why shampoo has instructions."

Beverly grumbled something as she pinched the bridge of her nose. "I need a drink."

"Me too," I answered.

"Well, before anyone does anything, we need to add more witch lights to the town," said Dolores. "A little more light can go a long way to help put away some of the fear. Then we'll come up with a plan to blast this wretched dome. The sooner the better, in this case. We need to move fast."

I frowned. "What are you not saying? We already know we can't get through without burning into a crisp."

"It's not just that." Dolores was quiet. "The last I heard of the wizards putting their magical dome over a town, it lasted for two months."

"Two months?" I had to pick up my jaw from the ground.

"Two months," repeated Dolores, "of the wizards killing here and there. But in the end, a lot of those trapped died of starvation. Well, it's what I've heard."

Ronin whistled and raked his fingers through his hair. "This is bad. Mark my words. They're going to turn on each other before the end."

I looked at him. "Meaning?"

The half-vampire shrugged and said, "Cannibalism."

Okay, gross. "Well, we're going to get this dome down before that." I sure hoped so because I didn't want to have to think about the people in this town going all zombie apocalypse.

I had a sudden torrent of crippling fear. Marcus and his two deputies were only three to face a town of wild, panicked shifters, weres, and witches. They weren't enough. He might be the strongest in this town in terms of physical strength, but what could one man do amid a few crazed thousand?

I had to get the dome down before the town went mad.

"Let's go, girls," said Beverly, ushering her sisters with her back to the Volvo. "We've got some light to produce," she added, pulling down on her shirt and looking frustrated. She was probably regretting that Boob-Booster spell, and I wondered how long it was going to last.

Dolores fisted her hands again like she wanted to take a swing at someone. "We're going to smash that dome. I don't care how. We melt it. Burn it. Crush it. Whatever. But no one sleeps until we do."

"I'll get the vodka, "said Ruth, surprising me.

I watched as the three sisters departed and made their way to the Volvo, my mind whirling on what Dolores had just said.

Yes, these Dark wizards had trapped us in their magical bubble, but the wizards had made one crucial mistake. They didn't know about me—more specifically what I could do that not many witches could.

"Tessa?" Iris stared at me. "You've got that look again. What's up?"

Ronin eyed me. "Yeah, something's up. You've got that big, wild smile, and you haven't had a sip of alcohol yet."

I grinned as excitement pounded through my veins.

I stared at my friends and then looked up at the dome. "I've got an idea."

CHAPTER
16

While my aunts had been busy getting light into the dome by adding more witch lights, and Marcus was engaged with extinguishing fights and suicidal attempts to pass through the dome, I was busy testing my theory. Or at least, trying to.

We stood at the entrance of Davenport House, my eyes tracing the wood grain from the front door. It gave the place a rich, organic glow, and my heart thumped on superspeed.

"You do realize that if it doesn't work, you'll end up frying yourself?" Ronin had his arms crossed over his chest, his usual sly smile replaced by a deep frown. "There might be some splitting too. Definitely splitting."

"I have to agree with Ronin," said Iris. "I'm not sure this is such a good idea. I mean, you've had some good ideas, even great ideas. But this isn't one of them."

"Can't you test it with… I don't know… a potted plant or something?" asked Ronin.

I looked at the half-vampire. "This isn't a teleportation machine. It's a ley line. Besides, I have no way of knowing if a plant would survive the trip since I won't be in there with it. It might end up as a pile of goo."

"Exactly my point," said Iris, worry tinting her voice. "It's too dangerous. How do we know you won't end up a pile of goo yourself? You might not be able to cross the dome."

"Yeah," agreed Ronin. "It'll be like hitting a brick wall at a hundred miles an hour. Splat."

I couldn't argue with that because I really didn't know if using the ley lines inside the dome was going to work.

My aunts had already left, hauling bags full of witch orbs they were going to distribute all over town.

"Dolores is going to drive while I get to shoot them in the air with my magical slingshot!" Ruth had expressed excitedly and shown me a giant, wooden slingshot with a leather pouch attached to the band. Hildo sat on her shoulder, his yellow eyes wide and looking just as excited as she was. "It's going to be great fun!"

Beverly tsked. "Not my idea of great fun. My idea of great fun is Lucio Rossi spinning me around over his naked chest while he sings opera."

I didn't want to, but I saw the visual before I could stop myself.

A minute after I watched the Volvo pull out of the driveway, I was voicing my theory to Iris and Ronin.

Iris crossed her arms over her chest and eyed me suspiciously. "Why did you wait for your aunts to leave before revealing this great plan?"

Ronin laughed. "She's got you there, sister. Got you good."

I clamped my mouth shut.

The Dark witch cocked a brow. "Because you knew they'd try and stop you. Deep down, you know this is crazy."

I thought about it. "I wouldn't say *crazy*, crazy... just a little unpredictable. It might work, you know." I always said there was a fine line between genius and crazy. It just so happens that my line was the invisible kind.

I cast my gaze over my two friends. Their nervous energy intensified my nerves until I felt as though I might jump out of my skin.

"Might work?" Iris was shaking her head. "You're going to risk your life on a 'might work'? This whole thing is a recipe for trouble."

I let out a long breath. "Listen. I get it. I really do. But I have to try. I might be the only one who can get through. You heard what Dolores said. We're going to need help. Lots of it. When I make it through, I'm calling in reinforcements."

"Which are?" asked Ronin.

"Everyone I can think of. The White witch court, the Dark witch court. The Gray Council. They don't know what's happening."

"That's true." Iris furrowed her brow. "If we're going to survive this, we're going to need their help."

I nodded. "So you see... I *have* to do this. We need to get this dome down before things escalate. Before things get out of control." I might have put on a brave face, but my insides were doing a jig with the walls of my stomach.

I wasn't an idiot. I knew this might not work, and I might end up either breaking my neck or in a pile of burnt ashes.

I swallowed hard. "I'll be back soon. This shouldn't take long."

"And if you don't come back?" pressed Iris. "What am I supposed to tell your aunts? And Marcus?"

The thought of Marcus sent a pang through me. I knew if I told him what I was about to do, he'd do his damnedest to talk me out of it. He'd probably tie me up. I rather liked the idea.

"I'll be fine. I'll pull out before it gets to that point." Not sure if I could, but it seemed to do the trick, and visible tension left Iris and Ronin's faces. I was going to have to test that theory too.

Ronin glanced at me with an arched brow. "You know which line you're going to use?"

"This one goes straight through to Hollow Cove bridge. I won't go far. I'll just be on the other side of the dome. Iris"—I glanced at the Dark witch—"see if you can find out anything about magical domes or these wizards while I'm gone. Anything that can help us."

The Dark witch nodded. "I'm on it."

"Okay. See you later."

I took a deep breath. Then, steeling myself, I focused my will and reached out to tap the ley line. A rumbling current of magical energy emanated out. I felt the ley line's magic charging like an enormous rushing river, flowing in me, in my mind, in my core.

And then I reached out, grabbed the door handle, pulled open the door—and jumped.

Bending slightly forward, I soared in the ley line like Tinker Bell on steroids. Images blurred as I sped ahead in a howl of wind and colors. Houses, streets, roads, and trees blurred past me as energy rushed through my head, my body, my nerves, everywhere.

Focusing, I willed the ley line to go slower, so I wouldn't miss the bridge at this speed and accidentally crash into the dome wall before I was ready—still not entirely sure I *could* go through it with a ley line.

I figured I had a few seconds to try and pull out once I reached the dome's border near the bridge.

Easy peasy, right?

We'd see.

A few moments later, my eyes found a brilliant globe of light hovering right above a red bridge and illuminating it with a soft, white glow.

Though still dark inside the dome, like it was midnight, I knew outside it was the complete opposite and probably high noon.

As I neared, I could see the bridge was deserted. Everyone had left after Gilbert's little temper tantrum. I was ticked that he'd run away scared, being the coward that he was. But I was grateful no one would witness this outcome, whatever it might be.

Now, I had a decision to make. And the dome's border was coming up fast.

Straining, I tried to push my senses beyond the black walls of the dome to see if my witchy feels could perceive the ley line's energy beyond the dome's edge. Just a trickle, a fraction—anything would be enough.

My heart sped up. I could feel it, just as I always did. There wasn't an abrupt stop, well, not that I could feel, anyway. It didn't feel any different than all the times I jumped a ley line, that continuous straight energy that propelled me forward.

Did that mean the ley line went *through* the dome? Its magic not impacted by the Dark wizards' trap?

Those were all excellent questions.

I pulled the ley line to a stop, hovering in the air like a superhero as I contemplated whether I could pass through without putting an end to my life. I happened to love my life at the moment. I didn't want to do anything to screw it up. But I also knew I might not have much of a life if we didn't get rid of the dome somehow.

The dome's black wall stared back at me, almost taunting, daring me to do my worst.

"You're on."

With my mind made up, I yanked on the ley line and pushed myself forward, gauging the distance and ready to jump out from the ley line the second I felt any kind of pain.

Five... four... three...

Focusing, I bent my ley line to go through the *very* solid-looking black dome wall.

Two...

Yeah, I was an idiot. Just like jumping out of a moving car.

One...

The wall came at me.

I held my breath and closed my eyes. Not entirely sure why I did that since I needed to see if I was going to hit a hard wall in order to haul my ass out of the ley line.

I braced myself, too late to turn back, or jump, expecting the buckets of pain.

But I felt nothing.

A second later, I yanked myself out of the ley line and landed right at the end of the bridge, where Hollow Cove ended and where Cape Elizabeth began. I opened my eyes and squinted at the bright blue sky and a brilliant yellow disk. It was a typical, sunny afternoon outside the dome.

I staggered, my heart pounding, my whole body alive with strain and adrenaline. What a rush!

A goofy smile spread over my face as I stared back at the black dome. I did it. I made it through the dome with my ley line, unscathed.

"Ha! Take that, you wizzies," I cried, throwing a fist in the air and twirling. Then I did a terrible representation of Michael Jackson's moonwalk. Thank God no one was around to witness that horrid interpretation.

Trouble was I wasn't alone.

CHAPTER
17

I turned at the sudden scrambling of feet.

On the bridge, just outside the dome, stood two figures. They were dressed the same, in heavy black robes with big black hoods that revealed nothing of the faces inside. They looked just like the three robed guys who had attacked me last night, which I had assumed were Lucifer's cronies.

Nope. These were the Dark wizards—the bastards responsible for killing four of our community and giving us this lovely dome.

My heart thudded as I took them in. There were only two of them. I could take on two.

The dome wall behind them shifted, making it appear like water before solidifying again, and then four more dark-robed wizards came through.

Okay. Maybe not.

"Nice trick," I told them, with adrenaline surging through me. "How did you do it? Is it the robes?" Not that I expected them to actually answer, but if they could step through the dome, maybe we could too. I just had to figure out how they did it, first.

One of the wizards laughed at the sight of me. I could see shadows of his features, gaunt and ordinary, inside his hood. His eyes sparkled with humor. Yeah, this situation was hilarious.

Of the six now standing between me and the dome, one stepped forward and drew back his hood. A long, white beard covered most of his weathered face. A few wisps of white hair drifted around his sun-damaged head.

With the others standing, their hands behind their backs, like soldiers at attention, I pegged the older wizard as their leader.

The leader's dark eyes pinned me. "How did you get through the dome?" he asked in a deep, resonant voice, with that same accent I'd heard from the other wizards. His tone wasn't cold or threatening but rather curious and slightly amused.

I scoffed. "Wouldn't you like to know?" I wasn't about to reveal my only advantage. Said advantage was my ticket outta here.

He tilted his head slightly. "What is this magic I sense?" He closed his eyes for a moment, seemingly taking in the smell or something. When he opened his eyes again, his gaze snapped to mine. I could all but feel the sudden intensity of his interest in me. "I am not familiar with it. Very curious. What kind of witch are you?"

Shit. Shit. Shit.

I had no idea if this old guy could recognize ley-line energy. But if he sensed it, I was done for.

One of the other wizards moved forward and said something to the older guy. I watched as his eyes widened in recognition. Not good.

"Ah," said the old wizard. "I know who you are now." Anger began to pour off him. "You attacked us."

I shrugged. "They started it."

"You killed one of us."

"Like I said, you guys started it." I kept my face blank, but my gut was spinning around and my heart beating so fast I could barely hear myself think.

Okay. Time to formulate a plan. I knew I couldn't fight six wizards. I'd barely made it out alive with three. These guys were powerful. Could I tap a ley line and jump before they could stop me? No idea. But what I did know was that I came here for a reason. I wasn't about to let these Dark wizards stop me.

I yanked out my phone, scrolled down for the Gray Council's number, and pressed it. I figured I'd try them first. After two rings someone picked up.

"Gray Council, how may I address your call?" answered a professional, bland male voice.

I took a breath. "Hi. My name is—"

My phone flew out of my hand and went crashing on the pavement, the metal and plastic shattering into pieces.

I glanced up in time to see the old wizard's hand disappearing into the folds of his robe. I could still feel the terrible power radiating off of his fingers—the same cold, ancient power I'd felt at the scene of the crimes, the same energy I felt when I fought more of these robed bastards.

"Enough with the Jedi tricks, will you?" I said, slightly afraid but more ticked that I'd just lost my phone. There went that plan.

Crap. Now what?

Focusing, I stretched out my witchy senses to the nearest ley line, feeling its familiar pulsing as it answered. I didn't pull on it or call to it, not yet. I had to keep it hidden for now, but it was there, just at the edge of my fingertips. One more hand gesture by the old wizard, or any of the others, and I was gone.

Without outside help, I didn't know how we were going to defeat these guys. I could ley line myself over to the next town and find a phone. But once I used that ley line, they would know. And I had the nasty feeling they'd alter the dome to make it so I couldn't return.

No. I couldn't take the chance. I wouldn't abandon my friends and family.

I had to get my butt back inside the dome. But first, I wanted some answers. The more I knew about their plans, other than wanting us dead, the higher our chances of defeating them.

I stilled, trying to calm my thrashing heart, and put my game face on. "You the wizard boss? The high wizard or whatever?" The old wizard blinked so I continued. "What do you want from us? Apart from wanting us dead, obviously. Why here? Why now? We're a small community. We don't bother anyone. Not even the humans."

I swept my gaze over the six wizards, not expecting them to answer, but the older one did.

"You harbor the beasts," answered the old wizard. "That in itself is a capital offense. Too long have these vile creatures made their beds with the *natural* magical community, sneaking, cunning, and manipulating their way in. But they are not like us. They are beasts. It is an act against nature. These beasts should and will be eliminated."

I gritted my teeth. "Wow. Okay there, Lord Sith. Can I call you Lord Sith? Great."

"It's Dragos," snapped the old wizard, and I could hear the trill in the R.

"Good to know. See, I disagree. We all live happily here, and we're all equal. Well, except for Gilbert, who thinks he's boss of everyone, but that's another conversation. No one is taking advantage of anyone here. We're family."

Dragos snorted. "How can you say that when your town chief is a monkey?"

The other wizards laughed, and I made out some sneers under their dark hoods.

My eyes narrowed as anger coursed through me. "He's a wereape, actually."

The old wizard shook his head. "What does that say about your town when you are led by a monkey?"

"He's not a monkey, Draco," I growled, feeling the need to defend my man. I could feel my fury seeping out of my pores.

"It's Dragos," said the wizard on the far left, clearly affronted that I'd already forgotten his leader's name.

"Right." Irritation welled in me. "Well, the chief happens to be my boyfriend. And a *real* man, not that I can say the same about you." I realized I should have kept my big mouth shut at the reaction on the old wizard's face. But

195

KIM RICHARDSON

there we had it. I'd always defend Marcus. Just like he'd always protect me.

The old wizard grimaced and rocked back as if I'd slapped him. Wish I had. "You lie with a beast? Have relations?"

I winced. Who said *relations* anymore? I grinned. "Best sex of my life." It really was.

Dragos twisted his expression in disgust, showing me his yellow teeth. He mumbled something in another language, or maybe not. I couldn't make it out either way.

"Kill her," said one of the other wizards, the tallest of the six. I couldn't see his face, but I could feel the scowl in his words. "She doesn't deserve to live. She's disgusting. She chooses an animal over her people. She's nothing but a whoremongering, shifter slut."

"You kiss your mommy with that mouth?" I asked.

The head wizard stared at me a moment, and something flickered in his eyes that had the hairs on my arms stand up. "She's nice to look at." His eyes rolled over me in a disgusting way, not unlike his pals the other night. "Healthy. Nice wide hips for childbearing."

"Yeah, I don't think so, creep."

Dragos sneered. "Yes, she'll do very well."

"In your dreams, grandpa. Not going to happen." I watched, ready to bolt as the head wizard folded his hands before him.

"Not all female witches are killed," he said. "Those we deem a good enough stock, we keep alive to bear our children. We have needs, after all."

"All the need you're going to get is the need for a kick in your meat twinkie." I just had to use it again.

I felt a pulse of his cold magic wash over me like it was trying to pull a layer off my forehead to get into my head. I'd already had enough of Lilith in there, so I wasn't about to let some old pervert in.

I could leave, but I still needed answers.

There had to be a reason why he hated the shifters so much. I could see it in his eyes, some memory that fed his fury, his hatred for all shifters and weres. And I was going to get it out of him.

"How old are you?" I'd start with that.

"Generations," replied the old wizard, which wasn't much of an answer.

I realized I was going to just to come out and ask the question. "Why? Why do you hate shifters?" I searched his old, wrinkled face. "What did they do to you?"

I knew I was onto something when I saw the twitch in his eyes—subtle, but it was there.

The old man raised his head slowly, his expression cold and calm, but I could now see the rage in his eyes, an old fury with a glimpse

197

of pain. Yeah, something had definitely happened to him.

"I was a young man when it happened," began the old wizard, surprising me. One of his members put a hand on his shoulder in an attempt to stop him from revealing too much, as though the memory was either secret or too painful. The old wizard batted it away. "It was ages ago, but I remember it as though it was only yesterday."

Now we were getting somewhere.

"I was a healer back then," he continued. "The village healer and wizard. I also answered to the king from time to time." A dark cast poured over his face. "And then one night they came."

When he didn't continue, I prompted. "Who came?"

His eyes pinned me. "The beasts. The werewolves. They came to our village at night and killed everyone." He shook with rage. "They killed my wife and my only child, my son. He was six years old." He took a breath and said, "I was on my way back from seeing the king's wife. She'd taken ill. When I got there, it was already too late. I managed to kill three, but most of them had left already."

"I can see why you hate them," I answered, "but it was long ago. I'm not very familiar with werewolves, but I know some of them do turn for the worst. I've heard of a disease that infects them, similar to rabies. I don't remember what it's called, but maybe they were infected." Though there was no way of knowing for sure. "They're not all bad. And most of the paranormals here in Hollow Cove aren't werewolves. They're werecats and werebears. Shifters."

"They're all the same. Don't you see?" said the old wizard. "Beasts. Animals that hide within humans. They get you to trust them, and then they turn on you. Kill you. And we will never rest until we rid the world of such creatures."

I shook my head. "You don't have to do this. Take the dome down and let's talk. Talk to Marcus. You'll see you're wrong about them." Look at me, a natural negotiator.

Dragos's smile was one-part evil and one-part amusement. "I think I will kill the monkey first."

The wizard on the right laughed, and I could see part of his thin face under his hood. He needed to brush his teeth more often too.

"Yes," continued Dragos, "take out the leader, and the rest will fall. Without their leader, they lose their purpose. They'll scatter. You'll see."

The thought of anyone hurting Marcus made something inside me snap. Call it feral. Call it primal. Call it whatever the hell you want. It was the overwhelming need to protect the man I loved. There, I said it. The dreaded L-word.

My anger flared, and I felt myself pull on the ley line. I reached out to its power, holding it there.

I glared at the old wizard. "We're not just going to let you kill us. We're going to fight back."

"We'll see," said Dragos. "First, we'll let the animals kill themselves. They always do. The longer they stay inside the dome, the weaker they'll get."

I frowned. "What the hell does that mean?"

My anger soared, and so did my connection to the ley line.

Its energy poured through me. I felt the murk of its power grow deeper. My body briefly lit up with a flood of tingling energy that traced along my limbs.

My eyes snapped to the old man. I didn't know why, but I saw the recognition in there.

"Ley lines," he guessed, that smile of his widening to match his eyes. His hands flicked, and I felt his power. Magic on his fingers grew and intensified around his hands like glowing blue eels. His control on his magic was impressive, but he was still a murderous old douche.

Shit. Time to go.

I didn't wait to see the extent of the old wizard's power. I wasn't an idiot.

I yanked on the ley line nearest me, pulling it along until it was right there in front of me.

And then I jumped.

CHAPTER
18

I stood in the entryway of Davenport House. Being a magical house, we had no need for candles to illuminate the inside. It was magically lit just as it always was. Take that, Draco, Dragon, Dragor, whatever.

A mix of panic and anger made me breathe hard like I'd just run around the block for fun, though I'd literally just stepped out of the ley line. My anger shifted to worry. I'd messed up my brilliant plan of calling for help.

It was time for Plan B. What was Plan B?

I realized I'd also made things worse. Marcus was now a target.

"Nice going, Tessa."

Without phones working, I'd have to look for him on foot. I had to warn him. I had no idea when they'd strike. Today? Tomorrow? Next month? But I wasn't taking any chances with Marcus's life. And something in the way the old wizard's tone told me that he'd be true to his word. He might be looking for Marcus right now. I had to find him soon.

But I needed to speak with someone else first.

"Hello?" I called out as I walked down the hallway.

Holding my breath, I stalked into the kitchen. Gleaming white cabinets and white subway-tiled backsplash stared at me. It was utterly deserted.

"Hildo?" I waited for the black cat to jump down from whatever high ledge he was hiding on, but he never did. Strange. Guess they weren't back yet.

I'd just have to look for them after I was done.

I moved to the single white door opposite the kitchen, which led to the basement.

"Dad?" I called out. "Dad? I need to speak with you. It's important."

I still didn't know how this whole communication thing worked. How Davenport House transmitted my message over to the Netherworld. Maybe it was like an email notification or something.

A moment later, the basement door flew open, and a tall man of medium build wearing an expensive suit, stepped out.

His usual white crisp shirt was wrinkled and untucked from his gray pants, which had two large coffee stains on them. His graying hair stuck out from all sides like he'd scratched or pulled at it over time.

"Did you sleep in your clothes or something?" I asked him.

The scent of rotten eggs wafted behind him as he stepped into the kitchen. "Of course not. Well, I'm here. What's so important? Is it Lilith again?" His voice was rushed and sounded tired. His silver, luminous eyes were accentuated by dark circles under them.

It was the first time I'd seen him a little disheveled like he was preoccupied with something, probably working tirelessly on the so-called trap we were supposed to use on the goddess. I'd forgotten to tell him.

Tiny daggers of guilt stabbed at me. "Listen, about Lilith. She wasn't responsible for the deaths of those kids. I was wrong. Maybe you should stop working on that trap for a while." When his eyes widened in dismay, I added quickly, "I'm not saying we're not going to need it someday. It's just… we have bigger problems right now."

My demon father frowned and watched me for a moment. "Bigger problems than a bitter, angry goddess of hell released into your world? One who clearly has set eyes on you?"

I shrugged. "When you say it like that, you wouldn't think so. But at the moment, yeah. We do." I quickly relayed the events about the Dark wizards, their mission to kill all shifters and weres, their magical dome, and their desire to kill everyone inside. Including me.

My father was quiet. "The last time we spoke, you were on your way to seek out Lilith. Did you find her?"

"I did. Did you hear what I said about the wizards?"

Obiryn crossed his arms over his chest and gave me a pointed look, reminiscent of Dolores. "And you found out that these wizards were responsible before or after you went to see her."

I got his point. "Um… after… About these wizards…"

"What happened with Lilith?" demanded my father. "What did you tell her exactly?"

He wasn't going to give up the subject of Lilith. "I kind of accused her of killing those kids."

My father's face went slack. "You accused her?"

"It was an honest mistake. How the hell did I know we had wizards?" Yup, that sounded strange coming out of my mouth.

"And she didn't kill you?" expressed my father. It was more of a statement rather than a question.

"I wouldn't be standing here having this conversation if she had."

My father shook his head, his eyes drawn past me to the kitchen. "It's worse than I thought."

I scoffed. "How can accusing a goddess while she was entertaining multiple dudes be worse than you thought? It's bad. Really bad."

I saw the fear touch the corners of his silver eyes, the uncertainty. "Because it just proves to me that she's formed an attachment with you," he said finally. "Because…"

"Because… what?"

"Because she must need you for something."

"Great." I remembered her saying I owed her a favor. It made sense. My father was right. It wasn't that she didn't kill me because she liked me and wanted to be friends. She needed me for something.

"What is it?" My father stepped closer, and the worry in his eyes deepened.

I let out a long breath and rubbed at my eyes, feeling the stress of the day weighing me down all of a sudden. "You're right. She said I'd owed her a favor."

My father hissed out words in another language, demonic probably, though I didn't catch any of it, and began pacing.

"I knew it," he growled. "I knew it was something like this. Why would she want to keep a mortal witch so close to her? Because she requires something from you."

"I can lend her some clothes, but I draw the line with my underwear." I laughed, trying to ease the tension. It didn't work.

My father's body and face hardened until he didn't quite look like himself. His silver eyes grew wider and glittered with a fevered intensity.

"This is no joking matter, Tessa."

"I know that."

"Do you? Because you're not acting like it."

Ticked, I took a deep, calming breath. The last thing I wanted was to fight with my father. I needed him. "I get it. Trust me. I was there. I saw her crazy eyes."

"Of all the beings in the world, you choose to anger someone as big, powerful, and irrationally vengeful as the goddess of hell? Deities take everything personally."

"I can see that," I answered. "Explains a lot."

"She is merciless and full of hate. It's a bloody miracle she didn't kill you."

I shrugged it off like it was no big deal, though, at the time, I nearly peed myself. "She hasn't killed me, so I'm taking that as a good sign. Besides, she hasn't asked anything of me." Not yet.

"Not yet," said my father, reading my thoughts. "But she will. Mark my words. And you're not going to like it."

"Figures." When did doing favors for deities benefit the doer? Never.

"Now," exhaled my father. He pressed his hands to his hips. "Tell me about this dome."

"It's like a giant magical net, in a way. Trapping us. It covers all of Hollow Cove," I answered. "You might be able to see the dome through the living room window." I moved to the living room, pulled back the heavy drape, and stepped back to give my father a full view of the outside. "It's around two o'clock in the afternoon."

My father looked out the window. "It looks as though it's night." He angled his head up. "I can't see the dome, but the lack of light is certainly something." He stepped back from the window, a frown on his face as he looked around the room. "What happens if someone attempts to leave the dome? Has anyone tried?"

"They suffer a horrible death by burning," I told him, and made a "poof" gesture with my hands. "No one can get through." Except for me, but I decided to keep my ley-line trip to myself for now. "Ruth tried to break a hole through it, but it didn't work. This dome, the magic is strong. My aunts are not familiar with it, which isn't great."

My father nodded, his face creased in concentration. "I'm also sensing some very powerful magical pulses—a throbbing, cold, seething energy. Different from what I'm accustomed to with this side of magic practitioners."

"Demonic?" I wasn't sure, but I thought I'd ask. "Could they be borrowing magic from demons?"

Obiryn shook his head. "No. It's old, but it's earthbound. Pure. Like the original magic from this world, or at least a fraction of it."

I felt my brows rise. "That's interesting. But whatever magic this is, it's keeping us from using our phones and calling out for help. Have you ever heard of the Guild of Dark Wizards?"

My father thought about it a moment as he raked his fingers through his short beard. "No, I'm sorry. I don't think I've ever heard of these wizards before."

I hesitated, not sure how he'd take what I was about to ask him. "Um. Is there a way you could call or maybe even send an email to our Gray Council? You know who they are. Right?"

"Yes."

I searched my father's face, his silver eyes hard. "Was that a yes you know them or yes you're going to call them? If the Dark wizards don't kill us all soon, they're going to wait until we either starve to death or kill each other. Is there a way you can get in touch with them? Tell them we're under attack by these Dark wizards, and ask them to send help?" With my father's restrictions on this side of the world, I wasn't sure he could, but I knew he had friends who could relay a message for him.

My father clasped his hands before him. "I can't promise anything, but I'll see what I can do."

I let out a breath, knowing this was his way of a definite yes. "In the meantime, I was wondering if you had any tips regarding how to take down the magical dome. The town is starting to panic. Marcus tells me that trapped shifters and weres react badly, worse than others when trapped. They're going to do something stupid. It's already started. So, if you have any ideas, I'd love to hear them."

My father looked back out the window before turning around at me. "I've heard of magical domes before but none of this magnitude. This is the work of years of studying and mastering enough controlled energy to put it all together. The domes we use in the Netherworld can fit a small group of people and are generally used as sound barriers when creatures or mortals are being tortured for information."

"Of course they are."

My demon father moved to the window and hauled it up. "It would be best if I could get closer." He edged as close as he could to the window without sticking out his head. "That magical pulse of energy is powerful. You say it began as a clear half sphere and then solidified?"

"Yes. That's right."

Obiryn's face went pensive. "Like the shell of an egg."

Strange analogy but whatever. "I guess. Sure, like the shell of an egg."

My father turned and looked at me. "You need to crack the egg," he said with a smile. It was the first time he'd smiled since he got here. I realized the loss of his smiles was on me. All my fault.

Though I took his smile as a good sign. "Does that mean we can crack the dome? Bring it down?" My heart hammered with excitement. We were onto something. I could feel it in my witchy bones.

"Yes," answered my father, lifting his eyebrows. "I believe *you* can."

I let out a breath of relief. "Thank the cauldron." Though I didn't miss his emphasis on me. This was the best news I'd gotten all day. "Okay, then. So, how do I do this?"

My father tucked in his shirt, apparently only now noticing his unkempt appearance. "Well, if it's anything like the magical domes I've used — I mean… other demons used, it's very simple."

"I like simple. I can work with simple."

My father buttoned up his jacket. He looked at me with calm silver eyes and said, "You'll

211

need to in…" My father's voice wavered and became too soft to hear, barely a whisper, like someone had turned off the volume.

"What? Say that again?"

My father's face wrinkled in a frown; his lips moved, but I couldn't hear anything. And then his body shifted, like it wasn't solid anymore, transparent enough for me to see through him to the window behind. He looked like a ghost.

He reached out, his eyes widening in sudden fear, and with a last flicker, he disappeared.

"Dad? What the hell just happened? Dad!"

I jumped to the spot where he'd vanished, moving my hands around like an idiot. But I found only air. That had never happened before.

"Dad?" I called out again, hoping he'd show up and tell me how to destroy the dome.

I ran to the basement door, thinking that's where he'd pop up. I shut it and opened it again. Then again. I did it about five times.

My heart hammered in my chest as I waited for my demon father to show up again. But he never reappeared.

After a few minutes or so, I knew something was very wrong. And I also knew who was responsible.

The Guild of Dark Wizards.

No way was this a coincidence. Somehow, they'd managed to remove the connection between Davenport House and the

Netherworld, that unique portal, if you will. I had no idea it could be done or how they did it, but they did. If they could do that, what else could they do?

Horror struck me as another awful feeling of dread hit.

"The ley lines."

I rushed to the front door and swung it open. I sent out my witchy senses, my will, reaching out to the familiar ley line that had been here since the day I had arrived.

But all I felt was the dull, cool air trapped inside the dome.

The ley lines were gone. Well, maybe not gone, but the ability to use them while trapped inside the dome had been removed.

"Bastards," I hissed. This was bad. But it was also partly my fault. If I hadn't pulled them to me, the old wizard wouldn't have sensed them.

And then the worst thought I could possibly imagine popped into my head. Fear bubbled up, bitter and numbing.

"Marcus."

I knew without a doubt he was next on the old wizard's to-do list.

I had to get to him first.

With my heart in my throat, I leaped off the front porch and tore down the street.

CHAPTER
19

It wasn't news to the world that I was in no way a great sprinter. I wasn't even a good runner or a decent candidate for a mild jog. My legs just weren't made for that kind of physical activity.

Let's face it. I'd gotten lazy with the ley lines. I could go anywhere I wanted and be there in a few moments.

Plus, without the Volvo, I had to submit to using my legs.

Which explained the heavy breathing, the giant cramps in my sides, and the stopping every thirty seconds or so, checking that my ankles were still attached to my feet.

Note to self: start working out more and stop drinking so much wine before bed.

Yeah, we all knew that was never going to happen.

Worse than my nonexistent ability to run, I had no idea *where* I was running to. Marcus could be anywhere in Hollow Cove.

Still, the closest place and the most logical would be to check the Hollow Cove Security Agency and go from there.

My lungs were burning, and my mouth was dry as I pulled open the glass door to Marcus's office and wobbled inside like a drunk. Long, dark shadows stretched out in the hallway. Yet I was surprised to see how lit it was. When I found the source of light, a hovering globe, I knew my aunts had stopped by and given Marcus a witch light.

"Hello? Marcus? Are you here?" I called out, expecting to see Grace glaring up at me from her desk, but the front desk sat empty.

I reached Marcus's office first. MARCUS DURAND with the words CHIEF OFFICER under it was stenciled on the window in black letters.

I pushed the door open and peered inside. Though everything was mostly in shadow, I recognized his desk stacked with papers next to a laptop, filing cabinets, and rows of bookcases that occupied the wall next to the desk.

Marcus wasn't here.

With a new surge of adrenaline, fueled by fear, I hurried out of his office, pushed open the front door, and ran down the street as fast as I could. Where was I going? Your guess is as good as mine. He wouldn't be lounging in his apartment, not when we were under attack.

I ran through the darkened streets, my legs cramping as my lungs strained to haul in a breath. But I didn't stop. I had to find Marcus.

The scent of smoke reached me. Shouts erupted from the shadows, and I slowed to get a better idea of where they were coming from. Yellow light glowed in the darkness, so I made a beeline for it.

What I'd first thought was witch light was actually the glow from a fire. One of the smaller witchcraft shops, Hex Appeal, which sold herbs, candles, and over-the-counter spells, was on fire. A crowd gathered before it, but no one was attempting to put it out. A few people ran past me. I didn't recognize any of them, though the fear on their faces was unmistakable. When I got closer to the burning building, I saw a few bodies lying in the street, not moving.

I turned at the sound of a cry and saw Marcus standing in the middle of the street, ripping his shirt off. His posture and bulging muscles, which I knew was a show of strength, said it all. He was about to go full-on King Kong.

But when my eyes found his target, my heart sank.

Four robed figures stood, evenly spaced, facing Marcus. One had his hood removed, and I could see his white beard and wrinkled face from where I stood. He pulled his hand from his robe, and I nearly lost it.

Shit.

Fear consumed me. I had a few seconds to try and get between Marcus and whatever spell that bastard wizard was about to spew. Marcus was somewhat resistant to magic, but this wizard magic was different, old, and I had no idea if the chief could resist it.

The wizards had managed to remove my ability to use the ley lines, but they hadn't abolished my magic. Still, with all that running, I wasn't in tip-top witch shape. I'd just have to do my best and hope it would do.

Just as Dragos flicked his wrist, I shouted, "Ventum!"

A gust of wind flew out of my outstretched hand and hurled toward Marcus.

It hit the chief on the side and propelled him sideways about ten feet. It did the trick.

Dragos's spell, a blue lightning bolt of some sort, hit the pavement where Marcus had stood seconds ago. After a hissing sound, a section of the pavement dissolved in a cloud of blue mist and foul stench.

I smiled, proud of myself. "Didn't see that coming. Did you?" I told the old wizard, whose face was blank and unreadable.

"Tessa, get back," ordered Marcus, moving back to his spot before the wizards, his chest muscles flexing.

"Not a chance. I've got a score to settle with these Nazgul wannabees." I came forward next to Marcus, panting. I wiped the sweat from my brow, trying to look calm and collected, but I probably came off more nervous and out of shape.

"We meet again, witch," said Dragos, that cold smile returning to his wrinkled face.

Marcus's attention flicked to me as I said, "Not by choice. If I had a choice, I'd be at home binge-watching a series on Netflix with my man."

Screams erupted behind me. A man's voice let out a ringing, defiant shout. I looked back to see crowds of paranormals running the streets in a startled panic, drawing my gaze to the hooded figures that chased them. The Dark wizards moved like liquid shadows. Too quick for even me. Their speed was unmatched. I blinked as they vanished and then reappeared fifty feet from where they'd disappeared. They moved... they moved like vampires.

I watched horrified as a female shifter ran, her speed impressive and probably a werehorse, but just when I thought she was clear, a wizard appeared in front of her.

With a flick of his hand, a beam of purple light hit her in the chest, and she went down. I didn't see her move again.

Five townspeople doubled back to the burning building in apparent panic, their flight erratic and rapid. High-pitched screams reverberated in the street.

I blinked as eight wizards materialized before the running horde. Like wraiths in the night, they moved like shadows, too fast for anyone.

With a roar of light and sound, a flash of blinding blue-and-purple sparks illuminated the street like fireworks as wizards flung their magic at them like automatic weapons.

I barely heard a cry as the five went down, never to get up again.

Rage filled me.

"They killed Jeff." Marcus's voice was rough, sad, and desperate all at once.

My mouth fell open in shock as I looked behind me at the bodies lying in front of the burning building. Only now did I notice Jeff's dark skin and his large, muscled body.

"Marcus... I'm..." That was Marcus's deputy and a close friend, which meant he wasn't thinking straight. He was too emotional. This was too personal.

His gaze never left the line of wizards. "I couldn't stop it. They move... they move fast. Like vampires. Something's happening to us. The dome... it's taking our energy."

"What?"

I looked back at the chief, his gray eyes wide with fury, shimmering with his motions and making him more captivating with the contrasting shadows of dominance and power.

But he had dark circles under his eyes that I hadn't noticed before. His face looked pale and tired. His cheeks were sunken like he hadn't eaten in weeks.

And then what Dragos had said to me came crashing back.

The longer they stay inside the dome, the weaker they'll get.

"Marcus," I ventured, moving closer. "We need to get out of here," I said softly. "Somehow the dome's draining you of your life force." I was willing to bet my life on that one. "We can't fight them like this. We need a plan. We have to come up with something. Let's go." Seeing how fast these robed bastards were, I knew I'd need help running, even with my adrenaline still soaring through me. I still had my magic. I could probably blast our way out. I had to, even if the fear in me was so tense I felt sick.

I'd defeated one of them. I could do it again, but I needed a place to think of a plan. And I needed Marcus with me. I wasn't leaving without him.

The chief's jaw twitched as absolute hatred and fury emitted from him. "They're going to pay for this."

More screams erupted behind us, the sound making my skin crawl and tighten.

"They will. I promise." I pressed my hand on his arm, tugging him with me, but he wouldn't move.

Marcus yanked his arm from my hold, visibly shaking. "No. I'm doing this now."

Damn. "Listen. You're not thinking straight. We need to *leave*." Either that dome was affecting his brain, or he was just lost in his rage.

The chief was a natural leader and protector. It was in his DNA to protect the town, which was his pack. If he had to give his own life to save it, I knew he would. He had to enforce his position by sheer will, and he answered to any threat to his town.

"Marcus," I urged, as another scream, a woman this time, echoed in my ears.

Marcus looked at me, his eyes haunted. He looked tired and old.

"Come with me," I pleaded, my voice shaking, knowing he wouldn't leave his pack, and knowing I might have to drag him by force. The image of Jeff's body kept flashing in my mind's eye. I would not let that happen to Marcus.

"Let's go, Marcus. Please." If we left now, we still had time to make a run and blast for it.

"You are not going anywhere, little witch," said Dragos, pushing away from the other wizards and coming forward. "I'm going to

221

keep you for my personal entertainment." He smiled, revealing a mouthful of rotten teeth. "But your... *friend* here. *He* is going to die."

A low, guttural growl emanated from Marcus's throat. The muscles on his neck popped at the mention of me being that old man's property. His lips lifted into a snarl. "You're wrong, wizard. I'm not dying tonight. You are."

"It's already begun," continued Dragos, staring at Marcus like he was an annoying fruit fly he wanted to swat. "The infliction has spread. Soon it will reach your brain and you'll wish you'd die."

"You picked the wrong town," growled Marcus.

Dragos sneered. "I always pick the *correct* town. I just look for the one with all the animals playing as humans."

The tall wizard on the left laughed, which caused his hood to slip, giving me a full-on view of his plain, forgettable features and his buckteeth.

"Like I said before"—Dragos's eyes flicked back to me—"I will keep you for later."

"Gee, let me see how I'm going to answer that," I said, planting my feet. "Oh, right. Fuck off."

Dragos's eyes widened. "Perhaps I will kill you, witch. Yes, I've changed my mind. All must die. Kill them both." His dark gaze pinned mine, and blue sparks dripped from his hand. "And we'll start with you first."

I narrowed my eyes. "Bring it."

CHAPTER
20

Shoots of blue energy came at me.

"Incoming!" I shouted, realizing too late that was the wrong word.

Whoops.

I tried again.

"Protego!" I cried, my body crashing into Marcus as I hurled up my hands and pulled on the elements around me.

A semitransparent half sphere rose from the ground at our feet and formed over our heads, just barely encircling us a split second before the wizard's magic hit.

Blue energy roared as it roiled and billowed, pressing against my shield. Heat seared my face like I'd stuck it in an oven. I flinched, and for a horrible moment, I thought it wouldn't hold.

But it did. For the time being.

I stared at it for a moment, realizing it was like a miniature dome in a way, but this one didn't hurt anyone. It was the opposite. It protected them.

I looked at Marcus as another beam of blue light hit my half sphere. "Hurry. It won't last long."

In one swift motion, Marcus unbuckled his belt and yanked off his jeans, ripping them at the same time. He stood in all his naked glory—and let me tell you, it was all kinds of glory—a fit, golden-brown physique, rippling in muscles because there was no room for anything else.

I moved away as far as I could, which was at the edge of my shield, so he wouldn't accidentally kick me in the face or something when he shifted.

Marcus's face and body rippled in a slithery motion with a flash of black fur, a snarl, a horrible tearing sound, and the breaking of bones. And then, in his place, stood a giant silverback gorilla, his dark fur peppered with gray.

With him being sick, he didn't have the strength to fight off all the wizards. But he'd have a better chance as a gorilla.

I stood in a half crouch, my hands at my sides. I met the gorilla's gray eyes and said, "Get ready."

"Gohh ome, Essa," he snarled, and I marveled at how far his conversational skills had improved since the last time I'd heard him speak in his beast form. "I sstaayy." His eyes gleamed with some sort of animalistic fury.

"No way," I said. "You can't possibly take them all on. You need me, fur ball."

The gorilla flashed me a mouthful of teeth the size of my fingers. "Krraazzy."

I grinned. "You bet I am."

A sudden change in pressure was followed by a loud, sharp pop, like the sound of a balloon bursting. Only this time my half sphere had burst.

Showtime.

Marcus and I exploded into motion.

The gorilla snarled and pounded his fists on the ground, making them pop and crack. With a mighty push of his back legs, the gorilla swung up and pitched at the wizards with abrupt speed.

A flash of dark robes caught my attention to my right, and I twisted around.

A wizard threw himself at me, and I had a few seconds to come up with a spell or power word to save my own skin. Only this time I knew my power words weren't very effective against these Dark wizards.

Good thing I had some demon mojo.

Though still a work in progress, I channeled my chi, my core, calling out to that dark power. Within me, the first hints of cold energy spilled from my soul and pooled into my body. I flung out my hands and hurled tendrils of black energy at the oncoming wizard.

I saw a split second of fear register in his eyes before it hit.

The wizard wailed as he collapsed to the ground, convulsing with Latin spilling from his lips as he desperately tried to counter my demon mojo. He jerked one last time and then went still.

I staggered with a sudden feeling of light-headedness like I was low on blood sugar or something. My demon mojo was calling for payment. And like all magic, I didn't have an everlasting supply. Eventually I would run out.

I heard a cry and the sound of tearing flesh. Marcus the gorilla attacked the wizards with voracious rapidity, his powerful body a killing machine on steroids.

Sparks of blue magic hit the gorilla in the chest. He was thrown back, and my breath caught. But he recovered quickly, and then he crouched low with murder in his eyes. He howled in fresh aggression and charged. In a flash of fury and savage strength, the gorilla soared a good ten feet over the wizard, landed behind him, and grabbed the wizard by the neck. Before the wizard could conjure up another spell, the gorilla snapped his neck like a twig and tossed him.

The gorilla turned toward me, his steps faltering. He staggered and went down on one knee, letting out a grunt of surprise. That attack had taken a toll on his strength. He couldn't keep this up. Not for long.

A quick count told me at least twenty wizards were here, probably more. We couldn't fight them all off, not just the two of us. We needed help, and I needed to get Marcus out of here before he ended up like Jeff.

The only safe place I could think of was Davenport House.

"Marcus!" I shouted, moving toward him as four robed figures rushed us. "Let's head back to Davenport House."

The gorilla leaped up and thrashed at a wizard with a terrible howl. He was lost in his own pain and anguish. His beast was in control now and it wanted to kill. I had to get closer.

"Damn it," I swore, running toward the gorilla.

I would have gotten there sooner if not for the robed figure who stepped in my way.

He moved with a casual and dangerous grace, blue magic coiling around his fingers like rings. He snickered at what he saw on my face, probably a combination of surprise and fatigue.

A brush of tiredness hit, courtesy of my latest power word and demo mojo. I rolled my shoulders, trying to force myself to relax. It didn't work.

Words emanated from the Dark wizard's lips in deep, languid tones. His confidence annoyed me. He took two strides forward and hurled both hands, sending a thunderbolt of blue energy rushing at my face.

Crap.

I hurled myself backward and hit the ground in a roll. The air moved above my head, and I had a moment of burnt hair smell shooting up my nose. Yikes. That was close. Too close.

His lips moved in a dark spell under his cowl, but I was ready.

I spun to my knees and pulled up every bit of power I could muster. Cold surged up. Ice throbbed in my middle. With my demon mojo still pounding through me, I hurled my hands at him.

Shoots of black energy burst from my fingers, twisting and stretching while catching the wizard on his left side. Black tendrils wrapped around him, blazing and bleeding into his skin. He howled in pain and fury, and then I heard nothing. I only smelled the acrid scent of burning flesh.

I stared at my hands, my demon mojo leaving me a bit short of breath. "You're awesome." If I could give myself a high five, I would.

I had to make a mental note of thanking my daddy dearest for this latest gift. Who knew it would come in so handy?

I barely had time to catch my breath as another black-robed figure sprang my way.

Couldn't a witch catch a break?

The wizard snarled, his hands taking on a sinister mien. He gestured with a flick of his wrist.

"Necare!" he bellowed, flinging his palms at me.

Blue rings of fire burst from his outstretched hands.

I ducked, but I wasn't fast enough.

Searing pain bit into my flesh, and I hissed as it knocked me to the pavement, my head thunking on the hard surface. That was going to leave a bump.

I lurched to the side, but agonizing pain flared up my back, my front, and everywhere. The pain struck deep. Doubling over, I curled into a ball as it spread through my bloodstream, burning.

A ghastly face came up above me, grinning a victory smile. I could see a flowing gray mane under his hood, a dark beard, and piercing dark eyes.

Boots studded behind me. Someone was shouting. Wizards? Paranormals?

"You're done, witch. Give up," said the wizard. "You can't win this. Might as well just let go and die with some dignity instead of playing at magic."

My power now raged inside me, my demon mojo throbbing and radiating out through my middle and my limbs.

"Screw you," I hissed, spinning around to my knees.

The wizard smiled and then hurled his magic at me, just as I flicked my wrist at him.

All I remembered was a blast of blue light as sound thundered in my head and ears before I found myself on the ground again, screaming in pain and not ready for the influx of power from being at the center of all that demon mojo. I gritted my teeth when pain flared as though my insides were aflame.

But I wasn't the only one in agony.

The wizard thrashed on the ground, his cries of pain drowning my own.

I wasn't done yet.

I took a deep breath, pushed through the pain, and stood on my feet. I staggered and puked. I was dizzy, though I wasn't sure if this was a result of too much demon mojo in such a short time or a mild concussion. Possibly both.

Wiping my mouth, I glanced away from the thrashing wizard on the ground and searched for Marcus. I saw groups of paranormals fighting back, fighting the wizards with everything they had. The sounds of battle blared in a combination of cries, shouts, and booms of magic, making my ears ring with constant pressure.

But I saw no sign of Marcus.

"What have you done!" raged a voice behind me.

I whirled around, still holding on to my demon mojo, keeping it close. Though the more I used my newest skill set, the more my body felt it had been beaten repeatedly by a two by four.

"You killed them," howled Dragos, a dark madness flashing in his eyes. Damn, he looked scary.

He stood next to a group of wizards, like the captain of a great ship. Ten of them, including the old guy. Their focus was on me.

I squared my shoulders, not daring to show them the fear inside. "It was either them or me. I'll always choose me," I told him.

"They were my sons!" Spit flew from the old man's mouth, his face darkened in rage.

"Your sons?" This was news to me. My gaze flicked to the two dead wizards on the ground and then back to the ten that now faced me. And then it hit me. The Guild of Dark Wizards were *all* Dragos's sons. That was gross and creepy all at the same time.

"Okay, I get the family resemblance." Not really. "So, this is a family business? You created your own guild with your kids. Why?

Did the other wizards not like you? They didn't let you join their guild?"

Dragos's fury was addressed at me, dangerous and personal.

The old wizard's face twisted up in rage. "Die, you witch whore." He moved his hand, but I was already moving.

Calling on my demon mojo, I flung out my palms, and a drip of black energy plopped to the ground at my feet. I'd run out.

"Whoops," I laughed. "Fire's out."

I braced myself for the old wizard's magic. In my panic, I sent out my will, trying to grab on to the ley lines but forgetting they'd cut my connection. I was screwed.

And then the wizards did something I didn't expect.

They took each other's hands like witches did sometimes when forming a circle or combining their magic. Only they didn't create a circle. They formed a straight line with Dragos in the middle.

I took a step back as the air was suddenly filled with crackling energy.

Blue energy coiled around each wizard and then shot out, connecting with the following wizard—or brother apparently—and spreading and spinning until they were all connected like they'd tied a magical rope around themselves. Ten pairs of eyes shone with the same blue energy, same magic.

233

And I shit you not, blue laser beams shot from Dragos's eyes, aimed right at me.

I knew I was a goner. No way in hell could I move fast enough to get out of the way of these laser-beam-shooting wizards.

I was going to die. Fear hit me in a cold flood. Did my life flash before my eyes?

No. Because all I saw was Marcus.

A flash of black-and-gray fur appeared from the corner of my eye.

The gorilla's body slammed into my side, pushing me out of the way and getting the full brunt of the beam right in the chest.

This wasn't the first time Marcus had taken a hit instead of me. But this time, I knew it was different.

Marcus fell to the ground in his human form, laying in a fetal position with smoke rising from his body like he'd been cooked from the inside. He was still. Too still.

And he wasn't breathing.

Forgetting the wizards and my imminent death, I rushed over and fell to my knees next to him.

Something about the way he lay there, his limbs twisted unnaturally with his chest still and not rising or falling, made blocks of fear hit me like a sledgehammer. The scent of burnt hair rose to my nose.

Hot tears bathed my cheeks as I reached out and shook him, crying, "Marcus! Marcus, wake up!" I slapped him across the face. Hard. And again, and again, until my hand ached.

But the chief did not wake.

CHAPTER

21

Numbness filled me. Shouts echoed in my ears, but I couldn't make them out. They were muffled, like words underwater.

"Marcus?" My voice rasped, my throat constricting as the tears fell. Desperate, I shoved at his chest and started to pound my fists on it, over and over again as hard as I could.

"Marcus! Get up. Get up!" I cried. "You can't be… I… Don't leave me…" I tasted the tears in my mouth. My chest clenched, and I couldn't get enough air in my lungs. Vertigo hit, and I clutched at his shoulders. I couldn't think. I couldn't breathe. This couldn't be happening.

Not my Marcus… please, God, no.

Finally, I heard the sound of laughter and glanced up. Through my blurred vision, I saw Dragos staring at Marcus's body with a satisfied expression on his wrinkled face while his sons laughed at me and at Marcus, like we were the butt of some joke. As though his life had meant nothing.

A rage like I'd never known welled in me. I saw darkness. I saw death. I wanted to kill the old wizard and all of his sons.

My fists trembled as a black fury filled my core. It tripled as their laughter increased at the sight of my defiance and my pain.

My demon mojo was spent. I had nothing left but my wits and my will to fight.

"He's dead." A smile of satisfaction blossomed over the old wizard's face.

"He's not… gone," I sobbed, unable to bring myself to say that word. *He can't be.*

"The beast is dead," repeated Dragos and cocked his head in a mockery of interest. "I felt his death. We all did."

My eyes filled as I slumped, staring at Marcus's gray skin, which was usually a warm golden color. My throat burned as I tried to speak, but the words wouldn't come. My breath escaped me in another sob, and my heart seemed to stop. I felt nothing but pain until it was all-consuming.

I felt my world shift with a nauseating spin. It was as though I'd lost a part of me, a part of my soul. A hole, a giant emptiness, threatened to throw me over the edge.

Grief slammed into me, and I struggled to breathe, not wanting to believe he was gone. Grief hard and cold, defined by gray eyes and that sexy smile I loved so much that I would never see again.

It should have been me. That beam should have killed me…

"Pathetic." Dragos smiled down at me like a malevolent, cruel god. "You shouldn't cry over him. He was just an animal. A pet."

I flinched as though he'd hit me. I opened my mouth to tell him off, but something stopped me.

The sound of crunching tires on the asphalt reached me. I turned to two gleaming headlights coming straight for us.

Instinctively, I threw myself over Marcus, shielding him with my body as a Volvo station wagon came tearing down the street and plowed into the line of wizards.

The thumps of flesh hitting metal and snapping of bones didn't even have me reacting. Music to my ears.

If I wasn't so numb, and despairing, I would have applauded the truly excellent driving.

Tires squealed as the Volvo fishtailed to a stop, extremely close to me and Marcus. The back passenger door burst open, and Ruth and Ronin jumped out.

"Hurry. Get in the car," urged Ruth, her blue eyes wild under a pink bandanna with the words THE MOON MADE ME DO IT stitched across it.

My hands clamped on Marcus's body, his skin icy to the touch as a hot madness took over me. I turned to the moans of crushed wizards, and I flicked my eyes to the three who lay prone on the street and the seven who were scrambling to their feet. "I'm not leaving him."

Frowning, Ruth hurried over to Marcus and pressed her fingers to his neck. "He's still alive."

I just stared at her, unable to formulate any words. I never thought of checking his pulse. I was an idiot.

Marcus is alive!

"But not for long. He needs medicine. We need to get him to Davenport House so I can begin working on a healing tonic that'll reverse whatever curse or spell he was hit with," said Ruth. She pressed her hands gently over mine and said, "Tessa. You need to let him go. We'll take him from here."

The startled cry that escaped my throat was my undoing. Huge raking, snot-tear sobs shook me, making my body tremble.

"Tessa. You need to let go," I heard Ruth say again.

I looked down at my hands peering under Ruth's, only realizing now that they were shaking and that my arms had locked around Marcus protectively.

"Ata witch," encouraged Ruth. "That's it. Let go of him. We've got him."

With a deep breath, while watching my hands as though they belonged to someone else, I let them go with a great effort of will.

"Ronin. Help me get him in the trunk," ordered Ruth, and she and Ronin each grabbed one of Marcus's shoulders while I grabbed his legs.

Together we gently placed him in the trunk. Thank the cauldron the Volvo's trunk was enormous because I clambered in after him. I hauled his upper body on my lap, cradling his head as Ronin and Ruth slipped into the back seat.

Iris turned around from the back seat, her eyes focused on mine, sad. "Tessa... I'm so sorry."

I blinked. Tears spilled down my cheeks and rolled off my chin. I held on to Marcus as though if I let go, I'd lose him for good.

"Here." Ruth handed me a green-and-red-checkered wool blanket. "Use that to cover him up. Try to keep him warm."

"Thanks." Tears blurred my vision as I pulled the blanket over his naked body, covering his large frame as best I could. But Marcus was huge, and the blanket looked like a bath towel. It was just enough to cover his chest and thighs.

With the window down, Ruth hung over the side of her car door and smacked the door twice with an open hand.

"Dolores. Step on it!" she howled.

Dolores slammed her foot on the accelerator.

Heads jerked back, and Beverly hung on to her boobs from the front passenger seat as the Volvo propelled forward, engine blaring as the car screamed down the street.

I was hit with the full-on creepy sensation of someone watching me.

And through the Volvo's rear window I saw a few figures standing next to the bodies still lying in the street where the Volvo had them plowed over.

The last thing I saw was Dragos's frown and twisted face as the Volvo took a sharp right turn.

We'd killed more of his sons. He wasn't going to let that go, but I didn't care. I didn't care about a lot of things at the moment.

I rubbed my hands over Marcus's shoulders and down his arms, trying to get his blood circulating, but his skin felt like it was made of ice—hard, cold, and numbing to the touch. I'd never felt anything like it before. He was so cold, too cold.

I felt as though my whole world was crashing down on me at this very moment. If I were to lose him, lose the best thing that ever happened to me…

"Don't you die on me, you stupid monkey," I cried and sniffed, tightening my hold on him. Tears fell down my cheeks, mixing with the snot tears.

"He won't," said Ruth, the sound of fabric pulling as she turned around to face me. "Not if I can help it. The sooner we get him to the house, the sooner I can treat him."

My lips trembled as I looked at her. "You… you can save him?"

Ruth's eyes shimmered. "His pulse is weak, but I'll do my damnedest."

It wasn't a definite yes, but I'd take it. Ruth was the best witch healer in Maine, maybe even in North America. If anyone could cure him, it was her.

"Speaking of the house…" I started. "Something happened to my father," I said, panic crawling at my insides at the memory of the fear I saw on his face. "He's gone."

"What do you mean he's gone?" came Dolores's voice from the front.

"We were talking, and he just disappeared as if something took him. So whatever the wizards are doing, they made sure the connection we had through Davenport House and the Netherworld is broken." At least I hoped that was the case, and nothing worse.

"Where were you guys?" I asked Ruth, but Dolores answered.

"At Gilbert's grocery store trying to help a group of shifters who were being attacked by those black-robed fanatics," answered Dolores, her eyes on the black road in front of her. "Stanley Dyson rushed over saying Jeff had been killed and that you and Marcus were in a duel with the Dark wizards."

I felt a pang in my chest at the mention of Jeff. "I didn't see it happen. I just saw Jeff's body lying there. Marcus… he just lost it."

"No kidding." Ronin stared at Marcus for a moment.

"I was trying to get him to leave with me." I shook my head. "But he wouldn't listen. The dome… it's doing something to the shifters and the weres. Draining them of their life force or something. It's making them weak and easier to kill."

"We know," said Beverly without turning around. "We realized something was very wrong when a group of werecats could barely fight back. Then Sarah Finnegan, a shifter, described the feeling of being sick, like having flu symptoms."

"What the hell happened?" asked the half-vampire.

The thought of the wizards' powerful beam sent a wave of rage through me. "They shot laser beams out of their eyes."

Dolores's head snapped in Beverly's direction, and Ruth's expression was troubled as she met Dolores's alarmed eyes in the rearview mirror.

"What? Like Superman?" Ronin leaned over the backrest of his seat. "You're kidding?"

"I wish I were. It was aimed at me, but Marcus…"

"Pushed you out of the way," answered the half-vampire. "Gallant bastard. And a tough sonofabitch. He's going to be fine, Tess. I know he will."

My throat constricted as I wiped at my tears, trying to think of something else to say before I lost it.

I held on to Marcus as silence descended in the car.

"What is *that*?" I heard Dolores say, and I turned to look out the front windshield.

A golden light winked in the surrounding darkness at the end of Stardust Drive. As we drove closer, the golden light grew in height and length, flickering as it reached high above the trees.

Dolores cursed. "Cauldron help us all."

"Oh no. No, no, no!" shouted Beverly.

I craned my neck as Ruth cried, "This can't be. Can't be. This can't be possible!"

Even from where I was sitting, I could see the tension in Dolores's shoulders as she slowed the Volvo to a stop in front of our driveway.

"Holy shit," cursed Ronin. "Damn. I thought nothing could touch it?"

Iris's face was pale as she stared out the window, a golden glow reflecting in her dark eyes.

Shock cascaded over me, startling me to stillness. I could not believe what I was looking at. It had to be a trick. It couldn't have happened at a worse time.

Davenport House was in flames.

CHAPTER
22

The fire roared, like the growl of a great beast. It rose in an explosion of heat and yellow-and-orange flames that engulfed the walls and chewed the beams. Davenport House was swallowed by hungry rising flames until I couldn't even see past the fire. All I saw was fire.

I'd felt a significant loss with Marcus just moments ago, and now I was hit by another.

Rage and sadness choked me. Everything I owned and cherished was in there. Photos, books, a gold necklace with a pendant my mother had given me when I turned twelve—one of the only things she'd given me—small memorabilia, things that could never be replaced. Stuff I'd gathered over the years was destroyed. They were worthless in terms of money, but they'd meant everything to me.

And then there was my father. Davenport House was a place where he could visit me and my aunts and have some sort of typical family gathering. Now he could never visit ever again.

"Hildo!" cried Ruth as she jumped out of the car and ran straight for the burning house.

"Ruth! Stop!" Beverly was out and running after her sister just as Dolores leaped out, leaving the door open, followed by Iris and Ronin.

Oh no. Hildo.

I stayed where I was, cradling Marcus while tears sprang anew as the thought of losing that cat at this moment was just unbearable.

"Here! I'm here!" came a faint voice from outside the car.

Ruth wiggled out of Beverly's grasp and ran to the tall maple tree on the front side of our yard. A tiny black shape sat on a branch.

Ruth reached out and the cat sprang into her arms. She collapsed to the ground, sobbing uncontrollably as she held on to her animal companion.

Damn, the waterworks started up again, and I turned to the sound of a strangled cry as I saw Dolores fall to her knees, her head snapped back as she wailed, and I felt my heart give a sudden thud. Beverly was the only sister left standing, though her pretty face was twisted in anguish. There was no mistaking the insurmountable grief that shook her to her core.

The loss I felt at seeing Davenport House burn was nothing compared to what my aunts felt. They were born and raised in that house — all their physical memories gone in one moment. Davenport House was family, in the not-real-family sort of way. And I cried for House, for that invisible magical butler who'd given me my special room.

"I don't get it," I heard Ronin say just out on the front lawn. "I thought this house was magical. I thought it couldn't burn or something?"

"It's not supposed to burn," came Iris's voice. She'd stayed at the edge of the front lawn, where it met with the street. "This isn't a normal fire. It's a magical one. And very powerful."

"The wizards did this," exclaimed Ronin, echoing my thoughts exactly. "Those bastards started this fire. They wanted to strike you, and they knew burning down this house would do that."

"It worked," I said, and both Iris and Ronin turned to look at me through the Volvo's window.

I blinked my blurred vision as I stared at the tall, yellow flames that engulfed that once beautiful farmhouse. My heart was heavy with fear and dread.

"Get back!" cried the half-vampire. In a flash, Ronin was pulling Dolores up on her feet and grabbing Beverly with his other arm as he hauled them back to the street.

With a great big shriek, the frame of Davenport House collapsed into a giant cloud of ash and a pile of burning wood.

Then, at that moment, I realized I was losing two things; I was losing my home and with that, the ability to save Marcus. If Davenport was destroyed, it meant Ruth's potions were burned and destroyed as well. Without them, we had nothing to help Marcus.

A thought struck me hard, making my limbs shake with adrenaline.

Ruth sometimes kept potions in the back shed. With Davenport House flattened to a crumpled mess, I could see the outline of the shed. The wizards had missed it.

And then I was moving.

With my heart pounding in my ears, I slipped from under Marcus's weight and carefully laid him on the trunk's floor before jumping out of the Volvo.

"The shed! Ruth, the shed!" I called out to her, adrenaline pumping as my legs found their strength again and propelled me forward with a speed I never thought possible with these flabby babies.

I met Ruth's gaze from across the front lawn. With the fire nearly out, we were back in semidarkness, but it was enough to see the recognition on her face. That's what I liked most about a close family. You didn't even need to utter the words for them to know exactly what you were thinking.

And then Ruth ran to join me, Hildo bouncing on her right shoulder.

Together we rushed toward the shed. I coughed as I inhaled smoke from the fire, which burned my lungs with each labored breath. My eyes stung and watered. I yanked the door open and stepped inside. Immediately, we were bathed in a soft glow.

"Magic," said Ruth with a shrug and then coughed. Her eyes were red and wet in the glow of the witch light.

"I'm sorry about your home, Tessa," said Hildo.

I reached up and stroked his head. "I'm just glad you weren't in there when they torched it."

"Oh, I was in there," answered the cat, his eyes narrowing. "I heard them chanting from inside while I was trying to take a nap. I thought they were kids fooling around, so I sneaked out the window to tell them to shut the hell up. That's when I saw the robes."

"So, there's no mistaking it was the Dark wizards?" questioned Ruth.

The cat hung his head. "I'm sorry I couldn't stop them. Their magic was beyond anything I'd ever seen."

I pulled my hand away. "They would have killed you, Hildo. I'm glad you had the sense to hide." I ran my gaze over the shelves and racks lining the four walls of the small shed, which were packed with an assortment of jars, along with unidentifiable objects, books, containers, and pouches full of all sorts of herbs, roots, candles, pendulums, and boxes of chalks. Piled on the tables sat a vast collection of cauldrons, shiny copper pots, ceramic spoons, and bowls that were perfect for mixing potions. Drying herbs and flowers hung down from the ceiling.

"Do you have everything here to save Marcus?" I knew time was running out for him, and I prayed to the goddess that something here could help him.

Ruth rushed over to one of the shelves. "Yes. I believe I do. We'll have to take this entire shelf of jars and containers," she said as she stepped back and gestured with her hand. "We'll have to do it in a few trips. Here." Ruth knelt and picked up an empty cardboard box. "We can use this."

"Okay," I exhaled, not having mastered the slowing of my pounding heart. "We'll have to hurry. Marcus is barely hanging on." The last words came out as a croak. I wasn't thrilled by the idea of having to run back and forth, but I was out of options.

Ruth's eyes pinched in worry. "I know," she said, in almost a whisper.

"I'll help," came Ronin's voice, and I spun around to find him, Iris, Beverly, and Dolores squeezed together in the shed's entrance, which was a strange sight to behold.

"We'll all take some," informed Dolores, her voice firm, but I could still hear a slight tremor in it.

Together, following Ruth's instructions, we all piled as many containers, vials, herbs, and even candles, as we could, in our arms. Ruth carried as many as she could in her box, and Beverly balanced jars and vials on her chest until we'd cleared that entire shelf.

I stepped out of the shed right behind Iris. "You'll need a safe place... with a stove or a cauldron to make your potions. Right?" I asked while I walked back to the Volvo as fast as I could without dropping anything.

"That's right," answered Ruth. Her gaze flicked to the charred remains of her home. The devastation on her face sent a pang of heartache through me.

Her sisters shared the same look as they all tried to avoid looking at their home while we rushed back to the Volvo, but their eyes were drawn to it. It was a shock—a huge one.

Dolores cleared her throat. "With the Dark wizards on the prowl, and with Davenport House gone, there aren't many safe places left in Hollow Cove."

Dolores was right. Davenport House was *the* safest place in town. Well, it used to be.

"And they'll be looking for us," said Beverly.

"Then we better hurry," expressed Dolores.

Iris dropped a small cloth bag, and I bent down to pick it up. "So, where do we go?"

"Martha's," answered Ruth, walking heavily with a defiant look in her eyes. "She's the only witch I know who has a working cauldron big enough to hold my potion-making."

All righty then.

CHAPTER

23

Marcus lay on a hot-pink couch with the backrest molded in the shape of a heart. The light of the candles on the coffee table cast harsh shadows on his beautiful face. Even in the dim light, I could see the black circles under his eyes darkening and spreading, his skin becoming increasingly clammy, pale, and sickly looking.

It was hard to watch him like that, so ill and on the verge of death. Marcus was the pillar of strength, the strongest of his kind, from what I'd witnessed. And to see him slipping away, all because he'd tried to protect me, was nearly too much for me to bear.

On my knees next to the couch, I reached out and brushed the hair from his eyes. It's no wonder I thought he was dead. His breathing was so shallow I couldn't even hear it.

"Hang on, Marcus," I whispered as another wave of grief hit me. I grabbed his left hand and flinched at how cool and hard his skin felt, like cold stone.

I heard something soft making contact with something hard followed by the loud curses that flew out of Dolores's mouth. "What's that damn swivel chair doing there!" she hissed, and I saw her tall frame limping toward the middle of Martha's shop.

We couldn't chance a witch light. It was way too bright, and the last thing we needed was to alert the Dark wizards to our whereabouts. So we were basically in the dark, except for the three candles.

"That styling chair is where it's supposed to be," answered Martha with annoyance in her voice. "You would know if you actually came into my salon once every full moon, hon. You could do with a trim."

"She has a point," said Beverly, staring at her reflection in one of the salon-styling station mirrors. "You need to tame that mane of yours. You look like the banshee of Killarney." She shrugged and added, "No. The banshee actually looked better."

Dolores let out a puff of air, a book hanging in her hand. "I don't care about my appearance right now. My vanity, unlike others, is not important. What *is* important is saving Marcus and our town from this wizard sect."

"Working on it." Ruth dropped what looked like yellow powder in the large boiling cauldron sitting in the middle of Martha's salon. Purple flames licked the bottom of the cauldron in some magical fire that apparently, didn't burn the wood floors it sat on.

Iris stood next to the cauldron, watching Ruth with admiration as she studied the older witch's skill at potion-making.

I heard a yowl and looked over at Hildo sitting on one of the stylish chairs, a large, bedazzled pink collar looped around his neck. His ears lay low on his head, and his tail slashed behind him. That cat was pissed.

But Martha wouldn't have it any other way.

"I say he puts on the collar," said the large witch as she'd thrust the pink, bedazzled collar at Ruth. "I made it especially for him. It's not asking a lot."

"But he doesn't *like* collars," Ruth had started, stroking her cat familiar on her shoulder. "Gives him hives."

"They really do," said the cat. "They're also very constricting."

Martha shoved the collar at Ruth. "He wears the collar, or you go find yourself another place to boil your spells."

There was no arguing with that.

And now Hildo looked like one of those poor pet celebrities, dressed up as dolls, whose sad eyes pleaded to go back to the breeder.

Dolores angled the book she had in her hand toward one of the candles. She flipped the pages and then slammed the book shut. "Is there a book in your establishment that has actual spells and information about magic other than beautifying spells?"

Martha gave her a look. "No. This isn't a boring library filled with dreary, mundane spells. Females and males come to my establishment to be beautified."

"More like mummified," muttered Dolores as she tossed the book on a side table.

Ruth mumbled a word I didn't quite hear, and I pulled my attention to her. A small cyclone appeared at the top of the cauldron and then lowered into the mix, stirring up the contents as though it was a giant spoon. That was a pretty cool spell.

Iris smiled as she leaned over the cauldron. "Wow. Can you teach me that spell some day?"

Ruth beamed. "Of course. It's straightforward… once you—"

A sudden crash came from outside on the street and I stiffened, holding my breath. If the wizards found us out now, it was all over.

The salon went silent. The only sound was the bubbling of the boiling cauldron and the flickering of magical flames at the bottom of the giant iron pot.

Ronin was at the front bay window in a flash, peering into the street.

"Ronin? What is it?" I whispered. "Are they here?"

Ronin lifted his hand to silence me and leaned his head toward the window. After what felt like minutes, he pulled back and turned. "They're gone. You can relax."

"Thank the goddess," said Martha, fanning herself with her hand. "I nearly had a stroke."

"We're sitting ducks in this place," I said, my voice a bit louder than I'd intended. "Not that I don't appreciate you letting us stay here," I quickly told Martha at her frown, "but sooner or later they'll find us. We need to come up with a plan. We need to figure out how to stop these wizards."

"All my books, my spellbooks I've collected over the years," said Dolores. "Books that were given to me by my grandmother. Old tomes that cannot be replaced. All lost in that fire. They burned down our home to send a message. They knew what it was and what was inside. What it meant to us. They want us to know who's in charge. But mostly who's more powerful."

"They might have disabled us a little, but I'm not giving up." I looked around the room. "There must be something we can use against them, something we haven't thought about yet."

"Like what?" asked Iris. "We barely know anything about this group, other than what Dolores told us."

"The head wizard is called Dragos," I said suddenly. "Does that name mean anything to anyone?" Every head shook. "The Guild of Dark Wizards is basically a family-run business. Like a Mafia crime family, only with douches playing with magic instead of guns."

"What?" expressed Dolores.

"They're his *sons*. All of them. All I know is that the wizards are the sons of Dragos."

"Damn, that's some potent seed," said Ronin, awarding himself a smack from Iris.

"What about his daughters?" asked Beverly.

I looked at her and shrugged. "No idea. If girls aren't allowed in his club, dead probably." Because anything worse was not something I wanted to think about at this moment.

Dolores's tall frame paced the room. "So, the guild is made up of his progeny. Wouldn't be the first time I've heard of magical practitioners wanting to keep the magic in the family."

"Isn't money supposed to be kept in the family?" offered Ronin.

Dolores nodded. "Same difference," she answered and fell into a concentrated silence.

But I couldn't keep silent anymore. "Ruth?" I asked. "Is the potion almost done?" My voice was harsh, and I regretted my tone. I hated to pressure her like this, but we'd been inside Martha's salon for over two hours, and Marcus was slipping away more every minute. He didn't have much longer.

Ruth let out a sigh and looked at me. "It would help if I knew what I was dealing with, what kind of spell this was. So, I mixed in my most effective counter curse and healing potions to make a super-duper healing elixir." She looked back at the cauldron and said proudly, "I call it, the Super-Twelve."

"Why that name?" Ronin spun around in one of the swivel chairs.

"Because. I used twelve counter curses and twelve healing potions."

"Shouldn't it be called the Super-Twenty-Four, then?" prompted the half-vampire.

Ruth gave him a frown. "No." And that was the end of that conversation. The witch who came up with the spell should be the witch who gave it its name too.

"Is it finished?" My heart thrashed in my chest, and I felt ill. The fact that her mixture had turned a black color that looked like tar or oil didn't bode well with me. I didn't think I could sit here any longer. I had to do something to help Marcus. Because if her concoction didn't work, I had to find another way.

The only other way I could think of was to kidnap that old wizard and make him give me the counter course or whatever to heal Marcus. And that wouldn't end well for either of us.

"Almost." Ruth tipped the contents from a glass jar that sat on the nearest beauty station, into the mix. She moved to the cauldron, her arms spread out dramatically. "Get back. This is going to kick."

An instant later, we felt a nearly soundless bang that made the house shake.

Red smoke coiled from the cauldron. The mixture hissed and bubbled, changing from red to green and ending finally in a pretty gold color.

Ruth's face was flushed. Her eyes widened as she turned to me. "It's ready." She grabbed a mug from one of the beauty stations, dunked it in the hot mixture, and rushed over to me and an unconscious Marcus.

"Wait. Isn't it too hot?" I asked, staring at the smoke coiling from the top of the mug.

"It's not. Don't worry. Lift his head," she instructed. "We need to force as much of the Super-Twelve as possible in him."

Trusting my aunt and doing as I was told, I moved over, scooped Marcus's head in between my hands, and lifted him. Ruth leaned forward, placed the edge of the mug to his lips, and raised it.

Golden liquid poured into Marcus's mouth. I was about to stop her since it was steaming, but before I could, she'd dunked the entire contents of the mug into the chief's mouth.

Ruth rocked back on her heels, the mug in her hands. "Okay. Okay."

"When are we supposed to see if it's working?" I asked her, searching Marcus's face but not seeing any changes.

"Give it a moment," answered my aunt. "The potion needs to mix into his bloodstream. If this curse or hex beam damaged any internal organs, it's going to take more time."

"Marcus doesn't have time. I need this to work." I let his head go gently and moved around him so I could grab his hand. "He's still frozen." Fear hit, making my body shake. "It should have worked by now." I knew magical healing worked a hundred times faster than the average human remedies. With Ruth's, it was usually instantaneous. If her potion didn't work right away, it meant he was too far gone. It meant we were too late.

My eyes welled with tears as I grabbed on to his hand, staring at his big, lovely hands that would never hold me again.

I sank to the floor next to the couch, my breath escaping in a sob. "It didn't work."

"What didn't work?"

My breath caught as I stared at Marcus. His beautiful gray eyes stared back at me.

"Marcus!"

Without thinking, I scrambled up and grabbed him, squeezing his body into mine.

"Ow," mumbled the chief. "Not so hard."

I released him and leaned back. "Sorry." I stared at his smiling face. He still had dark circles under his eyes, and his skin was still pale, but he was awake. I'd take that.

Ruth was next to us in a flash. She pressed her hand to his forehead. "He still has a fever. You're not out of the woods yet," she told Marcus, and then she added with a smile, "but I believe the worst of it is over."

"Thank the cauldron," said Beverly as she supported herself on one of the swivel chairs.

I felt a hand on my shoulder and turned to see Iris smiling at me. She gave a squeeze and then moved to stand with Ronin by the window.

"Welcome back, Chief," said Ronin, and Marcus gave a nod his way.

Stupid, happy tears leaked out of my eyes and I quickly wiped them away. I'd cried enough.

"What happened?" asked the chief as he hauled himself into more of a sitting position. I relayed the Volvo rescue and then what the wizards did to Davenport House.

263

"If we could take out the dome, the town would have a fighting chance," I told him, seeing the deep frown on the chief's face deepening every second. Yes, the wizards could most probably come up with another dome to replace this one if we managed to destroy it, but I was hoping it wasn't an instantaneous thing. More than likely it took several hours to produce a new one. At least I hoped. "It won't solve the wizard problem. I wish I knew where they got their magic. Where all this power comes from."

"I might be able to help you with that," said Hildo, and we all turned to look at him.

The black cat raised himself, stretched, and then sat back on the chair. "I forgot to tell you something," said the cat. "Something about the wizards and the dome."

"What?" both Dolores and I asked at the same time.

"First, you need to promise to remove the collar from my neck," hissed the cat.

"I promise," I said before anyone could respond and raised a hand at Martha's objection. If what the cat said could help us, I'd gladly burn the collar and dance around it with Hildo.

"A connection between the dome, the wizards, *and* the paranormals," answered the cat.

"I don't get it."

"The dome sucks out the weres' and shifters' auras, their magical life force, their internal magic, and then turns it into an energy the wizards can use, fueling them with powerful magic," elaborated the cat.

My heart thrashed with excitement. "Take down the dome, and the wizards would be easier to kill or at least seriously weaken."

"Exactly," said the cat, looking smug.

This was it. This was the answer.

I rushed over and kissed the top of the cat's head. "Hildo, *you* are a genius." I removed the collar and handed it over to a scowling Martha. I did not have the energy to deal with her drama.

The cat shrugged, lay down on the chair, and crossed his front paws. "Tell me something I don't know."

"This is good." Dolores peered over the cauldron. "Pity we can't call upon Obiryn. We could have used his help. With most of the town too sick or infected by the dome to help, I'm not sure how we can destroy it."

Infected.

"Wait a minute." I straightened. My father's words came at me again. "Before my father disappeared, before the wizards cut our connection," I told them, "he was trying to tell me how to destroy the dome." I flicked my gaze between my aunts. "I think he wanted me to *infect* the dome with my demon mojo."

It was the only thing that made sense. Infect the shell and the rest would fall. Well, something like that.

Dolores cocked her head in thought. "Contaminate the dome with your demon magic. You think it'll work?"

"Well, my demon mojo was the only thing they couldn't counter. My elemental magic didn't work on them, but my demon magic did."

"Yes." Dolores was nodding. "I think your father was right. It could work. The dome is constructed with powerful magic but still just magic. It can be worked around with enough power and skill. Perhaps your demon magic is exactly what we need."

"How are you going to do that?" asked Iris. "How are you going to infect the dome?"

I looked over at the Dark witch. "Like cracking an egg. I just need to get close enough so I can hit it with my demon mojo." I exhaled and said, "And if my father was right, the rest should follow."

"I'm coming with you," said Marcus as he pushed his large body forward. The strain on his face tore at my heart.

I pressed my hands on his bare chest and pushed him back. "You're in no shape to go anywhere, hot stuff."

The chief frowned. "You're not going alone."

266

"She won't be." Dolores raised her chin. "I'll be there."

"Me too," said Beverly.

"And me," added Ruth.

"I'm coming too," informed Martha, which really surprised me after the collar issue.

"You're gonna need backup." Ronin stretched and cracked his knuckles. "I'll be there to watch your back with Iris."

Something like a growl erupted from Marcus's throat. "You can't leave me behind. You need me."

"I need you to stay here and get better." As I searched his face, my chest welled with all kinds of emotions at the fierceness in his voice and on his face. "I know this is hard to hear, but you're not strong enough." A vein popped on his forehead. Oooh. He was mad. Proceed with extreme caution. "You can growl and snarl all you want, but you're staying here. And that's final." Not so much caution after all.

His ultimate duty and purpose were to protect the ones he loved, his town, and me. The fact that he wanted to protect me still, even as sick as he was, was a total turn-on.

"I can't risk you getting hurt again, or worse, killed," I told him as his gray eyes filled with anger. "I'll be too worried about you to focus on my job—to infect the dome. We might only get one shot at it," I added, hoping that would cool him off. "I don't want to screw this up."

Marcus looked away, his jaw clenching as the muscles on his throat and shoulders popped like they were competing with each other. "Fine." He crossed his arms over his ample chest. "I'll wait 'til I feel a bit better."

It wasn't the answer I wanted, but I'd take it. "Good." I exhaled, shaking out the tension and finally getting excited at the prospect of taking down the wizards once and for all.

I glanced over at my aunts and friends. "Let's do this. But first… I really need to pee."

CHAPTER
24

I'll admit leaving Marcus behind still weighed heavily on me. The guilt kept pressing on my chest, making it difficult to breathe. Worse was the fear for me reflecting in his gray eyes. But I knew I'd be too busy worrying about him if he came with us. I'd lose focus and screw up. Or worse, end up getting my ass fried by the dome.

It had been a hard choice, but it had been the right one.

I walked along the red wooden bridge planks, all the way to the edge of the dome. Dolores's witch light still shone as brightly as when it first emerged, adding some brightness to a gloomy task.

I needed that damned dome down. Not only for the people of this town but also for me. I needed my use of the ley lines back, and for that, the only way that would happen was if I got rid of the dome.

A distant scream erupted from the streets behind me, followed by a grunt and the wail of magic. It tore through the encroaching darkness as a long, piercing shriek steeped with sheer terror. These bastards were killing our townspeople. This needed to end now.

Behind me, my aunts, Iris, and Ronin tensed. Even Martha had shown up to give her support. I knew she didn't have much training in defensive magic like my aunts and Iris. Maybe she could threaten the wizards with a couple of magical makeovers and see how that'd go down. Yeah, that could work.

I took a deep breath and faced the dome's wall.

"You ready?" Iris joined me, looking more nervous than I felt.

"Nope. You?"

"Nope."

I smiled. I loved that Dark witch. "Listen. Maybe you should stay back. I'm not sure what's going to happen once I infect it."

"She's right." Ronin appeared next to Iris in a flash and grabbed her arm. I frowned. Damn that vamp speed.

"It might melt, just as it might explode and come down on us," said the half-vampire, holding on to his girlfriend protectively.

"Okay. But we'll be right over here," said Iris as she let Ronin pull her a good twenty feet away from me.

"Tessa. You better hurry," called Beverly, and I turned to follow her gaze.

A group of about twenty wizards was headed our way, their long, dark robes billowing around them like dark clouds. I watched the robed figures spilling down the street, moving with the speed and precision of predators.

"Right. No pressure." Gritting my teeth, I spun back around, trying to steel myself and focusing my will around that dark-force manipulation, that dark energy I could control, thanks to my daddy dearest.

Cold power answered, spilling from my core and coursing through my body to my limbs. It pounded in time to match my beating heart. I barely registered the energy that was emitting from me, making some of my loose strands of hair float up around my head.

"Hurry up, Tess," called Ronin's voice behind me. "They're coming."

"I'm trying," I snapped back. *Geez. Give me a break.* This demon magic was still very new to me, so it took a little more focus to get it going.

I choked down a surge of panic and forced myself not to turn around and run in the opposite direction.

"This has to work."

I drew in my will and focused on what I had to do, fixating on that dark dome wall. Then I ground my teeth together, reached out to my cold magic, and released it in a sudden burst of energy.

Using both hands, because why the hell not, I flicked my wrists high above my head.

Twin black tendrils shot out of my outstretched palms.

They hit the top of the dome, exactly where I'd planned. Well, at least my aim was good.

It was hard to see my black magic on that dark wall, but with the witch light's illumination, I could see a shadow of my demon mojo's tendrils, like the veins on a dark slab of marble or granite.

I held my breath and waited, searching for a sign that my magic had weakened the dome.

But after about a minute of waiting, nothing happened.

"Nothing happened," called Ronin behind me, echoing my thoughts.

"Ronin, I swear I'm going to castrate you if you don't stop," I growled, my irritation soaring to new levels.

My thoughts were rambling now as real panic struck. Why hadn't it worked? Had I read my father's intentions wrong? No. I didn't think so. So why didn't the dome react to my demon mojo?

Time for Plan B. And what is Plan B, you ask? Simple. A repeat of Plan A, only better.

A wave of fatigue hit, faster than before this time as I called upon my demon mojo. I hadn't had time to recharge or heal fully, though Ruth had given me a mug of her healing tonic. It got rid of some of the tiredness and soreness from my earlier fight with the wizards, but not all of it.

I needed to focus. I needed direction and better concentration, which was next to impossible when I heard Dolores's first defensive spell behind me.

I turned to a shower of lights in reds, greens, pinks, and purples as witches and wizards dueled. The sounds of battle boomed in a mixture of cries, shouts, and the surge of magic. It was like a show of fireworks and quite pretty. If lives didn't depend on me destroying the dome, I might have taken a moment to admire the view.

My aunts, Iris, and Martha formed a protective line in front of me—a solid, defensive wall of magic.

I saw Ruth dig into her bag and then throw a small vial at one of the wizards like she was a seasoned pitcher for the New York Yankees.

The vial exploded into a cloud of orange dust as it made contact. Perfect hit.

The wizard shook his head as he staggered, losing his balance and causing him to fall to his knees like a drunk.

Ruth threw a fist in the air. "Take that, you bad wizard!" Yeah, Ruth was ruthless when it came to insults.

Beverly stood with her arms out to her sides, her lips moving in a chant I couldn't hear as twin, eight-foot tornados swirled and spiraled into the wizards, pushing them back.

Next to her was Iris, a dark chant emanating from her lips as she, too, conjured some wind and blasted the wizards back after they'd been hit with the tornados.

Pink energy burst from Martha's outstretched hand. It hit an oncoming wizard. His robe blazed and then instead of black, it was pink with white polka dots. Confused, the wizard halted, staring at his hands, which were covered in glitter. I choked on a laugh as his hood fell, and his hair was pink with an eighties perm. Shock marred his face. Seemed like he was the vain kind, too preoccupied with his looks even to remember why he was here.

"Inmotems!" cried Dolores as she leaned forward with yellow flames spewing from her hands—elemental fire. Yellow light flooded around her as she hit one of the wizards. He staggered, and for a second I thought she'd had him. But the wizard straightened, countering with a shoot of blue flames.

Dolores waved her hand and knocked the flames quickly away. That was impressive to watch, but I didn't have time for that.

"Focus, Tessa," I said, panting and drawing in a breath.

A blur of movement caught my attention, and the sound of a voice articulating a curse reached me.

Crap.

I ducked and pitched myself sideways.

Pain tore at me in a blinding torrent of agony as if I'd slashed open my stomach and ripped out a clump of my guts. Darkness stained my vision and I tasted blood. For a moment, I was afraid to move. Pain would do that to a person. But then the pain subsided as the aftershocks of agony rocked through me and vanished.

I spat on the ground. "Ow."

I saw a flash of dark robes and braced myself for more pain, but it didn't come.

A blur of brown hair appeared in my line of sight. With a torrent of vampire speed, Ronin pivoted smoothly. With a swipe of his talons, he sliced the wizard across the neck, sending a spray of blood. And, of course, Ronin never got hit, not even a drop of blood could be seen on the half-vampire's clothes or his person.

He tossed the wizard like he was nothing more than a rag doll. "You better hurry, Tess. I don't know how long we can keep this up. Don't get me wrong. Your aunts are all kinds of awesome, but the wizards' magic is going to get through at some point."

"Right. I know." I scrambled to my feet and faced the dome wall again. Whatever I'd been hit with was still throbbing, making it difficult to concentrate.

Doubt clouded my mind until it threatened to overwhelm me, but I pushed it away. My father said *I* could destroy it, and I was pretty sure he meant by infecting it with my demon mojo. But I'd tried it, and the dome was still standing without even a scratch. I didn't even manage to make a dent. The damned thing was demon-mojo proof.

The battle sounds grew louder behind me, sending my stress level off the charts and my blood pressure dangerously high. My super plan of destroying the dome was crashing down on me fast.

We'd already lost Davenport House, and I'd come really close to losing Marcus. I didn't want to lose anything else—my aunts or my friends. No one. Not even a single paranormal in Hollow Cove.

So how could I do this?

I was missing something. I knew I was. I just didn't know *what* I was missing. How did I crack this damned thing?

And then it hit me.

My father had described the dome as an egg, well at least the shell of an egg. Maybe it wasn't about how much power I hit it with. Maybe it was about *where* I hit it with my demon mojo.

My heart sped with excitement at this new find. I knew I was onto something. If I followed my father's logic and thought of this dome as an egg, I knew the shell of an egg was strongest at the top and bottom. But they didn't stand well to uneven pressure. Like when you crack an egg on the side of a bowl.

I realized my mistake. I'd hit it at the top, where it was strongest.

I wouldn't make that same mistake twice.

"Tessa! Hurry!" Dolores called behind me, her voice strained.

Focusing, I called to my icy demon magic once again, feeling that cold power consuming my body. The cold surged up in greater amounts, feeding off my anger, my anguish, and my fears. Just like elemental magic, this dark elemental magic was fueled by emotions. And let me tell you right now, I was a bomb of explosive emotions.

Gritting my teeth, I let the demon power coil around my fingers, dripping down in droplets of black tendrils.

And then I flung my hands at the side of the dome.

The tendrils hit, and just like before they took on the shape of a veiny design. Only this time, they spread. I watched, both amazed and a little frightened as they branched out like spidery veins on the shell of the dome, climbing and spreading fast until I couldn't see where it ended or where it began.

The sound of a pop echoed around me, followed by a clap like thunder.

"Okay. Was not expecting that."

At that moment, a boom of sound ripped through the streets, shaking the bridge I stood on.

"Sweet sassy molassy."

My arms flung out to my sides as I steadied myself. If the bridge fell, Gilbert would surely bill me for that, and I'd be paying for it for the rest of my life.

Another blast came from somewhere high above my head. Then another blast. Over the pounding of my heart in my ears, I could hear voices shouting.

I looked back and saw groups of the Dark wizards standing in the streets, their fight forgotten with their hoods on their shoulders and fear reflected on their faces.

Another great boom of sound shifted the air and the floor of the bridge like a 7.0 earthquake on the Richter scale. A moment of absolute silence was followed by the distant noise of people shouting as it filtered through the streets and the surrounding darkness.

Dust fell from high above on the dome as another great boom assaulted my ears, followed by shouts and the pop of magic. The bridge shook with another blast, and a thunderous rumble echoed up through our feet. I heard a snap, and then one of the bridge's main cables broke free and came whipping over our heads.

I met Ronin's wide eyes. "Not sure this was such a good idea."

His face tensed. "Too late now. Looks like the dome is coming down. Wasn't that the point?"

"I just didn't factor in the dome actually falling on us. Or the bridge. Definitely not the bridge."

"I always said your planning needed some fine tweaking," teased Ronin with a smirk as another giant explosion rocked the bridge.

More dust fell from above. I looked up, peering through the cloud of dust. We heard a sudden loud crack, like when a frozen lake's ice starts to shift and thaw in late spring.

I stared at a point on the dome, high above my head. One large piece of the dome snapped off. And then another followed. Three more. Six more.

And like a domino effect, the dome's shell shattered and fell like giant, heavy pieces of concrete.

And coming down fast on all of us.

CHAPTER
25

I had a deer-in-the-headlights moment, when I just stood there like an idiot in imminent danger, my legs seemingly made of cement as the dome came crashing down on Hollow Cove.

We didn't have anywhere to go and hide, so I did what any witch would have done.

I crouched and covered my head with my hands.

But then something strange happened.

Peeking through my fingers, I saw the heavy blocks of the dome explode into dust seconds after they broke off from the surface. Then they fell like flakes of black snow.

I shielded my eyes from the sudden bright light. Streams of sunlight spilled from giant holes in the dome's ceiling and side walls. A warm wind blew in around us through the openings and lifted my hair.

I peered up into a bright blue sky, peppered with fluffy white clouds.

"Hi there, stranger."

I breathed in deeply, savoring the wonderous air. Glancing around, apart from the small cover of dark ash that littered the bridge, the streets, and even us, there was no sign that the dome ever existed. It only took a moment, and when I thought about it, the dome came down just as fast as it had gone up.

The loud humming of the dome's power faltered until it disappeared altogether.

The wizards' power, their connection to the dome that gave them immeasurable power—more like stealing power from the town's paranormals—was cut. They weren't all-powerful any longer.

"Guess your dad was right," said Ronin.

I smiled. "You guessed right."

"Well..." Ronin rubbed his hands together. His eyes dilated and flashed to black. He lifted his hands as talons sprouted from his fingertips, and he gave me a finger wave. Rolling his shoulders, he said, "I'm feeling good like it's my birthday. Is it my birthday?"

"It's your birthday," I answered.

"Excellent." Ronin clapped his hands once. His sharp canines flashed in a quick smile. "It's chow time!" In a flash of vampire speed, Ronin shot forward and in the blink of an eye was next to a surprised wizard.

"It's my birthday," announced the half-vampire, grinning with his canines sparkling in the light.

The wizard's lips moved in time with his fingers, no doubt in some attempt at a spell, but he was too slow.

Ronin pivoted smoothly. With a swipe of his talons, he sliced the wizard across the neck.

The wizard fell just as another wizard made a mad dash for Ronin, but the half-vampire was again faster. In the work of a moment, the robed figure was down on the ground, his head detached from his body and rolling off to the side, his lips open in an unfinished curse.

I searched the streets for my aunts, Iris, and Martha and found them at the other end of the bridge, facing a group of wizards. The wizards looked at one another, and I saw the hint of uncertainty and panic in their eyes. They were low on magical fuel.

In a storm of elemental magic, the witches exploded into motion, throwing curses and spells at the wizards like a volley of grenades.

The wizards fell back. It was working. With the dome—the amplifier for the wizards' magic—gone, they were just regular magic practitioners. Much easier to defeat, even to kill.

"Three!" I heard Ronin call out, and I found his black eyes staring at me from down the street. "I'll give you one hundred bucks if you can beat that. You in?"

I wasn't about to turn away a hundred dollars. I smiled. "I'm in."

I reached out and tapped into the ley lines, grinning like a fool as I felt their power reverberating through me.

"I'm back, baby."

I searched the streets for a wizard or two—hell, I'd even take three—and found them. I smiled my most evil twisted grin and said, "Game on."

Heart thumping with excitement, I rushed down the bridge just as a wizard stepped into my line of sight.

His light eyes narrowed as blue magic coiled around his wrists like snakes.

But I was way ahead of him.

"Fulgur!" I cried, thrusting my will behind my power word as I threw out my hand.

A bolt of white-purple lightning hit him right in the face, a bulls-eye hit right into his eye.

It had been a one-in-a-million hit, and I'd been aiming at his chest. Oopsie.

From the corner of my eye, I saw him fall and kept going.

I could barely see anything through the multitude of battling bodies, but I caught a glimpse of Ronin as he sliced the head off another wizard. Yet another came up behind him, but the half-vampire spun around and hit him with a succession of quick stabs. Buckets of black blood sprayed from the wizard's chest, but Ronin never slowed.

"Five!" came Ronin's voice rose above the sounds of battle. I could hear the joy and excitement reverberating in it. He was enjoying himself way too much. I wasn't sure if I should be worried or not.

With the bridge behind me, I hurried to reach my aunts. Adrenaline surged, mixed with an intoxicating high of magic. I halted just down the road as not one but two wizards advanced.

I shrugged. "Okay, I'll admit it. You guys do have some nice-looking robes. But I'm prettier."

One of the wizards threw his hand at me.

"Accendo!" I shouted as I flung out my hand, my head pounding with the effort. The ball of fire hit the guy in an explosion of yellow-and-orange flames. Then came a burst of ashes, all that was left of the robed wizard.

"Wow. I'm getting better at this," I told myself, wanting to pat myself on the back but realizing it would just come off looking awkward.

His companion was not impressed. "You fucking witch bitch."

"Yikes. Again with the name-calling. You really need to come up with some new material. It's getting old."

He sneered. "You promiscuous hag, you handmaiden of hell."

I pursed my lips. "Better. Wait"—I gestured to him then to myself—"did we just have a moment?"

Red-faced and sweat pouring, the wizard pulled a sharp dagger from inside his robe.

I stepped back, surprised. "Well, that was unexpected. You know how to use that thing? Here's a tip. Stick it with the pointy end."

"Seven!" came Ronin's shout from somewhere to my left.

I cracked out a laugh, which sent the wizard dude into a fit.

He yelled and came at me, his blade swinging.

I'll admit. I had zero experience fighting with sharp objects. I couldn't even slice a piece of bread without cutting my finger in the process.

But I was a witch. A Shadow witch. Why use daggers and swords when I could use magic?

He thrust forward. And when his blade was an inch from my chest, I pulled on the ley line, jumped in, and my body was yanked away in a blink of an eye.

I didn't go too far, just twisted and boomeranged the ley line back to bring me right behind the wizard.

He stumbled as his forward momentum never caught on something solid—me.

He straightened and I tapped him on the shoulder.

He flinched and spun around.

"Hi," I said, as I gave him a finger wave.

He frowned, stunned. "How—"

"Inflitus!" I thundered, unleashing my will as I thrust my hands at the wizard. A kinetic force hit him, throwing him end over end twenty feet back.

I ran over, my magic still coursing through me, to make sure he stayed down. But then with a grunt, the bastard pushed himself up, bending from the waist, clearly in pain.

"This is for House." And then I kicked him in the ass—literally.

This time, the wizard collapsed to the ground and didn't get up.

I might have gotten a little ahead of myself, but I couldn't help it. Jeff and many other townspeople were dead because of these wizards, and they'd burned down my home.

"Eight!" Ronin's head appeared down the street, grinning like a fool. And then I lost him again as he sped away.

I laughed. "This is turning out to be one strange day."

"And it's going to be your last," came a voice behind me, sending the hairs on my neck to stand.

I spun around, a power word on my lips. A wizard in his black-robed glory stood behind me. His hood hid most of his features, and I could just make out dark eyes. But it didn't matter. I recognized his voice.

"You're one of the guys who jumped me in the parking lot," I told him. "I forget names, sometimes faces, but never a creepy voice. And yours sets my creepy meter off the scale."

He pulled down his hood, and I cringed at his gaunt features and his pale skin.

"You should have kept the hood on. Trust me."

"You might have disabled the Dark Ring," he said, his face twisting in fury.

I made a face. "Wait. Is that what you call it? It's a really stupid name."

He grimaced. "But we're still going to take your town. Still going to kill every last *animal* in here."

I shook my head. "Yeah. I don't think so. Because, well, it's over. Look around. You've lost that edge. That power was never yours, by the way. If you could conjure another dome—I refuse to call it what you just said—you would have by now. Which tells me it takes a lot of time and effort to put one in place. Am I right?"

A dark chant spilled from the wizard's lips. When he lifted his arm, a ball of red energy hovered in his palm.

"Nice," I said, genuinely impressed.

And then he threw it at me.

I yanked on the ley line again, making me feel like The Flash as I was in one spot one moment and then in a different place the next.

The red ball hit the pavement where I'd been a second ago, leaving a liquidy, boiling mass.

I jumped out of the ley line behind him. "Boo!"

The wizard shrieked, actually shrieked like a ten-year-old girl. This was so much fun.

"Accendo!" I commanded in a controlled will of power. A small line of fire erupted from my hand and wrapped around the wizard like a flaming rope.

The wizard screamed, and in the panic and fear of burning, he tore off his burning clothes. He stood before me in his birthday britches.

I smiled. "Well, shit fire and save matches."

Just like his face, his skin was pale, his body gangly and thin, barely any muscle on it. And let me tell ya, it was *not* a pretty sight.

At first, he didn't seem to realize what had happened, and I laughed as I saw it finally reflect in his eyes and on his face.

"Took you long enough. That's right. You're buck naked, pal. No more nut covers," I added, swirling a finger at his nether regions.

The wizard glanced down at himself. He squealed again like a little girl and clasped his hands over his package, which he could have used two fingers to cover.

The man—well, if you could even call him that given what he was sporting, which looked more like a wet sock—went rigid. His face paled and his eyes lost their focus.

My grin went all the way to the sides of my face. "Not so tough anymore now, eh, tough guy?"

Without his clothes and his robe, the wizard was like a shriveled-up little mouse. As though being in the nude was terrifying somehow. What was wrong with a little naked?

Please. Marcus rocked his nakedness. No matter where he was or what he was doing.

"Not so fun when it's you doing the naked, huh?" I flicked my fingers at him. "Shoo!"

The wizard, still covering his man berries, spun around and ran in the opposite direction, bringing his knees up way too high as he ran, which made him look like a dancing skeleton in some animated movie.

I snorted. "That's the *whitest* ass I've ever seen," I called out, wishing Iris was with me so we might enjoy the view together. "It's practically transparent—"

Searing pain flared at the back of my head, and pretty black stars danced in my eyes. I took a step and faltered. Dizzy, I fell to my knees. I breathed through my nose, steadying myself. I blinked the black spots from my eyes and tasted the bile in the back of my throat before swallowing it back down. Whatever had hit me, it felt like someone had used a baseball bat to the back of my head.

When my vision cleared, Dragos was staring down at me.

CHAPTER
26

Damn, now I was in a pickle. The old bastard must have been floating because I never heard him coming. My gaze traveled to his hand. He had a big ol' rock in his wrinkled grip, the side stained with blood. My blood.

I rubbed the back of my head, feeling wetness on my fingers. "You hit me with a rock? You medieval lunatic."

Dragos's face and eyes were red; sweat poured down the sides of his temples, and he was breathing hard like he was having a heart attack.

"You killed my sons! How could you? They were my boys! My boys!"

I held up a finger. "Wait." With my left hand, I covered my left eye. "I'm seeing two of you. Okay. Now I only see one of you."

My head felt like it was splitting in two, and my vision blurred as the pain swelled. Maybe he hit me with a rock because he had no more wizard mojo? Could bringing down the dome have killed his magic completely? Maybe the old guy had invested too much of his power in that dome, more than his sons. Yeah, I was betting on it.

I scrambled away before he stoned me, and I pushed myself up on my feet, the back of my head throbbing, but at least the double vision was gone.

"Your magic is spent. Isn't it?" I told him, seeing the visible strain over his face and the hunch in his shoulders. That explained why he'd snuck up on me. Either that, or he didn't want to hit his son with his magic accidentally.

Dragos twisted his face. "You know nothing. A Dark wizard's power is everywhere and in everything."

"Keep telling yourself that," I said, pulling on my elemental magic around me.

The old wizard snarled and tossed the rock. Drawing himself up, he came at me, fists swinging.

I was so shocked that for a moment I just stood there with my jaw hanging open like an idiot, staring at grandpa wizard coming at me like something out of my worst nightmares.

The pain that followed sobered me right up, though.

His fist came out of nowhere and hit me on the right breast. If I hadn't planted my legs at the last minute, it would have thrown me to the ground, and then I'd have been finished.

My right breast throbbed, and I covered it with my hand. "You hit me in the boob? Really? What kind of sicko are you?" Getting hit in the boob hurts like a sonofabitch.

"Argh!" cried Dragos as he threw himself at me again.

"What the hell?"

The one self-defense class training I went to years ago vanished. Moving on instincts alone, I twisted around and kicked out, making contact with the side of his leg. Dragos staggered and went down.

"Ha!" I straightened, proud of myself. "Seen that move in one of Chuck Norris's reruns on YouTube." I don't know why I wasn't using magic. Guess it was just one of those weird events that took me, and I just had to go with it.

Rage rippled over the old wizard. "You killed my sons."

"You already said that. But I wouldn't have if you hadn't attacked us first and killed some of us. This is your own damn fault, *Draco*."

Dragos kicked out with his leg just as I kicked out with my own.

Our shins connected in mid-strike, sending a painful throb in my leg up to my spine and making my teeth clatter.

I dropped my leg just as the old wizard came at me with another side kick. I swung out my leg and heard a loud crack as we hit our legs together at the same time, our calves this time.

And again, we went at it, like some D-rated kung fu movie. It was the weirdest thing, but I couldn't stop. Obviously, neither one of us had any idea what the hell we were doing.

But I was done dancing around this old maniac.

As he came at me with another swing of his boot, I yanked on the elements and shouted, "Ventum!"

A powerful gust of wind blasted him in the chest, and he went spinning back, hitting the hard pavement thirty feet away and landing in a tangle of robes and limbs.

"I think I'll stick with magic," I told myself, eyeing the bundle that was Dragos.

After a moment of indecision, I stalked forward. He wasn't moving. I'd struck him hard, but he'd hit the pavement harder. And at his age—possibly hundreds of years old—he'd probably broken more than a hip in that fall.

I crept closer. He lay on his right side. When I neared, I leaned over and saw blood trickling out of his left ear. I wasn't sure what that meant, but I knew he wasn't getting up soon. Maybe never.

"Serves him right," I muttered and straightened. I heard a shout up the street and I turned.

Something hard slammed into my legs below the knee, taking them out from under me and sending me to the ground.

I barely had a second to brace my fall as something heavy climbed over me. He moved fast, sliding his hands around my throat and locking them there with strength that shouldn't have been possible for a man his age.

"I got you," snarled Dragos, assaulting me with foul, rotten breath. "*I* got you, witch. You're going to die."

Blood rushed to my face, and I couldn't breathe. I couldn't call out as darkness crept along the edges of my mind. Dragos kept squeezing. The more he pressed, the more I felt myself falling.

That old bastard wizard was going to kill me. How did that happen?

Tears leaked out of the corners of my eyes as I tried to focus. Panic filled me. I hit and pulled at his hand around my neck, trying to pry his fingers apart, but it was like trying to bend steel with my hands. His grip on me was iron-tight.

Dragos pulled me closer until his nose was almost touching my face. "Stupid, stupid witch," he sneered, his breath like carrion on a hot summer day. "I told you, you were no match for me. You're going to die now." Beads of sweat shone on his forehead and nose. A few drops fell on me.

Damn. I was going to have nightmares for the rest of my life.

"Screw. You," I wheezed, my voice hoarse and low as my head pounded with the effort.

Dragos pressed his knees into my chest, crushing my throat. "Die, bitch. Die! I got you now."

My concentration vanished. God. That. Hurt. I heard Dragos's laughter, and he squeezed harder as black spots marred my vision. It was impossible not to panic in this kind of situation. The lack of air started to wear me down, and I couldn't think clearly.

Through my obscured vision, I saw Dragos's lips move, but I couldn't hear what he was saying over the pounding of blood in my ears. This time I *was* going to die.

A golden arm flashed before my eyes.

I heard a loud crack, like the sound of a skull fracturing, and Dragos flew off of me and disappeared somewhere to my left.

I rolled to the side, taking in huge gasps of air and causing my lungs to burn like I'd swallowed acid between the dry heaves that left my lungs screaming in pain. I took another breath and then another. My muscles relaxed, leaving only my pounding head and the taste of something metallic in my mouth. My neck throbbed. It felt broken, though I knew if it was, I wouldn't be able to move.

I wiped the tears from my eyes and turned to the sound of flesh pounding on flesh.

A muscular man in a pair of pink, bedazzled sweatpants was kneeling over Dragos on the ground, pounding his face in with his big manly hands.

Marcus drove his fist into the old wizard's face, over and over again. It didn't look like he planned on stopping. His expression was blackened with fury.

"Marcus," I wheezed in barely a whisper. Damn my throat hurt. "Marcus, stop," I tried again.

I didn't think beating someone to death—even though he deserved it—was the way to go.

Gray eyes met mine. They were filled with rage and fear that I'd nearly died. He froze at whatever he saw on my face. With his left hand, he held Dragos by the neck of his robe, his right fist angled high for another blow to the wizard's face.

He closed his eyes for a second, and I saw him take a visible calming breath. Then he tossed Dragos to the side like he was discarding an old cloak.

I blinked, and he was there, pulling me up into him and holding me close. My face was buried into his warm chest, his musky scent familiar and intoxicating. His muscular arms wrapped around me protectively and hardened with tension. His hold was locked as though he never wanted to let me go. He pulled me closer, my breasts crushing into his chest and my legs bumping into his muscular thighs. His body shook with the last of his rage, his fear of losing me. I'm not going to lie. It felt awesome.

I was caught in his arms. I couldn't move. He had caged me. And I was not complaining.

The world around us disappeared. It was just me and him, no more wizards, no dome. Minutes passed. I had things I wanted to say, but I didn't. We'd have time for that later.

And then he angled his head and kissed me. The taste of him on my tongue was magical. It had my lady regions pounding to match my beating heart.

After a moment, Marcus pulled away, his gaze blazing with desire. "You scared me," he said, his voice rough with a need that had my heart pumping and my knees weak.

"That makes two of us." I frowned. "I thought I told you to stay put."

The chief shrugged, rubbing his hands up and down my arms. "I was never one to take orders. I give orders. I don't take them," he said with a cheeky smile.

I shook my head, smiling. "You're so macho." Such a turn-on. "I kind of like it."

Marcus turned his head and his gaze fell on Dragos. "Besides." He pointed a finger at the old wizard who still hadn't moved. "That one was mine. I owed him a few punches after what he did."

I totally got that. "I like the pants," I said, eyeing the pink sweats with the words "Kiss Me" in glitter on his butt. Martha's, no doubt.

The chief smiled. "I thought you would."

Two wizards approached, dragging their feet with their eyes fixed on Marcus and me like they were about to bolt in the opposite direction.

"Oh, look," said the chief, letting go of me and pushing me protectively behind me. "More playthings."

"Hang on." I watched as the two wizards walked over to their father. With each of them taking an arm, they hauled him upright and began to drag him away. Dragos's bloodied head hung down over his chest, and he was barely recognizable with both his eyes swollen shut.

"I should stop them," said Marcus, rolling his shoulders in his signature move before a fight. "They can't get away with this."

"They didn't," I told him, stepping aside so I could get a better view. "We beat them. They're humiliated, and now they're leaving."

The sound of tires crunching pavement pulled my attention to the right. Three black

SUVs came speeding down the street. The vehicles' tires squealed as they made an abrupt stop next to the wizards. Doors popped open and three more robed wizards came out of one of the SUVs and helped the other two drag their father into the back seat.

A mob of angry townspeople shouted and came rushing at them. All they needed were some fiery torches and it would look like a scene from *Beauty and the Beast*. Some faces I recognized, but others I didn't.

The wizards all climbed into the SUV. A flash of something in black sailed above one of the SUVs. Even from a distance, there was no mistaking that mischievous grin.

Ronin jumped up and down on the roof of the SUV with Dragos in the back. Then he began to tap dance. Who knew?

Engines roared to life, and the three SUVs sped forward. Ronin leaped off the SUV, stuck the landing, and took a bow.

"It's always a show with that guy," said Marcus, though a smile twitched the sides of his mouth.

I watched as the three vehicles sped down the street, following each other. They rushed up onto the Hollow Cove bridge and took a sharp right turn that led out of our town and back into the mainland before disappearing.

The crowd cheered, and I recognized Ronin's whistle somewhere amid all the cacophony of voices as the town came together in happy wails and cries of victory. It was finally over.

And then the cries of joy changed, and the townspeople began to chant, "RO-nin, RO-nin, RO-nin!"

The half-vampire had the biggest smile on his face I'd ever seen, lifting his arms to encourage the chant of his name.

"We'll never hear the end of that one," I said.

"That's it. The town's gone mad," said Marcus, and I broke out in laughter. It felt amazing.

I felt an arm wrap around my waist and found Marcus pulling me closer.

"The other communities will have to be warned about the wizards," said the chief. "We might have scared them off for now, but that doesn't mean they might not try another, smaller, and more vulnerable paranormal community. I'll need to make a detailed report on what happened here and how we defeated them."

"But you can't tell them about my demon mojo," I warned. I was not ready for the paranormal community to know about who my father was and what was in my blood. The Dark wizards were bad enough, and in theory, they weren't even here for me. But as soon as word spread about my heritage, only a crap load of bad would surely follow.

Marcus pulled his eyes away from me and looked at the cheering crowd. "I'll leave that part out. But we can set a system in place. Some Dark witches can control mid-demons to use their powers to break the domes if they were to appear again."

"That could work." It would be challenging, but even Iris could control a demon to use its power.

Marcus's fingers twined with mine, warm and rough. "You think they'll show their faces again? These wizards?" His eyes traveled to the spot where the SUVs had disappeared.

"I don't think we've seen the last of them," I said, knowing that they'd probably regroup, spawn again, and one day they'd be back. "But they're going to have to think twice about trying anything again on this town."

Though somewhere in my gut, I had a feeling if Dragos ever showed his face again, it wouldn't be with another dome. No, they'd probably try something else.

But we'd be ready for them.

CHAPTER
27

We walked along Stardust Drive, the scent of smoke and charred wood hanging heavily in the air as an ugly reminder of what had happened here. The cloud of smoke had turned the sun into a bleakly glowing orb.

It seemed on every street, a house was burning or left in smoking frames. Most of the burnt homes seemed to be chosen at random by the wizards, no real strategy, just unlucky. It would take weeks, perhaps months to rebuild and fix the damage that the Guild of Dark Wizards bestowed on the town.

But some buildings were lost forever.

I stared at what had once been the most beautiful house in all of Hollow Cove. The charred ruins had only a few blackened beams sticking out from the rubble, like a skeleton of a giant beast. The front lawn was a mess of dirt and ash where the grass had been burned to a crisp, along with the hydrangeas, Ruth's favorite rosebushes, the lilacs planted generations ago, all of it.

I stopped when I was about thirty feet from the burnt rubble with Marcus still hanging on to my hand, seemingly afraid to let go. Not that I minded. He was like my rock right now, my grounding force, and I needed it.

The rubble that was left of Davenport House was made worse in the daylight; it made it true somehow. Under the darkness of the dome, it had felt more like a bad dream.

At first, I didn't even realize where I was going. I just walked and kept on walking. It seemed my aunts had had the same idea as the three of them joined us on the sidewalk.

They all looked worn out. Ruth's bun had become undone, and her white, disheveled hair brushed her shoulders to make a curtain around Hildo who sat on her right one. I could see red and pink glitter in it, and a few twigs. Her long, black skirt was torn in several places like she'd been attacked by a pack of wildcats.

Beverly's usually tip-top appearance and clothes were in disarray. Her tight jeans were covered in rust-brown stains and earth. Mascara streaked down her cheeks, and she had a cut on her lower lip like she'd been hit.

Dolores looked like a mad scientist who'd been locked away in a mental institution for over a decade and had dug her way out. Long strands of gray hair had come apart from her braid and were sticking out on ends, some floating about her head like she was still operating magic or possibly radioactive. Her clothes were covered in mud and soot, and her dark eyes sparkled with that crazy I'd seen before: right before she spelled your ass, her mouth twisted in an ugly grimace.

The three sisters looked like they'd fought a great battle and won, though their faces said otherwise.

They shared a defeated sadness in their eyes, one they could never recover from or fix.

I swallowed hard, a pang crushing my heart. "Will you rebuild Davenport House?" I asked no one in particular. Marcus, who was still holding my hand, squeezed it.

"Sure," answered Dolores, her face shifting as she thought about it. "You can always rebuild a house."

"But it'll never be the same," said Beverly.

"Never be the same," repeated Ruth, a tight pain in her voice.

"You can even make it appear exactly the same if you wanted," continued Dolores.

"But it'll never be magical," concluded Beverly.

"Never magical," echoed Ruth.

Without another word, the three sisters picked themselves up and walked over to Martha who stood with another group of townspeople, one of them Gilbert. I wasn't surprised to see he hadn't a scratch on him. The little shit had probably stayed hidden in his shop the whole time.

I spotted Iris and Ronin next to his black BMW 7 Series parked at the curb, and she gave me a sad wave. Then her face froze, her eyes widening at something down the street. She looked back at me and mouthed the words, "Oh. My. God."

I followed her gaze, and my heart gave a jolt. "Oh, this ought to be good."

"What?" asked Marcus. I felt him turn to see what I was looking at, but I never tore my eyes from her.

Lilith, the queen of hell, strolled up Stardust Drive.

Her lean figure was perfectly enclosed in a tight leather black ensemble of bustier and pants. The bustier pushed her breasts up to her neck, and she'd finished off the look with red knee-high boots and a wicked gleam in her eyes. She wore her red hair in a slicked-back low ponytail, which only accentuated her gorgeous, otherworldly features.

All she was missing was a whip, and she was good to go to a BDSM party.

"What is *she* doing here?" Marcus's low voice brushed against my neck, and his grip on my hand tightened. His posture went rigid, like he was just about to go into beast mode.

There were only two reasons why the goddess of night would come to our town. One, she was here to turn me into a pile of ash, or two, she was here to collect her favor.

"She's here for me," was all I said. There was nothing else to say. A sense of wild panic hit me. I had a crazy moment of insanity to flee, where I thought I could make a run for it. But no matter where I went or where I hid, Lilith would find me.

Lilith walked forward with a red-lipped smile. "Ah, Marcus. Aren't you a sight for sore eyes?" Her red eyes sparkled. "Are you into sex with a bit of pain?"

Oh, hell, no. "Marcus, could you give us a minute?" I let go of his hand and nudged him back. When he didn't move, I pressed. "Please. Can you see if my aunts need anything?"

Reluctantly, the wereape moved off, but he didn't go far. He stood in the middle of the street with his arms crossed over his large chest and his gray eyes fixed on Lilith with a predatory glare.

Lilith watched him for a moment. "Shame. He definitely looks like he'd enjoy a bit of pain with a *lot* of sex. Yum." Her red eyes met mine. "Have you tried erotic flogging? It's a real trip."

"Why are you here, Lilith?" If she didn't stop staring at Marcus like he was a lollipop she wanted to suck on, I was going to do something foolish. Again.

Lilith made a face. "What's the matter with you all?" She cast her gaze over my aunts and the other townspeople out in the streets. "Why all the gloomy faces? Why do you all look like someone died?"

I stared at her incredulously. I pointed to the pile of ash where Davenport House used to stand. "Because someone kinda did. The wizards burned down our family home."

The goddess stared at the burned rubble that used to be Davenport House. "The Guild of Dark Wizards."

My lips parted. "How did you know?"

She cocked a perfectly groomed brow. "Do I really need to answer that?"

"Right. You're a goddess."

She beamed. "I knew you were a clever one." She laughed, and part of me wanted to kick her in the mouth.

"What do you want? I'm really not in the mood." I realized this was not the way to speak to a goddess. Hell, I probably should be on my knees, begging her forgiveness for accusing her of the kids' murders. But I wasn't a beggar, and I wasn't about to start now.

"You owe me a favor, my little demon witch," said the queen of hell. "I'm here to make sure you make good on that favor."

I shook my head, feeling the exhaustion of the days hitting me all at once and making me feel sick. "You really do know how to pick your moments."

Lilith flicked a finger at me. "Is that a little sarcasm I'm detecting?"

I said nothing.

"I get that you had your hands full with these wizards." Her red eyes pinned mine. "Am I to assume they were the ones who killed those boys you accused me of?"

I swallowed. "That's right. They were. Sorry about that." There, it wasn't much of an apology, but that's all she was going to get.

Lilith kept her gaze on me, and I felt a chill crawl up my back and settle on my neck. "Well. I'll get straight to the point." Her face was still and went hard. "I need you to help me kill Lucifer."

She could not have dropped a bigger bomb. "Uh... what?" What the hell was I supposed to say to that?

"You're going to help me kill Lucifer." Lilith wrinkled her face and leaned forward. "Is that a yes? Doesn't matter. You can't refuse." She shrugged, pulled back, and swung her long ponytail over her back. "I'll just kill you if you do."

309

"Figures." I tried to wrap my head around what she just said, but it felt crazy. "You want me to help you kill Lucifer?"

"That's right."

"And how am I supposed to do that? I'm mortal. He's not. He's the king of hell. I'm just a witch. See where I'm going with this?"

A smile spread on Lilith's face, terrifying and beautiful. "I have a plan. You in or not?" She waited patiently, her hands on her hips, the smile on her face evidence that we both knew I didn't have a choice.

Kill Lucifer.

"Sure. Why the hell not." Yup. I was going to die.

Lilith's red eyes widened. "Fabulous. I knew you couldn't refuse. I'll be in touch."

I felt numb and in despair all at once. I wasn't sure that was even possible. Here I was doing a favor for a goddess. Said favor was to kill the king of hell? What was wrong with me? We all knew that wasn't going to end well—for me, that is.

The only good thing was that my aunts were too far away across the street to hear any of that exchange, though Dolores's frown might have been an indication she'd caught a few words. Either that, or she was a gifted lip-reader.

Marcus? Hell, I didn't even want to look at him. With his expert hearing, I had no doubt he'd heard it all. I was going to get an earful in a few minutes.

I let out a long breath. I felt done in. Exhausted. But what kept me from collapsing on my knees like a puppet whose strings had been cut was the fact that Marcus would heal from his infliction. He would live. He would live and we'd have our lives back—until I was killed by either Lucifer or Lilith.

Speaking of the goddess, I noticed she'd halted on our driveway, staring at the ash remains of Davenport House. If she started to pick through the rubble for a souvenir, I was going to strangle her.

And then she did something truly remarkable and genuinely unexpected.

Lilith splayed her arms to her sides as words spilled from her lips that I didn't understand.

A wind blew, carrying the scent of spices as Lilith slowly raised her arms. Clouds of ashes, pieces of burnt wood that could have been siding of a part of the interior walls, all rose from the ground. The wind picked them up with a wailing shriek, forming a cyclone of broken wood, shattered plaster, and shingles as it spun them into a spiraling curtain that rose sixty feet in the air.

At the sudden blast of white light, I shielded my eyes from the glare. When the light subsided, I looked back, and my jaw dropped.

"Great, googa mooga."

311

A massive farmhouse with a black metal roof, white wood siding, and a glorious wraparound porch supported by thick, round columns stood where it had always stood since the day it was built, hundreds of years ago by the first Davenport witches.

It looked perfect, unscathed, as though a fire never scorched its insides, never burned it down to glowing embers. I couldn't see a single scorch mark on the white-painted siding. Nothing. It looked like it was *newly* built.

I stared at the rosebushes and Annabelle hydrangeas that had died in the fire but now were in full bloom (not in season but who cared). Red geraniums and purple petunias draped from the flower boxes that hung over the porch's rail, just like before the fire.

I stared at it all—at the broad, birch front door with a stained-glass window portraying the image of a witch flying on her broom next to a full moon, and to the metal plate next to it with the words THE MERLIN GROUP.

The hum of magic reverberated in the air. Davenport House's magic. It was all back. As though the Dark wizards had never touched it. Never burned our house to the ground.

I turned at the sounds of hysterical clapping and sobs and spotted my aunts hugging and crying into each other's arms.

My eyes burned as I looked back at Lilith, who was admiring her handiwork. "You...

How… Wow. Unbelievable. That was impressive," I said, shocked at how numb my mouth felt.

"I know. I'm amazing." Lilith spun around and winked at me, a strange smile on her face.

I shrugged. "But why?"

The goddess turned back and surveyed Davenport House. "They don't make houses like this anymore. I'm not ready to see it go."

My brows rose. There was a lot more to this goddess than she let on.

And with that, in a pop of displaced air, Lilith, the goddess of hell, who'd just reinstated our family home, vanished.

CHAPTER
28

White clouds tracked a blue sky, and the sun shone as a bright yellow disk. I took in the smell of lilacs, freshly mowed lawns, and the crabapple trees that were in full bloom. Their light-pink and white flowers filled the air with a sweet aroma.

It was high noon, and the streets of Hollow cove exploded with life as all manner of shifters, weres, half-breeds, and witches strolled the streets, young and old, hopping from one festivity to the other.

High above my head, across Shifter Lane from lamppost to lamppost, hung a giant sign:

THE ANNUAL HOLLOW COVE PIE FESTIVAL.

Yup, it was happening.

With a smile on my face, I strolled through the festival, my head swiveling as I tried to see everything at once. I'd never attended a pie festival, so I had no idea what that entailed. My pulse was throbbing at the excitement of discovering new things.

A pack of teenage weres—werecats, if I wasn't mistaken—was throwing pies at an unfortunate, angry-looking Cameron, who stood behind a large bull-seye sign, like target practice. A sign above his head read PIE THROWING CONTEST.

Damn. He must have lost a bet or something.

Cameron's eyes found mine, and I ducked my head in behind a tall male and sneaked away before he saw me smiling.

When I raised my head, I faced a loud group of paranormals, primarily male, cheering on two very naked werewolves, wrestling in a twenty-by-twenty wooden box filled with what looked like squished raspberry pies.

"No way," I laughed. Who knew there was such a thing as pie wrestling? No idea you had to be naked to participate either. But I liked it.

Witches stood in front of booths that displayed their homemade jams, pies, an assortment of different kinds of candy, chocolate-covered berries, edible love charms that you wore around your wrist like bracelets, and baskets filled with home-baked goods and magical surprises.

I caught a glimpse of a bunch of kids stealing some of the chocolate-coated berries and pocketing handfuls of candy whenever the witches weren't looking. They were most probably spelled against thieves, but I wasn't telling.

I pulled out a five-dollar bill, gave it to the witch, and grabbed a bag of those chocolate-covered berries. I popped one into my mouth and moaned as the delicious chocolate melted on my tongue, leaving a perfectly round blueberry for me to chew.

"Wow," I said, my mouth full. "I have to get Ruth to make these."

Having finished all fifteen chocolate-coated blueberries in one go—yes, yes, I did—I strolled forward until I reached another challenge. The words PIE EATING CONTEST were written in big black letters on a stack of wine barrels.

Ronin sat behind a table between the skinniest female I'd ever seen and possibly the largest male I'd ever seen. Their hands were tied behind their backs as they bent over and ate pies with only their mouths, like their lives depended on it. It was the strangest thing I'd ever seen.

"You can do it, Ronin!" cheered Iris, in the crowd, a proud grin on her face. She pumped her fist in the air and cried, "Eat that pie! Eeeat it! Eeeat it!"

God, I love this town.

It was colorful and bizarre, like walking into a circus fun house. You could never tell that only four weeks ago we'd been viciously attacked by the Guild of Dark Wizards. It would take time for the town to heal—years, most likely—but it *would* heal. It had already begun.

Funerals were held for our fallen community members, and I made sure I attended every single one of them, even if I didn't know the person. I made sure I was there.

Lilith had given us back Davenport House. After she'd left, I'd rushed inside, not to verify if the magical refurbishment had continued— which it did—but more about checking to see that the door to the basement was still operational as the gateway between our world and the Netherworld.

When my father had shown up, looking just as he'd been a few hours before, I knew the goddess had truly restored Davenport House to its former glory with all its magical bells and whistles.

My aunts had been so overcome with happiness and gratitude that I didn't have the heart to tell them about my deal with Lilith and helping her to kill Lucifer.

It sounded absurd when I thought about it. What could *I* do? Lilith was a goddess and had rebuilt our magical house in under a minute. And if the rumors were true and Lucifer was more powerful, I was doomed.

After Lilith had given us Davenport House back, my aunts had changed their tunes.

Strange how they were praising her, too, especially Dolores, who couldn't stop glorifying the queen of hell every chance she had.

"Wasn't she clever?" Dolores had said. "That control on her power... magnificent. A true proficient in the arts. She is, as you know, the first witch."

"She is fabulous," Beverly added. "Great style. Great hair. Great body. She could be me."

Ruth giggled. "I think I'm going to name my next tonic after her—the Lilith Mix."

We'd been lucky or blessed. I couldn't say which. But even with Davenport House restored, my aunts safe, and Marcus healed, nothing lifted my spirits.

I'd made a deal with Lilith to try and kill Lucifer.

Four weeks had passed since our agreement, and still, the goddess was a no-show. No way in hell had she forgotten about me. She was probably still making arrangements. The thought of it all made me ill. I knew it was only a matter of time before she showed up again.

I pushed the morbid thoughts away and continued my walk until I came face-to-face with my quarry.

On a raised platform was a long table. The large cloth sign above the table read BEST PIE AWARD. Seated at the table were three participants. First was a woman of considerable size and a frown that could put Dolores to shame, which I'd never seen before. Next to her was Ruth, and at the end was none other than our town mayor, Gilbert. He shifted as he adjusted his bow tie and brown corduroy jacket, and I spotted two pillows propped under him.

I sneered. "Maybe you should have asked for the high chair," I muttered.

I was still waiting to see if Gilbert would bill me or my aunts for the damage the wizards had caused in town. Though technically *his* fault, Gilbert loved to make everything our fault.

Standing off to the side, all straight and important looking, was a female and two males. All three were whited-haired and stern-looking. Judges, I'd bet. The forks in their hands said it all. They were the tasters, the judges, and the executioners.

Placed before the three contestants were the pies they'd baked for the contest. They couldn't be any more different.

The woman's pie crust was the darkest, stuffed into a white baking dish. Ruth's pie had a golden crust, sat in a copper-colored baking dish, and was the smallest of the three. Gilbert's pie crust had an intricate design, like feathers, that I could see from where I was standing. It was also the fluffiest of the three pies, sitting in a blue baking dish. He wore a confident grin, that smug stance that no one could ever beat him. He sat there looking like he'd already won.

I narrowed my eyes. Ruth had stayed up all night baking pies, trying to pick the right one. The kitchen smelled like a bakery, which I thought was great. There was pecan pie, apple pie, pumpkin pie, key lime pie, cherry pie, lemon meringue pie, sugar cream pie, blueberry pie, raspberry pie, banana peanut butter pie which was Hildo's favorite, and others I couldn't guess. Knowing Ruth, she had probably tried to invent a new kind of pie for the contest.

Everywhere I looked, pies had covered every hard surface of the kitchen. Pies even lined the dining table, with a few more on the couch in the living room.

"No good," she'd said around eleven o'clock last night as she'd stuffed a fork with a chunk of what looked like apple pie in her mouth. Her white hair was wrapped around the top of her head in a messy bun and held by two forks. The apron she wore over a long, blue skirt and white blouse was spotted in flour. So was her face. But the spots of her skin that weren't covered in flour were red. She was stressed out, her cute face wrinkled in a frown. She was going to give herself a heart attack over this competition.

"I'm sure it's amazing," I told her, knowing just how great her cooking was.

Ruth shook her head, her eyes tight. "No. It's tastes like a regular apple pie."

"And that's bad?" I looked over to Dolores and Beverly for help, but they both shrugged, like they'd been here before and knew I was wasting my breath.

Dolores handed Ruth a glass of red wine. "Here. Have a sip before you give yourself a stroke."

Ruth batted the glass away. "I need to focus. I can't focus with wine."

"She does this every year," said Beverly. "She'll work herself into a state."

"Over a pie?"

Ruth swiped a pink spatula in my direction. "Not just any pie. It has to be *the* pie. The one that wins over Gilbert's."

Aha. Now I got it.

"He's won for the last eleven years in a row," said Ruth, and I remembered her mentioning it a few weeks back. "And he makes sure I know about it. Just once, I just want to win. And to see his face. Oh, I've dreamed about it."

I glanced at the hundreds of pies, no kidding, that covered the kitchen. "Which one will you pick?" My eyes found what I believed was a pecan pie. It looked abandoned and sad that no one was going to eat it. So I grabbed a fork and stabbed at it.

Ruth rubbed her eyes with her free hand. "I don't know. But it has to be better. Special." She tossed the spatula into the sink. Her face pulled down into a frown, and then her bare feet slapped the dark hardwood floor as she ran out of the kitchen and disappeared into her potions room.

"Is magic allowed?" I asked, swallowing a massive, chunk of pecan pie. Yum.

"Absolutely not," said Dolores. "They put measures in place if a person tries to tamper with the judges' taste buds. Every pie is put through a magical detection. If magic is found, the contestant is immediately disqualified."

"Ruth would never cheat." Beverly grabbed the glass of wine meant for Ruth and took a sip. "She wants to win this on pure merit."

"Pure taste." I fetched myself a wineglass and filled it up with the bottle of Chianti that my aunts were drinking. I took a sip. "Hmm. This is really good with pecan pie." I took another sip. "So, what happens if she wins?"

Beverly smiled. "We'll throw a party."

Of course. "And if she doesn't?"

"She'll mope around for a few days," answered Dolores. "But she'll be fine. She's used to it. Used to not winning."

"And Gilbert always wins?" I asked. "Seems strange. Don't you think?"

"Everything about that little shifter is strange," said Beverly. "But I get your point. You think he cheats?"

"Maybe. Not with magic, but I wouldn't put it past him if he somehow manages to bribe the judges." I was almost sure he did. Yeah, I bet he did.

Dolores's free hand curled into a fist. "If that's true, we would have found him out. The truth is... that miserable owl makes a damn good pie."

Beverly shrugged. "Who knew?"

I'd gone to bed after that, feeling sorry for Ruth, who I was sure was going to spend the rest of the night and early morning trying to beat Gilbert in his pie making.

My phone vibrated in my pocket. I yanked it out to find Marcus had sent me a text.

Marcus: *Dinner at my place tonight? I have something special for you.*

Me: *Does it involve nakedness?*

Marcus: *Always.*

Me: *I'm in.*

I laughed by myself like a crazy person. I felt eyes on me and glanced up to find Marcus standing where the pie wrestling was still happening. He stood with that smooth contained power. Knowing him, it was probably a precaution, to stop the weres if they went overboard with the wrestling.

His gray eyes bore into mine, his gaze intense, which sent my body on fire. He looked at me as though I were naked. And when he grinned, well, I practically flew over with my imaginary broom—the Horny Witch 2000—and tackled him.

Lust flared inside me like a well-lit cauldron. I was hot. He was hot. It was all very hot.

Damn. If his eyes and smile could practically melt my panties, imagine what the rest of him could do.

Marcus had become really quiet during Jeff's funeral, and I gave him his space to deal with his loss on his own. I didn't want to be one of those women who kept nagging at her man to tell her everything. I didn't even grab Allison by the hair when she cozied up to him after the funeral, rubbing her hand up and down his arm, though I had imagined her head exploding more than once.

He hadn't fully recovered from the wizards' cursed beam. He was still on the mend. The dark circles under his eyes were clearing every day, and his skin was regaining its golden color. According to Ruth, he was still not out of the woods and needed to drink that Super-Twelve elixir every day for another four weeks. Which he'd followed to a T.

And I'd been right about Marcus. The chief had heard every single word I'd exchanged with Lilith. He'd told me so much as soon as the goddess had vanished, but his frown spoke volumes. Thank the cauldron he'd been busy interviewing people for the new deputy post, so he hadn't had time for *that* conversation, though I knew it was coming.

"Is it time yet?"

I pulled my eyes away from Marcus. Beverly appeared next to me. Her perfectly styled blonde hair brushed against her shoulders as she neared. A short blue jacket and jeans accentuated all her curves. Her red shoes matched her red lips as she smiled. She looked amazing and back to her pre-boob-spelled self.

I smiled at her. "Nice to see that you're back to your *normal* bosom self. Any man who made you feel like you had to alter a part of your body wasn't a real man. And he was definitely *not* the man for you."

Beverly shrugged a shoulder. "Oh, that. That's nothing."

"It's the opposite of nothing." I'd wanted to ask her about this Derrick who'd made her feel this way, precisely what had transpired between them, but she kept dismissing it like it was no big deal. I knew better, though. I knew my aunt.

"Have I missed it yet?" Dolores appeared next to her sister, her long, black skirt swaying along with her long hair. She cut an impressive statuesque figure; she really did.

"Not yet," I told her.

Beverly let out a puff of air. "I need a drink," she said and disappeared into the crowd.

"You know, you could have participated in some of the competitions," said Dolores. "I'm sure Gilbert wouldn't have objected, especially not after his *involvement*."

I laughed and shook my head. "Nah. I wouldn't have entered anyway. Besides, it's much more fun being a spectator. Do you know what pie Ruth picked in the end?" I asked my tall aunt.

My aunt shook her head. "No idea. By the time I went to bed, she'd baked over a hundred and twenty pies. Your guess is as good as mine."

My eyes moved over to the platform and settled on Ruth. She sat straight and bore a tiny smile on her lips.

"Wait… is she smiling?"

"Shh. It's starting." Dolores practically elbowed me as she moved closer.

The three judges, forks in tow, formed a line and then one by one, tasted a piece of each pie. Then they all moved off to the side of the platform, hunched in conversation.

My heart was thumping with nerves for Ruth. When I looked back at her, she still had that smile on her face.

After a minute or so, Gilbert jumped off his chair and grabbed a microphone from the ground behind him. He tapped the microphone with his finger.

"Is this on? Can you hear me? Hello? Hello. Great." He took a breath and turned to the crowd that had gathered around the platform. "Welcome to the Annual Hollow Cove Pie Festival and this year's Best Pie award. The judges have tasted and have selected a winner." He gestured to the judges, and the female judge came forward and handed him an envelope.

Gilbert snatched the envelope from her, and balancing the mic on his chest, he tore it open. He cleared his throat. "It is with great pleasure that I accept this award—" His face screwed up and then changed color. "What is this? This can't be? No..."

"Who won, Gilbert?" shouted Dolores.

Gilbert blanched as the envelope fell from his shaking fingers. His gaze traveled to the table. "The winner of the Annual Hollow Cove Pie Festival... is Ruth Davenport."

I threw up my hands and screamed like a banshee. So did Dolores.

Ruth stood as the three judges gave her a gaudy-looking trophy of a golden pie.

Gilbert chucked the microphone down like a child throwing a tantrum. "Impossible! No pie is better than mine! No pie!" shouted the town mayor. "Everyone knows *I* bake the best pies!"

"A little humbleness goes a long way," I told him, though he never heard.

He grabbed a fork from inside his jacket—I swear he did—and rushed over to Ruth's pie. He stabbed his utensil in her pie and took a bite. His eyes widened. "This is... good... really good." He took another mouthful. "What's in it? It's apple pie... but there's something in here. It's not sugar..."

Ruth held her pie trophy like it was a pet, stroking it gently. At first, I wasn't sure she was going to tell him, and then, "Maple apple pie."

"Maple apple pie," repeated Gilbert, tears streaming down his face as he kept on eating. "It's good." He sniffed. "Really good. It's... better than mine."

Ruth beamed at the very rare praise from Gilbert. She caught me looking and gave me a thumbs-up. Loved my Aunt Ruthy.

"Girls!" Beverly came strutting, her hips swaying and kitten heels clicking the pavement.

"What is it, now?" said Dolores. "A butt lift? Lip implants? A foot filler? A bra-line back lift?"

I had no idea if such a thing as a bra-line back lift existed, but I wasn't about to correct my aunt.

Beverly's green eyes shone, and she looked happier than when she hit the sale rack at Macy's. This ought to be good.

She thrust out her hand to us. And on her ring finger was the biggest diamond I'd ever seen. It looked like a Ring Pop, those candy rings you got as a kid when it was acceptable to eat your jewelry.

"Girls." Beverly beamed, wiggling that diamond ring at us. "I'm getting married!"

And here we go again.

Don't miss the next book in The Witches of
Hollow Cove series!

ABOUT THE AUTHOR

Kim Richardson is a USA Today bestselling and award-winning author of urban fantasy, fantasy, and young adult books. She lives in the eastern part of Canada with her husband, two dogs and a very old cat. Kim's books are available in print editions, and translations are available in over 7 languages.

To learn more about the author, please visit:

www.kimrichardsonbooks.com

Printed in Great Britain
by Amazon

74699042R00201